The Craze

The Craze

Paul Southern

W F HOWES LTD

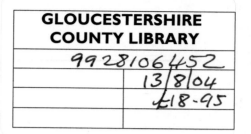
This large print edition published in 2004 by
W F Howes Ltd
Units 6/7, Victoria Mills, Fowke Street
Rothley, Leicester LE7 7PJ

1 3 5 7 9 10 8 6 4 2

First published in 2003
by Century Books

A CIP catalogue record for this book is available
from the British Library

ISBN 1 84505 693 0

Typeset by Palimpsest Book Production Limited,
Polmont, Stirlingshire
Printed and bound in Great Britain
by Antony Rowe Ltd, Chippenham, Wilts.

For Tasneem

PROLOGUE

No matter where you are in Manchester, you're only a road away from being mugged, a house away from being burgled, a pavement away from the next stolen car. The great arteries that lead in and out of the city, roads like the A34 and the A6, don't usually let you hang around long enough to discover this but, with delays as long as they are, and car-jackings on the increase, they're working on it. With Roman vision, they point directly south, to the suburbs, to Cheshire, to the world beyond the M60 ring road. That motorway, purposely built to fence the natives in, marks the demarcation point. You enter at your peril. If you're sensible, you won't bother.

Recently, the surgeons have given the city a face-lift. Along the Wilmslow Road corridor, chic eateries and upwardly mobile-phone bars vie for public space, their Tate Modern designed floating chairs the perfect fit for media airheads, phone rangers and art-house luvvies. But it's all cosmetic. Thinly applied make-up for a city on the mortuary slab. If you were to hail a taxi in Chinatown and, fuelled on high-octane perfume and the latest designer drugs, inhale the neon line of Wilmslow Road, through the bustle of Rusholme and Fallowfield to the outer-outer London borough of Didsbury, you'd think the world was one long party stretching into the night. The road is thronged with a million couples, riding the passion wagons of youth. Headlong, they rush into their twenties with the knowledge that there'll be more to come. The outrageous fortune of being young.

Never stray from the path, Little Red Riding Hood was told. Did she live in Manchester? The roads that lead off the dream run of Wilmslow Road, off the A6, off the Kingsway, off Princess Parkway, off all the major thoroughfares, these roads are the *real* Manchester. Down the old terraced Victorian streets and crumbling estates, where life is not so much hard as impossible, starved of the oxygen of hope. Here, they breathe the fug of despair, so close to the doors of potential, the universities and libraries, but so closed to them.

Take the east of the city, a sprawling mass of disused factories, miles and miles of terraced housing that suffocates the little life that breathes there. Clayton, with its unfinished faces and battle-hardened old women, Beswick and Collyhurst with their tower blocks and concrete dereliction, Gorton with its effluvia of white-trash council estates washed up and dying. A compass of unending deprivation, an ocean of the great

2

unwashed. What sorry flotsam it brings. The mountain bike generation. No need for face-masks and balaclavas here. This is a real war zone. Everyone wears the pallor of the dead. The women. The children. The dogs. All born of the deprived and dispossessed.

And it gets worse. There are areas in this city to which Gorton beckons like a Promised Land, a Paradise in the making. The descent into Manchester's hell ends elsewhere. Moss Side and Longsight. Gateways to the Underworld. The real Inferno. And, flowing between them, the slender line of Wilmslow Road, a river of milk and money. A shop window for every pimp, shooter and dealer in town. A no-man's land, where the gorgeous and glitterate rub shoulders with gangland kings, oblivious to the hoods and crooks breaking into their cars, to the runners on every street corner, waiting their chance.

In Manchester, opportunity knocks for those who wait. The shattered glass of a million parked cars, the snap of a thousand back doors being taken off their hinges, bear testimony to the rich pickings on offer. Just ask the thieves. The kaleidoscopic network of back alleys could have been designed with them in mind. Theseus would have struggled to navigate their maze of getaways. Fuelled on crack, the world has few fears. The gutted properties that even Manchester's most heartless landlords wouldn't rent out are now crack houses or opium dens. There's one on every

3

street. Smackhead City. A city on the edge of night.

And, with the summer clocks set at one, that night had come. A clear and crescent moon hung over Longsight Rail Depot like an open noose. George Malone, sitting alone in his Portakabin, looked out across the tracks and sighed. A car door slammed somewhere in the distance. He turned back to his table, scattered with newspapers and tea, and a copy of the Good News Bible, and cast a wary look over the passage he'd just been reading. Psalm 2. *Why do the heathen rage?* Why, indeed?

He pulled up his chair. Time to think. But, as he did, he caught the sound of human voices on the night air, stretched and thin. Their advent bothered him more than the words. This was *his* time. The last train from Piccadilly had passed an hour ago, the shunters all gone home. Slowly, he made his way to the open door and peered outside. The voices were louder now, rising like mist from across the old access road. There was a thumping sound, too; a slow, ominous thud. Something was wrong.

Nervously, he descended into the gloom. The tracks disappeared into darkness. One, two, as many as he could count, like blackened fingers. Step by step, he was drawn across them. He lit his torch. The cuffing sound had ceased. The voices, no longer muffled by the heavy, summer air, were clearer still. A man's, certainly, and

4

maybe a woman's. He was getting closer. And closer. He felt his heart pick up where the thumping had stopped.

One beat. Two beats. Three. Then nothing. From out of the darkness a murderous scream split the night air. Torn from a throat, piercing the sky, it killed his courage. And the palpitations began.

He flashed his torch, instinctively, fear driving him to unexpected voice.

'Who's there?'

But there was nothing. No scream. No sound. Nothing but the smell of diesel hanging limply in the air.

He held his breath.

He'd reached the embankment overlooking the old access road, the road that led down to the Dead Shed, where all the suicides were brought and counted. The sweat ran down his face like rain. In the shallow hollow before him, there was movement. Grey movement in the dark. The palpitations in his chest grew stronger. Panic rising. There was somebody there.

Instinct again.

'What are you up to?' he shouted. 'This is private property.'

In an instant a spark lit, arced in the moonlight like a shooting star, then fell to earth. There was a second of hiss and flame, then a blinding supernova roaring into being, fire dancing in the night. A figure, framed in the glow, scuttled spider-like over the fence to the road. No ghoul then, but flesh and blood. George gave futile chase, the familiar, dull ache spreading up his arms and legs. But, as he reached the fire, he drew up sharply. His senses were assaulted by something far worse; a smell that left him wheezing for clear air; a smell that made him want to throw up.

It was no ordinary fire. A great sheet of tarpaulin spat rockets into the sky. George kicked at the greasy canvas where the flames licked, kicked hard to put them out. But his boot cracked into bone. There was something in there. Or someone. The voices? *Oh, God.* Struggling to get out. The heathen calling. He took his jacket off and flapped it around madly, but the flames rose to meet him like Passover. It hadn't rained for weeks and the ground sparked like an electric storm. Fuelled by desperation, he tried one last time. One last kick. *Please.* Thud. The fire roared. And the innards spilled out.

George's face blanched despite the heat. *Jesus Christ.* He was right. It *was* someone. A young woman, her body spitting fat, the shreds of her skin writhing like tongues. His stomach finally gave way.

Retching and stumbling, he heaved himself up and ran down to the fence. Desperately, he tried to scale it, just about managed to squeeze his head over the top, to a section where the barbed wire had been flattened by an old carpet. But he was too late. The figure had gone. There was nothing but the headlights of a distant car. He heard its engine splutter into life, then the eyes winked out and vanished.

The last spark of hope gone, George Malone was left to assemble what little of his world remained, trying to picture what the young woman looked like before the fires consumed her. Heavy blows had pulped the back of her head. There was agony in every tortured shred of skin and bone. He'd seen pictures like this before. Documentaries on television. Victims of concentration camps, of far-flung wars. Nameless victims slung out all over the world. And that world was now here. In Longsight. In Manchester. Touching him directly.

He wept, for her and for himself, and made his way back to his cabin, to his papers and his Good News Bible. To what used to be home.

Within thirty minutes, the police had sealed the area and the questions had begun. Within hours the body was gone, too. Darkness had closed in. It would be left to the pathologists to make sense of it all, to explain the little details George had missed.

The woman's marriage finger had been removed and her tongue cut out.

Both were missing.

CHAPTER 1

For as long as anyone could remember, the Craze had been part of their lives. There was no escaping it. It spread like plague through Manchester's twilit streets, infected every house and home from Cheetham Hill to Cheadle Heath. Spread like mutant DNA, each strain more virulent than the last. The Craze. How else to explain the mugging of a wizened Second World War veteran at Belle Vue Dog Track last Saturday night, or the knuckledusting of a frail, old lady coming home from bingo? How else to explain the production line of cars lying strewn and gutted under thick palls of grey smoke? Or the sixteen-year-old beanpole shooters playing Al Capone in the nearest off licence, the junkies lining Stockport Road like the army of the Undead, the green fields of Irish youth, face down, floating in a bog of booze after the twelfth round had ended? Or the boy intruders on crack cocaine, their fat trash whore mothers pimping their white arses to Moss Side Yardies, and the growing gangs of Paki-boy gunrunners from Cheetham Hill and Longsight, holding up their own corner shops? How do you explain it,

8

to Johnny Public, that they'd more chance of getting their car pinched (whether they're in it or not), their face smashed, and their house ransacked, than in *any* city on the Eastern seaboard? What do you tell them?

You tell them the truth.

Beneath their feet, the compressed magma of social deprivation churns daily, breaks out on to the surface with volcanic force and increasing regularity. The fault-lines are shifting, one area lifted by council regeneration, another sinking again into poverty and crime as council overspill pours into the heathen breaches. Gang warfare erupts along the earthquake zones, internecine feuds fuelled by greed and pathological insecurity. One day, one fine June day, the whole lid will come off and Manchester will burn in fires hotter than the Kalahari bush.

The Craze. Jamie Farrell had known it all his life. Had grown up with it. As had Darren Finch next door, who'd shot the eyeballs out of his dog, then tried it on a school friend. Or poor Sandy Sloane over the way, whose legs were broken by a black BMW one Friday night. Her husband Gandhi, banged up good following another failed armed robbery, discovered she was sleeping with everyone at his old boozer and got her steamrollered. Broke both her legs. Didn't stop her, though. Sandy did most of her best work on her back.

For Jamie it began when he was ten. He pinched the purse of some old Paki on Hamilton Road, punched her as she struggled, and flew off into the badlands of the Anson Estate. He'd crossed the line. And had been vaulting it ever since. But with his teens ending, the line was disappearing from view. The Craze was killing him. And it was getting worse.

Night on Northmoor Road, the hard boys were spilling out on to the streets. He was with Billy Whizz, intravenous on cocaine, sitting in a stolen Astra. Life could not have been worse. The moon hung high in the pale beyond. Billy egged him on: Drive. So he drove. Faster. And faster. Faster towards Kirkmanshulme Lane, over ramps that threatened to plough the car into the hereafter. What the fuck point was there in having them when the car you were wrecking wasn't even your own, and the thrill of shaft and axle breaking beneath you was as near to love as you were ever likely to get?

Bang. The car soared like an angel into the night sky. Bang. Over ramp into ruin. Headed straight for the junction of Stanley Grove. And the blinking red eye. Billy screamed, nearly blew his head off, told him to run it, run it, run through the fucking thing. Jamie put his foot through the floor and closed his eyes. Horns blared and the screech of wheels concussed the air. Fucking hell. They were through. Through with everything. He'd success-fully failed his emergency stop. And all with Billy Whizz beside him.

The Craze was born. Beautiful and simple. Better than any drug. Trying to capture that moment when your whole life lay suspended over the world, when the rope was hung out for you, waiting for you to slip your head in, but you tied the knot all the same. A moment when consequences receded so far away that nothing on God's, or anyone else's, earth mattered at all. Jumping that red light was beautiful. Death and the brake pedal. It was for Jamie the beginning and ending of everything. As near to anything as he'd ever get. Two had died already. A pile-up in Denton, their faces up in lights on Granada News. What a way to go. The reporter said it was a tragedy for the families. Jamie knew the families. It wasn't. They were shit-bags. No-one gave a fuck about them. Still, he was envious. They'd died in fire and glory. And he was still here. There was only one way to beat them. Kingsway. Not even Billy Whizz had managed that.

Kingsway was four long miles of joy-riding heaven, a dual carriageway stretching from West Point in the north to Didsbury in the south. The ultimate challenge. Junctions every four hundred yards, six sets of lights. Six ways to kill yourself. On a hot Manchester night you could top a hundred down there. If you dared. Terence. Billy. None had got as far as Fog Lane. Something always got in the way. A pedestrian staggering across the dual carriageway with armalite pizzas from Signori's, a tyre bursting, jack-knifing them into the reservation, or two fat slags pissing in a gutter. They should have rammed their fucking fat arses.

Kingsway was the big one. Jamie'd get it one day. Or one day it'd get him.

CHAPTER 2

The sun came up, gradually, meniscus by meniscus, emerging from the rim of the world like a waking titan. Giant marmalade fingers poked through the net curtains of a second storey room in a run-down Victorian tenement, running themselves gently down its single occupant. A girl, changing. She slid her long legs into some jeans, quickly applied a smear of purple lipstick and some black mascara, and was out of her flat in five minutes. Hair upright, dancing behind her, she raced across Dickenson Road and felt the warmth of a June day on her neck. Shazia Ahmed had only one thing on her mind: shoes. She needed shoes for London.

She headed towards Longsight Market. Its wooden stalls and hastily erected canvas tents were scattered over the tarmac like the camp of a medieval army. It was the perfect place to get them. She knew what she wanted. Flat soles. Nothing fancy. There must have been a hundred people there already, the din of morning hanging in the air over them. She passed the stalls of the Asian traders and aroused the usual looks, her long legs targets for their darting eyes. A mouth like a battering ram had kept them at bay so far, but for how long? An Asian girl in a one-bed flat, with Diana Ross and a mirror for company, you didn't want trouble. Not from anyone.

She scoured the racks of Abdul's Ladies Fashions and found a pair she liked. Then, grabbing a strictly forbidden bacon sandwich from Christo's Butty Bar, she was off down Dickenson Road, and into the morning. The Victorian terraces looked almost kindly in the sun, their roofs shimmering expectantly with the promise of the new day. Windows wound down on passing cars, the thumping techno of eager dealers a reminder that Manchester was indeed a 24-hour city: for some professions.

She approached Birchfields Park in good spirits, thoughts of London high in her heart. She picked the fingers out of her pockets and stared at her small gold ring. Her engagement ring. She knew it wasn't real, but she didn't care. All that glitters, well, the reverse was true. And Damon did love her, she was sure. He was going to take her away. And she drifted along the road and imagined she was with him now. But before she got any further, she was beeped by a passing black cab, heading the opposite way. She ignored it and kept on walking. It didn't do to look. But the taxi stopped and the driver stuck his head out.

'Shazi, wait!'

Familiar. It was her uncle. Mamoo Azad. Bad news at the best of times. She threw the remains of the bacon sandwich away. The car swung round in a well-practised arc and pulled up beside her.

'Get in, Shazi, we need to talk.'

She eyed him warily. He looked unwell. *Seriously* unwell. He was sweating profusely, beads of it lining a week's growth. His eyes were bloodshot, too, scored with searing red tributaries. More than a fever, she thought. His thirty-something years looked like sixty.

'What about?'

He stared at her. And she at him. His lower lip trembled.

'Please, Shazi.'

'I'll be late for work,' she lied. Unflinching.

Mamoo Azad was trouble. *Big trouble.* It followed him like a vengeful fury. Tales of his drinking were preached like parables in the community. Half a *ghora*. One of the new breed. Spent his adult years in a drunken stupor, summoning just enough energy to seethe at the injustice of a world that had given him two mentally subnormal children and a wife he couldn't stand. Shazia hadn't seen him for over a year. She doubted another one like that would bother her much.

'Please, Shazi.'

His face twitched anxiously, the sweat sticking to it like syrup.

She rolled her eyes and knew she was done for. Family and all that. She got in.

The taxi sped on towards Wilmslow Road, the air inside suffocating her. As she stared out, she felt him looking at her through the rear-view mirror, waiting for him to start.

'It's been a long time, eh, Shazi? You've no words for your uncle?'

She turned and looked at him.

'No, Mamoo, no words, not today.'

He was frowning. Agitated. Something 'big' was wrong.

'I saw your mother last week, Shazi, she wants you to go home.'

The first surprise.

'I think it's a bit late for that, don't you?' she said, alarmed.

A pause. Azad went on.

'She says your father wants to make up. He says he's sorry for what he's done.'

Shazia stared harder at him. A second surprise.

'Not as sorry as I am, Mamoo.'

Then pausing.

'It's over, Mamoo. He only wants one thing. Get me married.'

She sat back.

Azad liked Shazia, he liked her a lot. Where his other nephews and nieces were set to become doctors and dentists and that kind of thing, doing all that was expected of them, Shazia had dropped out. A kindred spirit. Yes, she was gobby, yes, she was a handful, but so what? He liked women like that, not kowtowing to his every whim and being decent to him like his bloody wife. If only he'd have met someone like Shazia – a white Shazia, maybe

– he wouldn't have ended up like this, scratching around for a living, with debts hanging over him. And what debts. He'd have met fire with fire.

'We've made up, Shazi,' he continued, 'your mother and I. I'm on the straight and narrow now. Your father even speaks to me.'

Now, that *was* hard to believe, Shazia thought. Not after he gave the carpet his blessing, throwing up over the Kaaba rug. They'd come to serious blows then. Mainly her father's. He'd banished Azad from the house, from ever visiting; had taken his enormous sledgehammer fists to his face when he deigned to show up again, asking for pennies for cigarettes, begging like the poorest fakir in Lahore.

'I don't think so,' Shazia said, matter of factly. 'He hates you.'

Azad looked at her, turned up Hathersage Road, past the hospital. His lower lip hung even further. It was true.

He tried again.

'You should see him, Shazi, you belong at home, you've been too long away, you know.' He paused. 'Your mother cries all the time. It's destroying her. Your brothers and sisters want to see you. They ask after you, Shazi. Why don't you call him?'

She looked out of the window.

'I can't,' she said. 'Not after what he's done. Tell him no.'

Azad pulled up, stopped the taxi by the old Victoria baths, another grand old building waiting

16

to be made into self-contained luxury flats or student halls of residence. He remembered taking Shazia there as a little girl. The property developers were everywhere, transforming the city into one giant glass-fronted art gallery. Well out of his reach. Unless his horses came in. And what were the odds on that? After last night he was all but ruined.

'Anyway, why are you so bothered?' Shazia continued after a pause. 'Is that all you wanted?'

Further silence. She pulled a stick of gum out. And softened.

'Mamoo, what's going on? You look terrible.'

For a moment he wavered, and a strange expression crossed his face. He seemed on the point of telling her. Then relented.

'I thought you'd given it up, Mamoo.'

It killed him to hear it, she knew. But everyone knew. He couldn't change that.

He shrugged.

'I can't, Shazi. I can't.'

And he said no more. The taxi started up again.

'Where you want to go, madam?' he asked suddenly, in a mock-Pakistani accent.

Despite herself, Shazia smiled.

'Wilmslow Road. I late for work,' she mimicked.

And so she was. She stared out of the window, lost in thought. Her mother. Her father. And she blanked her uncle completely, and failed to notice his anxious glances in the rear-view mirror, his regret of things not said.

17

After a few minutes, they pulled up on a double yellow. Wilmslow Road was heavy with traffic. She skipped out quickly and popped her head through the glass.

'How much?' she said, continuing the game.

But the jokes had gone and Mamoo Azad looked like he'd done when she met him. Ill. He struggled to get his words out.

'I saw you a few months ago, Shazi. Outside Sanam. With a *ghora*.'

Silence. The air was prickling. So was she.

'So?'

'It's hurting your father, Shazi. You know the community talks.'

She nodded slowly.

'Some parts more than others, obviously,' she agreed, looking directly at him.

He smiled. Fire with fire. Just what he liked.

'You do what you do, Shazi, but it won't come to any good, you know. Drink and white boys. It's not a good mix.'

And he stared long and hard at her, wishing he could say more.

'Ring your mother, Shazi. Before it's too late.'

And the cab pulled out into the stream of traffic, soon lost to sight.

CHAPTER 3

The white Golf thundered down the Kingsway like a rocket. Stolen from Northmoor Road, Longsight, in the early hours, it already resembled a Daytona dragster: bruised chassis, fenders missing, several of its windows knocked out for safety. A police patrol car had been on its tail around 4 a.m. but had soon lost it in the maze of cul-de-sacs and screened roads that wove through Wythenshawe's council estates. It had ridden red lights on Princess Parkway, Wilmslow Road and Stockport Road, neatly jumping the curbs and scattering a number of pedestrians in the process. The car was burning up, its occupants coming off a crackhigh. And now the red smudge of dawn that had greeted its new ownership was turning into a fireball of a day.

Taking a handbrake skid left and on to Burnage Lane, and neatly revolving 360 degrees in the process, the car sped up towards Green End. Wheels spinning all ends up, it orbited the round-about twice before launching itself up Errwood Road. With practised skill it vaulted the pavement, dodged the railings guarding Cringle Fields, and rallied across the scorched grass till it took a great thump against a tree. The branches shook violently and shed a green confetti upon its white bridal roof. Its two occupants staggered out, eyes streaming with tears, noses streaming with chemicals. They torched the car. More incandescent heat. Now running, they made for Stockport Road.

This had been quite a night for Jamie Farrell. Two cars and two grand. A bit out of the ordinary, even by his own graceless standards. Tall and lean, and with an eye for Manchester fashion, the ear studs, the gold tooth, the hooded designer anorak (stolen, of course), the brand-name trainers (ditto) and the mountain bike, he had followed the well-worn path of most crime graduates from Gorton and Longsight's sprawling council estates. Shoplifting, vandalism, petty extortion, joy-riding, shop burglary, house burglary, street muggings, dealer. He'd passed with honours.

It was the only world he knew, and the only world that counted. No need for education when he had every qualification worth having: the ugly mug, the shaven head, the muscled frame, the piercing Neanderthal stare. He had *the look*. Passers-by took one glance through darting eyes and correctly assumed this man was a mugger. No need to stamp 'thief' on his forehead. You just knew. And last night he was showing everyone why. He was back in Longsight. Back with the shit-bags and smackheads. Joyriding with Terence McMahon. They'd done a number of jobs together

20

in their early teens, running for dealers, break-ins, the usual starters. They had a brothers' history between them. Terence, too, was on his second of the night when they discovered and broke into the Golf. A Golf on Northmoor Road? You *are* asking for it. Jamie insisted on them knocking the windscreen out before bombing down to Wythenshawe on 'business'. You couldn't yet smoke your mobile phone, unfortunately. Some things still had to be done face to face. The police car caught them speeding down there but speed was no substitute for savvy, and it took only a little of Terry's local topography to have them away before the 'copter came out. Easy.

They drove into the night, reckless and stoned. And, as they did, the Golf seemed to drive into the sky above. The street lights, like a blur of Olympic torches, lined the route for them, to the thousand galaxies that beckoned them upward. Hotwire joy-riders teleprinting the word *dream*, emailing heaven and oblivion. Jamie loved it, though he was barely conscious enough to take it all in. The stars stood out like cats' eyes, swimming in the pool of the firmament. They winked, danced and disappeared as the tide of amphetamines swept back and forth over him. While Terence drove, anywhere and everywhere, in symbiotic union with the car, feeling the violence of the engine, the inhalations of the throttle, the scream of rubber, Jamie felt the moment above and about him.

And so riding the breakers of dawn, the fore-runners of a new day, they careered into the morning. Jamie and Terence, now at the end of the rainbow, began sweating with fear and vulnerability. The crack in their invincibility had become a fault-line, widening with paranoia and hate. When Terence crashed the car into a tree he was aiming for home. It took him several moments to realise his mistake, by which time Jamie's auto-alarm had shaken him from stupor and dragged him screaming into life.

'Get the fuck out!' he yelled.

Terence, strong in body if not in mind, grinned.

'We're out of fuckin' fuel, pal. She's sound.'

Jamie stared at him.

'I'm not hangin' round to find out, mate. C'mon. Get the fuck out!'

As they ran off, the car provided a fitting metaphor for the night's events, the splutter of need, the smoke of anticipation, the loud bang of fulfilment. And then the blaze. And the slow diminution of fire.

They came to the McVitie's factory on Stockport Road. They pulled their hoods over their faces and then swung into Levenshulme like gunslingers in a distant Western. They should have been doing houses now in Heaton Chapel; the itch was still there and it was the perfect time. No-one expected it in the morning. Certainly not the 'stay at home' wives off shopping at Tesco, or the 'late back from dropping the kids off' type. But they had money in hand and there was time for that later. Time for everything. And besides, Jamie's interests had widened considerably since those far-off days. Rather than making a career of hanging round Costcutter on Mount Road, he'd taken his golden opportunity in life. He didn't tell Terence. Terence was a fuckwit, good for some muscle in times of trouble but completely unreliable. Stupid unreliable.

They sauntered down Stockport Road, past the antique shops. The smell of chocolate hung so heavily in the air, they could almost taste the syrup; Mr McVitie's great globules melting in the heat. Traders with bronzed arms and craggy faces wire-wooled and varnished the treasures of yesterday. The sounds of lathe and hammer, the chippings flying like confetti into the air, the mugs of tea and coffee stacked high on old tables, all preserving the ancient order of things. Work, marriage, stability. The old lies. Treasures for the elevated young things from Didsbury, with their Saturday-morning enthusiasm and chequebooks.

All lost on Jamie and Terence, oblivious as they were to the stained-glass craftsmanship and barley-sugar table legs. They walked into a Balti take-out, something a little more accessible. The skewered hunk of kebab meat spat and spun in the window, the faintly nauseous smells of grease and fat assaulting their senses. No need for a menu here. How many ways can you sell shit? A white-aproned kid behind the counter looked up. He had craters of acne like star clusters on his cheeks and forehead. This was the only work he could get.

'Okay, lads, what can I get you?'

Practised, rehearsed, confident, just as he'd heard his father say it.

Jamie eyeballed him.

'We'll have two kebabs.'

'Anything else?'

Jamie shook his head. An older man had entered the kitchen, with a machete and chicken carcass in his hands. Jamie watched the butchery, the callow insouciance of the killer, the flesh being hacked to pieces and splayed across the table.

'Nice day, isn't it?' said the kid, hopefully.

Terence looked up from the window ledge where he was sitting. His slitted eyes and cobra's hood seemed poised to strike some venomous retort. He hated Pakis, preached their destruction with the messianic zeal that only Gorton's white-trash council estates could harbour. His head was almost clear, certainly clear of anything like conscience or intelligence.

'Fuckin' brilliant, mate.'

The kid carved some sculpted flesh from the rotating skewer of fat.

'Onions, salad?' he asked.

Jamie nodded. He was joined at the counter by Terence. Terence shook his head. The boy looked from one to the other, at their shaven heads and glazed eyes, and was glad to hear the reassuring sound of Amir's machete behind him.

'One with, one without, is that right?'

Jamie shook his head, Terence nodded. The kid looked confused.

'You don't want them?' he asked Jamie.

'Salad, I want salad. No onions.'

'And you? What do you want?' he asked, addressing Terence.

'Me?' said Terence. 'I want onions, no salad.'

He gestured to the boy, confidentially, and leaned over the counter. The boy maintained his distance.

'Not too much onions, Paki, I don't like too much onions.'

The kid turned round and said something in Urdu to his friend. He was worried, and for good reason. As he did so, the right side of his face exploded with pain, a giant clubbing blow making him drop the kebab and leaving him flattened on the counter. Jamie, joining in, smashed his fist into the other cheek, shattering the ready-to-burst yellowheads there. The boy groaned.

At the commotion, the man in the back shouted out and sprang forward. In two deft leaps, and agile as a circus acrobat, he vaulted the counter. The air was sliced a whisker away from Terence's ear. The bastard was wielding his machete. Jamie swore in panic. He hadn't expected such hasty retaliation. Before another arc could come sailing through the quivering air, he charged. And ran into rock. The

25

man was a brute, and had the fire of vengeance in his belly. One flailing swipe of his giant hands caught Jamie on the back of his head and he felt his legs buckle under him. On the back of last night's sleeplessness, with his mind not yet alive to the day's reality, it nearly floored him. And when he heard voices, many voices behind the counter, speaking in tongues, his thoughts turned to one thing: self-preservation.

'Fuckin' leg it, Terence, leg it.'

But Terence was already out, flying into the day. Jamie followed hard on his heels but not before the air was again split behind him. Arms flung out like tentacles, he reached for freedom, almost taking the window of the door out as he made for the exit. Brown faces and white eyes eyeballed him back as he stared through the tinted glass. They'll toast for this tonight, he thought, and his mind was already racing for purchase, thirsting for revenge. The imprint of the acned boy and the man with the machete were indelibly marked in his mind; in his humiliating retreat, he lashed out in the only way he knew. Abuse. He pointed at them, and drew his hand slowly across his throat.

'Fuckin' Pakis!'

When he caught up with Terence near the Palace night-club, more than vengeance was on his mind. In the mêlée he'd lost a grand's worth of fifty-pound notes. They could be scattered all over Stockport Road by now, he thought, but most likely they'd been pocketed by those bastard Pakis. Terence was all up for going back with some scallies he knew on Broom Lane, local hard boys who could be relied upon to meet fire with a flamethrower. But Jamie thought not, thought that revenge was best served cold; cold in the shape of steel. And he had the faces of his victims photograph-clear in his mind. He never forgot a face, never forgot a trick, and he knew just the person who'd shoot the next one.

'I'll see ya, later, Terence, ta-ra now. Don't do nothing.'

And he upped and went, back up Stockport Road, back to Longsight.

CHAPTER 4

The refuse of the night before was only just being cleaned up. Swept into every litter-filled alley by the gentlest of breezes, a million doggie bags and cardboard take-outs took flight. Cramped cheek by jowl along Wilmslow Road, over fifty Indian restaurants once more opened their doors to the sounds of a new day. This was Rusholme, the filling between Moss Side and Longsight. The land of curry and spice. Chillied rubies and golden peppers. Opals of rogan josh. Turquoise and amethyst sweets from the Jewel in the Crown. Whole new dishes for the flies and hungry dogs.

Shazia took stock of the pavement outside the Al-Biswan. The shutters were up and Ali was there, as usual, looking half-cut and being important. He puffed away at a Gitanes cigarette and nodded in the general direction of his watch. She rolled her eyes and went in.

'You're late again, Missy, did you get pissy again last night?'

He'd started early.

'No. Not this time.'

'You're always pissy, Missy. I've seen you. Behind the bar when you think I'm not looking.'

He followed her round the restaurant. She ignored him. Checking the float, she tried to snatch a black coffee from one of the waiters, then parked herself on a black stool. She half expected Ali to try and sit on her.

She smiled at him sarcastically. His trademark seventies Burt Reynolds moustache was flecked with spittle. Even at the worst of times he was hard to take seriously.

'You pocketed some extras last night, Missy?' he continued.

She shook her head, slowly and deliberately.

'Nope, they're in the dish. Twenty-four pounds fifty-three.'

He frowned.

'Fat Umer says not, Shazi. He says you've been a bad girl again.'

Shazia took a first swing of coffee and looked up. He wasn't kidding. She looked across the restaurant to the open-plan kitchen. A plume of tobacco smoke sent Hiawatha signals to the ceiling. Caught in the fug beneath them was Fat Umer, the odious hint of a smile curling across his chins.

'He should know, should he, when he's back there? He should stick to what he's good at.'

She stuck two fingers up at him. The bastard. It was not a good start to the day. Ali looked at her. And she at him. They knew the score. She needed the work. He needed her *to* work. She brought in too much. Constantly on display. The businessmen at lunchtime, fresh from their board-room torpor, rained tips down on her like manna, imagining her dark, compliant body in all sorts of Kama Sutra fantasies. The students, piling in at closing time, nicely tanked on twisters and beer, bringing the tone down so low that, for a while, the Al-Biswan became a Gorton Kebab House, spent their parents' wages hoping for a sniff. And the families who came in at the weekend, the serious families, the college lecturers, the social workers and the Asians, they wanted a piece of her, too, if only because she was the only one there who didn't look like she'd spit in your food.

So Ali needed her, at least for a while.

'If you have, Shazi, I'll find out,' he whispered. 'Then you'll owe me, Missy.'

There was no mistaking that. Ali had a fuse shorter than your thumb. It didn't do to cross him. Jobs were not so much lost over a broken glass or dirty knife as wrenched, disembowelled and torn grunting from you. He had too much invested in the place to let some gobby girl sell it down the river. Too much time and money.

Built in a day when his moustache was truly in fashion, before every Tariq, Amjad and Imran had dreamt of turning Wilmslow Road into the mad curry mile, he'd dreamt of an empire to rival the Raj, a chain of tandooris extending across the wintry north of England. He'd struggled with crippling debts that had forced his wife into selling her dowry, and he into making fictitious charitable collections for Indian orphans; getting his relations back home in Rawalpindi to send him ever more hopeless pictures of street children which he'd tearfully hand round to the late-night inebriates. He'd had his arms broken by Great White loan sharks in the dead of a Gorton night, fended off the Inland Revenue, the Environmental Health and the Insurance Investigators. All for the love of his restaurant. No girl was going to lose him all that.

He watched her get up and help the waiters set up tables, then thought about his eldest son. He chuckled to himself. He'd have his hands full there, surely. A husband would have a tough time bending *her* to the will of Allah. He was having enough trouble bending her to his. This spat with Fat Umer, for example. It had been simmering and curdling like a bad masala for months now. He'd had to pull them apart several times already. Bad for business. Bad for everything. If he was honest, he wasn't keen on the fat boy, either. He looked, well, unhygienic. All that sweat everywhere. Who knows what was in the Ras Malai?

The great rotating ceiling fans whirred softly as the sticky June heat and the flames from the kitchen scorched the air. Shazia was sculpted in fire, framed by the glow of the tandoor. Her ponytail bobbed and danced like a dervish as she squared up to Fat

Umer, pointing and gesticulating wildly. He'll have bad dreams about that, Ali thought.

The first happy eaters had entered the pleasure dome. A couple of policemen in shirt sleeves, carrying their hats. Ali sat at the window with his filtered jug of black coffee. Here he had all he wanted. Coffee and cigarettes and a view of the world he loved best. A well-practised routine. He could mingle with the customers and watch over the staff. Ali's mad eye, flickering across its socket, missed nothing.

It turned out to be a good day. City slickers, with their Mercedes mentality, a few student-looking types, and an office party of twenty-somethings celebrating someone's leaving. The staff all joined in at the end and gave practised smiles to the soon departing. Mints all round and a few discretionary winks to the girls. So long as they weren't Asian, what was the harm? It was good for the lads' morale and gave the *ghori* a taste of something hotter than their watered-down Saag Gosht.

Shazia was down to her last stick of gum already. She was out the back, shift over, kicking through the empty boxes. She thought about Mamoo Azad, in his cab, twitching to tell her something. And about London and Damon. And she stared up into the sky and watched the vapour trails of vanishing jets scoring its high serenity from east to west.

Then woke up.

With a loud metallic clang the door from the kitchens opened. Wreathed in smoke, one of the chefs emerged. No need for detective work, the bulk of the man needed little pronouncement. Fat Umer. She turned to face him, groaning inwardly. He wiped his sweaty palms on his apron, bloodied and charcoaled.

'What do you want?' she said. 'You're in the way.'

'You fucking *kunjaree*,' he whispered, shutting the door behind him and pointing his fingers at her. 'They're laughing at me in there.'

She feigned a smile.

'They've got a lot to laugh at.'

His face soured.

'Oh, piss off, Umer, what do you expect? What do you go and tell Ali for?'

He smiled.

'Because I've seen you do it, you bitch. You always keep a bit back. A bit for Daddy, eh?'

She stopped.

'Daddy? What the hell are you talking about?'

The puddles of fat were rippling along his jaw. He was shuffling towards her.

'I think you know,' he said.

She stood her ground.

'You don't scare me, Umer. Don't forget. I know what you're *really* like.'

And she did, too. The magazines.

Umer spat like a snake, writhing in rage. Months of frustration, of humiliation, were oozing out of

33

his pores. And, for the first time, Shazia did feel a flicker of fear. Her throat tightened; escape over the boxes and up the wall of the yard was all but impossible. Ali had erected so much barbed wire and broken glass after the last robbery that you'd need a tank to get out.

'Touch me and I'll scream,' she threatened, summoning all her strength.

But she was too late. The scream died on her lips. Umer was on her like a wolf, with a speed and agility that took her completely by surprise. He caught her flailing arm and brought his great weight down upon her, forcing the breath from her lungs. She clawed and tore and bit but no words came. His hand was clapped over her mouth. The blood coursed through her veins. Delirious with panic and fright, she was trapped. And then a hammer blow to the side of her face made her reel till the sky above seemed flecked and stained with blood.

Umer was on fire. The constant wriggling beneath him, the straining of muscle and body and the heaving of passion ignited a tempestuous spark within him. The flames that habitually burned only for boys were now licking and dancing over a female for the first time. Anger and weakness and guilt drove him on. He felt his hidden point stiffen and rise. Sensing the danger, Shazia redoubled her efforts to get free. She bit hard on anything her teeth could sink into. Clothes. Chest. Skin. Hands. As hard as she could.

Then heard the scream, blasting with pain. Screaming louder and louder till her head exploded.

In the distance she thought she heard voices. She was shouting so hard it was hard to tell. Then, as another blow smashed across her temple, she felt the weight pinning her down shift to the side and she could breathe again. Clear air. Freedom. Her lungs could move. And she could hear.

'Get the fuck off her, Mister!'

The voice cut through the air like a drawn scimitar.

'Get the fuck off her!'

And, for once, Shazia was glad to hear it.

'You crazy bastard, you crazy fucking bastard.'

Ali. Her brain exploded with relief.

The chefs and the waiters tore at Umer's arms and legs, punching him to quiet. His giant frame heaved like a monstrous heart. Time stood still. Where do eyes look when there's nowhere to turn? At the monster before them or at the monster in themselves? The waiters avoided Shazia's as if to look at them were to make them culpable, too. Instead, they stared at Umer. He was holding his left hand up in supplication, and the mangled remains of his little finger.

'Look,' he said, realisation dawning.

Ali wiped his face and eyeballed the heaving jelly before him.

'Mister, if you come near my restaurant again, I'll take the others off for you. Now piss off.'

The shock of the moment froze Umer's mouth into a dentist's 'open wide'. The round well of his lips parched and dried in the summer air. His brain reached for meaning in a moment that had none. Eyes staring uncomprehendingly, they fixed on the only tangible thing in that whole world. Not on Ali, nor on the chefs and waiters who were party to his madness – these were vague and watery like the milky clouds. Nor on the boxes and the yard where he'd spent many a starry night talking and gambling with the boys at the end of a long shift. No. Fat Umer's eyes rested on Shazia Ahmed, and they burnt with a hunger and a fire even as he was led away from all that he'd known.

When he'd gone, Ali helped her up. She wiped the hair from her eyes. Blood smeared across her hand.

'How do I look?' she said.

He winced.

'You're a lucky girl, Missy,' he said, 'Umer's a big man. What did you say?'

'Does it matter? He's mad.'

She began to pick up the boxes and cans.

'What are you doing?' he said.

'I've got to finish off these . . .'

But Ali laughed.

'I don't think so, Shazi, look at the state you're in. You better go. My heart can't take this, you know,' and he patted his ticker dramatically.

'Go?' she said. 'Go where?'

Ali shrugged. And looked at her.

'Take some time off, Shazi. Till things calm down. If you go on like this you'll get us all banged up. Maybe worse.'

And his eyes narrowed.

She stopped and picked her hair-band up, head reeling. As she walked away, her hair a whiplash curtain trailing behind her, through the kitchens and the restaurant and into the heat of the day, Ali's eyes followed her. Despite himself, he chuckled grimly. Definitely not for his son, he thought. The girl was a menace.

The world was setting about its business. Wilmslow Road teemed with life. Flies gathered over fruit and vegetables, children batted them in a frenzy, itching and crying in the stifling warmth. Traders and waiters stood in shirt sleeves at their doors, chatting and laughing. For them, the day's potential seemed limitless, with hope on the breeze and expectation in every look and smile. It would unfold slowly, stretch infinitely into a night of promise. But for Shazia, the magic of the morning and the market was lost. Tears threatened to pierce the bulwark of her eye.

Students in shirt sleeves and sunglasses eddied past her, Sony Walkmans growing out of their ears. Black guys in dark BMWs coasted down the road like sharks. Net junkies menaced the highways of the ether in Internet cafes. The deals were being cut and pasted before you had time to think. And everywhere mobile phones, the indispensable

37

fashion crime accessory, the louche epitome of media cool, providing shades of anonymity sunglasses could only dream of. Slickers, slackers, the real dealers. London calling.

Shazia bit her lip. She entered a public phone box, took up the receiver and dialled. There was the familiar answer machine message.

'Damon,' she said softly, 'I didn't know if you'd left, yet.' Pause. 'I'm off work a bit earlier.' Pause. 'I'll see you soon.'

She rang off, the receiver still in her hands, hardly daring to dial again.

Outside the box two elderly women set up camp. And waited.

She dialled. And, for the first time in over a year, she heard her mother's voice.

'Mum, it's me.'

She should have just hung up.

Silence. Then the tears. And the dreadful truth. She had been long away. Why hadn't Mamoo Azad told her?

She left hurriedly, needing to see Damon more than ever. Soon lost in the crowd, she vanished, the tide of people swallowing her up. Looking up into the sky, the vapour trails had all but gone. The way ahead was clear. To London.

Fat Umer had just about decided it.

CHAPTER 5

The bus crawled along. Roadworks again. No sooner had one part of the A6 been dug up than another needed treatment. Cancers of disrepair spreading like contagion through the city. Had it been a patient in a hospital, there would have been but one diagnosis: condition terminal. This was not a council redevelopment area, not a Wilmslow Road. This was Longsight.

Jamie Farrell stared out of the window, at the bustle of the streets, and caught his reflection in it. He was shot to pieces. The lids drew down like steel shutters and he realised that he needed sleep badly. He alighted from the bus near the Asda superstore, into the full glare of the day, and headed up Stanley Grove towards Mount Road.

He passed the old park where he used to play, running his hand along the railings. He could touch the tops of them so easily now. He remembered how they'd dwarfed him as a kid, how he always struggled to climb them, to reach their steel tops. Kids were doing it right now. Little things with jeans and trainers on, baring their torsos like miniature Tarzans. They jumped, rode on each other's backs, manfully tried to haul themselves over. Eventually, one succeeded. Balancing himself on the precipice of the railings, he beat his chest like a savage, while the other little savages danced around him and tried to bring him down. He jumped, arcing into the air, his face alive with passion, then fell to earth. The moment lasted less than a second, but in dreams and memory it was there forever: the first exultation, the first triumph. Jamie knew. He remembered.

He passed the phone boxes on Stanley Grove and marvelled at their appearance. Gleaming steel. Too important to vandalise. While the supermarkets and shops round the corner were alive with graffiti and barbed wire, these electronic sentinels were unmarked. The little kids on bikes saw to that. Minor leaguers pinch-hitting for the big boys. Dealers' delights. He'd used them many times himself.

He whistled to one of them in the park, a regular little tyke.

'Ashley, you working?'

The kid nodded his head. His jug ears stuck out like Mickey Mouse's; his front teeth were missing.

'You know Billy?'

The kid nodded.

'Take this to him. Quickly.'

In the blink of an eye a stick of chewing gum was produced, a ten-pound note folded inside.

The boy grinned and turned and nonchalantly walked off, the sun streaming after him.

Jamie watched him go and squinted, then continued on his way.

The house off Mount Road was no different from the others. Overgrown and untended at the front, it boasted the usual accessories: Sky dish on the roof, a ginnel barred by a steel gate at the side, and one of those bulldozer-proof metal doors the council are so fond of providing for residents in 'problem areas'. The pavement outside, now baking in the morning heat, was scored with dog shit. The street itself, waking to violence once more. Little kids with crewcuts and ear studs threw stones at one another, rode their mini mountain bikes round strangers in a grotesque parody of their older brothers. The girls called one another *tart* and *slag*, threw skipping ropes at one another, ate ice lollies, kissed the boys, eyed their pregnant fourteen-year-old sisters with nothing but envy.

Jamie knocked on the door and shouted through the letter box.

'You in, Mam?'

Silence.

'Mam, are you there?'

There was the clatter of pots and pans in the distance. And a woman's screech.

'Jamie, is that you?'

He heard the patter of feet.

41

A peroxide blonde in her late thirties opened the door. She had tight ski pants and a skimpy top on. A cigarette drooled lazily from the corner of her mouth. She had nothing on her feet.

'I've just been in the garden, luv. Do you want a brew?'

Jamie grunted.

'No, Mam, I can't stay.'

'We're just back from Tenerife. What do you think of the tan?'

Jamie studied the flesh, the deep brown puddles of it round his mother's neck, the deeper sagging of her breasts threatening to catapult from the sling of her top. He felt sick.

'You look fine, Mam.'

'Come and see Patrick. He's out back. He'll want to say hello.'

Jamie sneered.

'Come on, luv, just a moment.'

The back yard had been recently flagged. There was a barbecue set up. It all looked rather different from the knotty clumps of grass and mud he was used to. He hadn't seen his mother for months. He couldn't say he'd missed her, either.

'Patrick's done it, luv, what do you think?' she asked, anticipating his look and going over to a muscular navvy type lounging in a sun chair.

'All right there, Jamie?' the man said, holding up a can. 'Can we get you anything? There's beer in the fridge.'

Patrick had his arm round his mother. Jamie prickled.

'Have you heard from Dad, Mam?'

She extricated herself from Patrick, and stamped her fag out on the flagging. She looked vexed. The same questions again.

'I haven't, son.'

She saw him bite his lip and look round, confused.

'It's too late, Jamie. I can't wait forever now, can I?'

'What about parole, Mam?'

'He's been knocked back, Jamie, you know what he's like.'

'You've seen him, though?'

'Don't spoil the day, Jamie. Come and sit with us and tell us what you're up to.'

Jamie stared at her. He knew what the score was.

'You haven't, 'ave you?'

'Jamie,' she said and bristled with injustice and intent, 'don't start with me. You don't understand. The things I've been through. The times I spent pulling my hair out when he didn't come home, when the police came knocking, when his mates came round expecting favours. Your father's in there for a reason. A very good reason. You think I'm going to sit round watching myself get old and grey? Is that what you want?'

Jamie's mind whirred with a thousand retorts but he couldn't get one out. He needed sleep or he needed coke. Fast. His speech slurred as he tried to make himself heard.

'I don't want you to fuck this shit, Mam. He ain't my fuckin' dad.'

The air went dead. A momentary calm. Jamie's mother looked from one to the other of the two men in her life and, for the umpteenth time, felt more than a little dirty. She stood there exposed, Patrick's piece of flesh, cooking on the spit of his desire, roasting in the summer's heat before him. And now no more than that in the eyes of her baby, the son she never saw. She loathed herself for it.

Patrick stood up, bronzed and waxed arms glinting like pistons on the engine of his torso. His bald pate, shaven and ruddy, threatened to let off a jet of steam, bursting with hostility. He bore down on Jamie like a slow-moving ship. But Jamie wasn't scared. He wasn't the intruder here. This was still his patch and his mother, sensing the latent violence, the paralysis of hurt now broken, tried to force her way between them.

'Pat,' she said, 'leave him.'

But Patrick muscled her out of the way, expertly, the way he always handled her, with a doorman's gusto.

'Don't mess now, Michelle, I'll sort 'im out. He's a cheeky bugger. He's nothing to us. He'll more than likely be seein' his Dad soon enough, any roads.'

Jamie watched his Mum's reaction and understood. This wasn't his patch at all. It never had been. He watched her futile struggles with Patrick's arms, the taut leaden cords twisting her round like a doll. Her face wasn't twisted with rage, leaping to the defence of her son, nor was it torn between the two men. It was sweating and sullen in the searing heat.

'Is that right, Mam? I'm nothing to you? Just like Dad?'

'No, Jamie, that's not true,' she protested, 'you're everything to me.'

'Then leave him,' he said, and gestured to Patrick. 'You always shack up with guys like him. You should be with Dad. What the fuck's this guy, anyway? Some dirty fuckin' gypsy Irish git. He's messin' you around, Mam. He's only here for the dinner you put on his plate. If you want to know what he's really like, call down the Old Bull. He's at it every night you're not with him. You ask the girls down there. You're a bleedin' laughin' stock.'

The fist came sailing through the air like a steam-hammer and caught Jamie on the temple, a great shuddering blow. Only instinct saved him from the follow-through. Only instinct would preserve him. He dived on Patrick and arrowed a short, sharp punch to his groin, the kind of hernia-inducing punch he'd learned from a police sergeant at Longsight station. Patrick groaned, unsuspecting and slightly dazed by the pre-lunchtime cans he'd downed. They rolled on to the patio like drunken men, a mass of limbs, uncoordinated and brutal. The real violence of the streets.

Of this particular art Patrick was an acknowledged master. He hadn't built up a fearsome reputation in all the Paddy dives of Longsight, Levenshulme, and Gorton, without exercising every Irishman's Saturday-night prerogative, the piss-up and the scrap. Patrick could tear houses down if the mood was on him. Jamie, taut and lean and muscular as he was, was too used to the quick head-butt and debilitating punch. How many times had he used fear and his shaved pate to do the work for him? His mugging victims had been carefully selected: drunks, students, old women. And the drugs were killing him. Killing his mind. Killing his body.

Patrick's weight crushed him till he had him pinned on the ground.

'You fuckin' cokehead, do you think you're any better? Nobody'd piss on ya if they had the time to do it. You're a fuckin' no-good thief. You've never been here to see ya mother, either. Now, go and piss off. Go on. Piss off out.'

And he dragged Jamie up and out through the house, with Michelle screaming in tow, hollering in fear and embarrassment.

'Patrick, let the fuckin' boy go, will ya?'

She chased them into the streets. The kids there turned to the din and watched the spectacle with no little amusement. How many times had they seen this kind of thing? Jamie answered the only way he could. Eluding Patrick's grasp, he spat full in his face. And ran. Ran as far and fast as his legs would take him, ran like he did when he was little, aimlessly, and to clear his head. He left his mother and the pealing yells far behind him. Better to go out with a bang, anyway. And thoughts of a bang made him think of Billy, and he imagined Patrick's face forced to chew on Billy's gun and being blown into a thousand little pieces.

He ran back past the park. Back past the kids on the railings. This was the way of the world, the way it always had been, a life of escalating violence and diminishing returns. They were all poor tykes round here. He grew up knowing it. All roads and all avenues, every tower block and cul-de-sac, led to despair. Every dig, every score, was a slender epiphany that relieved it, punctuating the life as the needle punctured the arm. All roads led here. They brought you peace. When the madness took you, when life was just too much, they brought you succour. Eternal forgiveness and no confession needed.

The memory of his mother's vacant flesh, of the scything Asian with the meat cleaver, of Patrick's clubbing hands, they all span before him till they became one maddening desperation and he sought the one consolation. Memories of the previous night's million stars turning and pulsing above

47

him. Memories of cold steel in his arm, slicing into him. All would be better soon. For the fires of revenge were being stoked and tonight would be a furnace of madness. This night, at last, he felt the Craze would take him.

CHAPTER 6

The room was more a crypt than a bedroom, more a morgue than a place for the living. Its high walls stretched upwards to the ceiling sky like the arches of a subterranean vault and left unarticulated the dim plaster patterns above. It was wooded from oaken beam to oaken floor, Victorian splendour carved in every cornice and picture rail. In such vastness the spartan furniture seemed to shrink: two small Tiffany lamps set beside a large, wooden bed and a genuine nineteenth-century mahogany bureau reclining along one bare wall.

Along the others a selection of Atkinson Grimshaw prints were arranged; moonlit vigils in Roundhay Park, solitary women carrying wicker baskets down narrow and ruminative country lanes. The mood was sombre and chill. Fashionably floral curtains hung heavy, like weighed anchors, and blocked out most of the light of the new day. Through windows that never opened, the sounds and smells of summer were but dimly felt. But who needed them after last night?

49

Dru Round lay back, smoked a spliff, and thought about it. What a night it had been. His star turn at the DeepDrill. His first big chance. He'd had everyone on the floor. On his terms. Avoiding the gay poison: shallow double entendres, the cretinous and simpering trannies-with-attitude routine, the nauseous sexual innuendo. It made him sick just thinking about it. Years ago, he'd camped about like the rest of them. Now he was going straight and it was paying off. Granada TV on the phone. Channel 4 interested.

And last night had been a great success. Not just his own performance, either, but for what came after; the boy who hung on his every word like he was some kind of prophet, whose taste in torture rivalled his own Caligulan excess. He'd ruffled the blond locks in the back of the black cab as it sped down Wilmslow Road, past the clubbers filing into all-night end-of-term raves, spilling on to the streets in drunken abandon. His cock was already tearing at the seams by the time they reached his flat in Didsbury.

He'd been toying with the idea of stuffing that boyish face into his lap in the back of the car, of having those bee-stung lips caress him up and down his length and shooting into his mouth, but the eyes of the Asian cab driver were on him all the way, some kind of fanatical kill-Rushdie type, he thought, with his Saddamite moustache and piercing brown look. You couldn't be too careful. Vexed, he felt like confronting them, flexing his muscle and showing a bit of gay steel; felt like punching them back into their sockets and banging his head on the steering wheel. But he'd bit his lip. Hard. Now was not the time. Now was the time to dream. He had plenty of stuff back home to bring him down. And he'd traced the rest of the journey in his mind, to the moment when he'd be free of them.

The cab pulled up. Without a word he paid. But, as he did so, he realised his hand was being held fast. The eyes he'd struggled so hard to avoid now met his fully. In his intoxicated state, the brown pools threatened to dissolve into nothing and, their orbit appearing not so very far from his own, he found the particulars of the face almost handsome.

'Keep it,' the driver said.

'Keep it?' Dru asked, bemused.

The driver nodded.

'I'm finished tonight, you're my last fare.'

For a moment nothing made sense, but the blond boy whispered in his ear and laughed and Dru understood. He just hadn't expected it, that's all.

'All right,' he said. 'Come on up.'

The driver switched off the engine and got out. He was big and broad, and more than a match for the pair of them. Their silent passage to the top-floor flat, up the landings of the detached Victorian house, was as near to a religious experience as Dru had ever had. He felt the potential of the moment, alive in every muscular movement, though numbed and sweetened by the last kiss of marijuana.

Oh, it had indeed been a good night. The blond boy was as willing and submissive as any camp queen but without the usual drawbacks; he didn't mince and squeal and make Dru want to vomit all over him. Not at all. His taut bronzed skin would have graced any fashion magazine, his body hewn from the iron trunks and limbs of Adonis, each muscle defined and articulate. The Asian cab driver evidently found him to his taste, too, for he set to kissing him with missionary zeal and wilful abandon. He'd taken his own clothes off hesitantly, almost embarrassedly, but there was no need. He boasted an enormous cut meat, thick and handsome.

While Dru forced himself into the boy's mouth and made him swallow him whole, he knew the lad was getting even more satisfaction from the battering-ram assault up his anus. Grunts and chokes escaped from his cock-filled mouth till he seemed to forget that there was anything in front of him at all, and all he could think of was the searing heat inside. Dru silently came in his face and mopped the cum on the blond's undefiled hair. He was angry at being upstaged but elated at the erotic potential. He grabbed the boy's meat in his right hand as the Asian pressed down on the young man's haunches. He pinched and pulled at it till it spilled its goods on the bed. The Asian gave a grunt, too, as he released his load. Something that size could fill a bath, Dru thought.

Hours later, with the cab driver gone and the boy asleep on his bed, Dru brought his gear out. The serious stuff. He roused the boy, who turned over and squinted up at him in the almost lightening room, the pale shadow of dawn. Dru caressed the face, the hair, ran his hands across the hairless chest. He felt strangely reluctant to say anything, and meekly held up the leather hood and cuffs, the ones he liked best.

'You or me?' the boy asked. 'I'm tired.'

'You.'

When they finished, Dru felt dead, too. And mutilated. He detested himself, detested the shocking weakness of his body. He tried to banish the waves of guilt which swallowed him up, the feelings of uselessness which inevitably caught up with him and left him stinking and rotten to the core. Standing now in his room, punishing himself for being this way at all, he strangled thoughts of doing serious damage to the boy. He'd read about that kind of thing on the Internet, had paid to watch it take place, and had been amazed to see himself taking part. Each concession to his darker side was a guarantee there would be more to come. More pain, more hurt, more guilt.

He led the boy back to his bed, the bed where the Asian had skewered him, and keeping the hood and cuffs on him, bent him down over it. The boy's moans spurred him to greater lengths as he burnt his way into his hole, making him suffer as he wanted himself to suffer. He came suddenly, felt all his loathing spread up and into the boy, felt momentarily purged and free. When he'd packed the boy off in a taxi, with crude money and silence, the guilt erupted once more and he smoked some more dope to vanquish the terrible and shocking realisation that he should have killed him.

Yes, it had been a good night, after all. Dru opened the curtains and was startled by the blaze of blue which warmed and lightened him. A new day again. He looked round his room, pacing it naked. He saw a little card on one of the bedside tables. He picked it up and smiled. It read 'Thanks' and was followed by a name he couldn't quite make out and a phone number he obviously could. The taxi driver's.

CHAPTER 7

The tears were just drying on Shazia's face when Damon Ruff walked in. She'd been sipping a Coca-Cola on a black leather stool, waiting for him, idly squeezing the last drop of lemon into her empty glass. The clock on the wall said 2:15 p.m. and he was already fifteen minutes late. She half expected him not to turn up. He'd done that before. But there he was, and despite herself, her heart lifted. The events of the day were momentarily forgotten.

Damon Ruff was a student, and a poor one at that. The two were not always the same thing, leastways in Manchester where London luvvies come for their three-year sabbaticals, to party hard at Mummy and Daddy's expense. He studied graphic art or something like that, Shazia could never be quite sure. To be honest, it never really mattered. He loved her and she loved him. What more could she want?

She watched him as he made his way over to her, his fringe flopping down over his face like Hugh Grant's. He'd already managed to drop his wallet and bang his knee on the leg of a plastic stool.

55

'It needs cutting,' she said.

'Sorry, sweetheart, I came as quickly as I could.'
He gave her a peck on the cheek.

The young Asian behind the bar, who'd been eyeing her up for the last twenty minutes, turned his nose up. She was conscious of him staring down it all the while Damon spoke. Daft Tep.

'Shazi, what's up?' he asked. 'What happened to your face?'

The flesh had darkened from Umer's clubbing blows. She pursed her lips and smiled awkwardly. Time to change the subject.

'Remember what you said a few weeks ago, Damon? About London?'

He gulped a mouthful of saliva down and nodded.

'Well, I've thought about it now. I want to go. There's nothing for me here any more.'

Her face, so recently flecked with tears, wept sincerity. Her lips, pouting and purple, rose and fell like an ocean swell. It was a moment that called for manly certainty, and Damon did his best to oblige.

'Sure,' he said, doubtful.

Her eyes round with purpose, oases of hope in a desert of longing.

'I've thought about it all. I could get a bar job down there, like you said. And you could do your design. You said you'd got the contacts, didn't you?'

Damon's heart sank. Today was going to be a long one, he thought. His mind wrestled with the

56

terrible admission that his only real contact was his mother, that he'd actually flunked all this year's exams, and that he'd been asked to resit them all in September or fail outright. It was a sobering prospect, and once again called for a manly response.

'Sure,' he said again. 'I just need a while to get myself sorted, that's all. When were you thinking of?'

Encouraged by his certainty, she went for the jugular.

'Tonight,' she said, and stared into the bright light of the day, half imagining herself in London already.

Damon's face blanched to the colour of snow. He nearly choked on the ice-cube he was sucking from her glass. This was more than trouble. He'd only suggested the whole thing to make her feel better. He was sick of the late-night phone calls, warning him off, and the looks of white-robed strangers out on Longsight Market: What are you doing, *ghora*?

'Tonight?' he asked. 'Isn't that a little bit sudden, Shazi? Why the rush?'

'I need to get away.'

Big emphasis on need. It sounded pretty final.

'You *were* serious, weren't you, Damon?'

He felt her eyes boring into him, trying to ascertain his mood, his conviction. To be honest, he was doing the same thing himself. What exactly were his feelings for Shazia? He looked long and hard at her, at her lustrous eyes and prominent lips, and realised a *big* factor here was her looks. He liked to pretend it wasn't but it was. There was no avoiding it. They had nothing in common. He was just getting started on this thought when Shazia kicked him under the table. Manly, remember.

'Okay,' he said, 'let's do it. We'll go tonight.'

Fuck.

He wondered where that had come from. And sat dejectedly. Taking responsibility, he kissed her passionately on the lips. To make himself feel better. The Asian behind the counter turned his nose up even further and muttered strange blasphemies into the steam. The prophet wouldn't be too happy about this.

'There's a train at ten tonight,' Damon said, ruffling his hair the way she liked. 'You are sure about this, aren't you?'

But he knew already. Of course she was. Her heart was leaping at the prospect. She was thinking of all the fine times coming, away from family, and the Al-Biswan, and Fat Umer, already preparing a new world on the shores of the old.

'Of course I am,' she said and looked at him. 'I love you, Damon. No-one's been as kind to me as you have.'

He squirmed.

As they stood up to leave, a police siren wailed high into the heat of the day. Another drive-by in Moss Side, or break-in in Longsight. No-one batted an eyelid, least of all the black boys on Great Western Street with their cars and Uzis. The days of account were still a long way off their calendars, the pull of a trigger away from oblivion, the lure of a deal away from a million. Shazia and Damon left together in a shower of confetti disguised as litter.

They walked down Wilmslow Road and turned into Park Crescent. All that was left of the old entrance to Victoria Park were the two battered and graffitied gateposts. The gates had long gone. Too many tramps pissing on them, too many kids kicking them, too many young lovers etching their temporary infatuations on their wooden beams.

'We came here when we were kids,' said Shazia, circling one of the old gateposts.

Damon shuffled his feet and thrust his hands deep into his pockets. Neither of them spoke for a few minutes.

'What happened?' he asked, finally.

She raised her eyes quizzically but knew very well what he was talking about.

'I've been fired. There was a problem with one of the chefs.'

Her voice sounded hollow, even to herself. She looked at Damon, at his fringe, his face, his tight T-shirt, and wondered what was different about him today. He seemed so distant. She sighed. She shouldn't expect too much. He had been loyal. All a girl could really hope for in these days of quick draws and bodily exchanges. More reliable than all the others, anyway. And her mind darkened, terrified that she might be on her own again. She looked into the blazing sky and saw birds reach the distant reaches of sight, gliding into infinity. That would be her, swooping down to London, going down to Buckingham Palace, eating ice creams in Hyde Park, watching the boats on the Thames. Amina's fiancé studied down there and he said the place just never stopped. It ate you up. You could just forget who you were and melt. Melt into the summer air, become somebody new again. Forget the pain.

Damon was still shuffling distractedly, as if he had things to do. She thought she might tell him everything, all that she desperately wanted to tell him but couldn't. The shame of the past hung over like a pall, threatening to crush her. But her angel spoke to her. Best to leave well alone, Shazia Ahmed, there'll be time enough to right the wrongs. There's always time.

Damon was staring at the gateposts and thinking about London.

'Shall we get your stuff, then?' he asked, trying to sound hopeful and organised, but with his brain whirring like a dynamo.

She stopped momentarily and caught his arm.

'Damon, there's something else.'

There was *always* something else. In her heart, she knew it. How much more could she ask of him? But Damon was prepared; he felt his heart couldn't sink any further.

'I rang my mum earlier. My dad's been taken ill. I said I'd go and see him.'

He was wrong. It could. Right into his stomach. Summer cupped its breath. The sound of cars being swallowed up.

'You're kidding,' he said slowly. 'Tell me you're kidding.'

And, for once, there was real irritation in his voice. Despair, even.

'I thought you were trying to get away from them?'

'I know,' she said, 'but my mother's desperate. I have to go.'

Damon groaned. *Desperate* was the word. It was getting worse.

'Shazia, listen to me. You're not thinking properly. The last time you saw him, you needed a police escort to get out. Your father's lost it. Look what we've been through. The flat, the hiding, the phone calls. How many times have we been warned? These guys aren't kidding, you know? Your father's out to get you. And me.'

She looked pained.

'I know, Damon, but he *is* my father. If he's poorly then I have to see him.'

Damon stood up, all the way up, and looked down on her pitiably.

'You're crazy, Shazi. No good will come of it, you know?'

And he made as if to walk off.

Shazia tried to grab him by the arm but he evaded her clutch. He was right. It was madness. Her father's moods were dark. Yet there was still that nagging voice in the back of her head, calling her back. That bloody sense of duty. Bloody *izzet*. Would she ever forgive herself if she never saw him again?

'I just need to see if he's okay, Damon. Please. You get everything together. I'll meet you later.'

Damon stared sadly at her. It felt like the ending of things. There'd be no more romps on his three-springed sofa at this rate.

'Shazi,' he said earnestly, 'let me come with you. You can't go on your own.'

But she shook her head. That was impossible.

They walked back to Wilmslow Road, back into the indifference of strangers, back into the real world. Shazia stared at her hands, at her long, brown fingers, and caught the gleam of gold between them. The sun burned it brightly.

'Look, Damon,' she said, and held up her marriage finger. 'This is all I have in the world. You're all I have in the world. Please.'

And he stared at her and the cheap zircon ring he'd bought her last autumn, and felt guilty. And not just because it was cheap. Darker clouds rumbled behind that, and he heard once more the rain falling on the window in Shazia's flat, and he was silent.

'Okay,' he said eventually, trying to banish the memory.

And she leaned over to kiss him.

'It's ours,' she said, 'it's our engagement ring. We're going to be married, remember.'

And she wasn't kidding. He felt the distance between them open like a fissure. Damon was facing an altogether unfamiliar world of responsibility. He looked down at the ring and felt numb. Too young, he thought; his father had made the same mistake, and paid the price. He wasn't about to do the same thing.

'Sure,' he said, 'but let's get to London first. I'm going to sort a few things out. I'll see you at the station. Quarter to ten. Don't be late.'

And he gave her a kiss on the lips and touched her hair.

'Shazi,' he said, as he walked away. 'Be careful.'

She looked after him as she'd looked after them all, departing from her life like she was marked EXIT. She stuck a stick of gum in her mouth and chewed vaguely, watching the figure of her lover vanish down Denison Road. She looked again at the gateposts and tried to read some of the graffiti on the stone. At first she couldn't find it, and thought maybe the wind and rain had worn it away, but, no, there it was, near the base of the left-hand post: *SA 4 PS Forever*. Written on a cold December day some four years ago. Carved in a black scrawl, she'd committed herself to eternity. With a baby growing inside her and the boy she loved beside her. She choked back the tears. She should have told Damon, of course, but that would come. Like her mother said, she'd be lucky if anyone'd look at her again.

63

He was all she had. What mattered now was London.

'Damon,' she whispered to herself. 'Please be there.'

And she looked up at the sky, the great wide heavens, for a sign that he would be.

CHAPTER 8

Azad Riaz sat smouldering in the back of his taxi, wondering where it had all gone wrong. There were plenty of clues. He could have picked any day out from his last, fruitless almost forty years on Earth. One, however, loomed larger than all the others, burned hotter than the giant magnifying glass of his memory. It was the sorry day he met Intikhab Khan.

He remembered it clearly. Intikhab, card sharp of the western world, had spotted him at Raffles Casino on Portland Street and stopped him from blowing another ton of stolen money. Had taken him under his wing and told him to stop wasting his time with all the other losers off the taxi ranks; they were small-time Teps, forever gambling the wives' housekeeping away. Told him to watch him, instead: the Desert Storm. Told him if he hung around, they'd both be very rich, claiming he'd learned some tricks in Yemen and Saudi with the sheikhs and sultans, sipping sherbet and cocaine on the terraces of the *nach ghar*. And he had, too. They cleaned every strip joint from here to Wigan Pier. Hard times turned to great expectations. The dreary monotony of the day, sweltering in black cabs, gave way to nights of magic and promise. Azad felt like Omar Sharif. Pretty girls aplenty flocked to his arms for one night only. Sat on the seat of his moustache. Just the way he liked it. Money bought him all the happiness he'd ever dreamed about. And more.

And then the rot set in. Intikhab's luck ran out. Allah had given them tools to destroy his enemies. Now Allah was taking them away. They'd been shown the truth. Every man's fate was fastened round his neck, the scroll of his misdemeanours spread before him. They'd built up debts of biblical proportion. Debts they could never hope to repay. And worse was to come.

Azad made a terrible discovery.

It seemed gambling wasn't the only un-Koranic habit Intikhab had imported from the mysterious east. Beneath that traditional exterior, the broad, Saddamite moustache and dark impassive glower, he'd developed a Westerner's licentiousness, too. Worshipped at the temple of Sodom. It would have turned any man's goat.

He took to cruising round Canal Street, picking them up. English boys. Fair on his dark body. Azad was appalled. And worried, too. One of his own prostrating himself like that. 'The wish of those who follow their lusts was that ye should turn away from Him,' the malvi had said. Just as he thought about filing for divorce, however, Intikhab came up with another plan.

An audacious plan. And Azad found himself listening again. No longer thicker than thieves, they would just *be* them. The plan was simple. They were going to hold each other's cabs up, stopping conveniently at prearranged locations and frisking the frightened passengers, swearing at them in Punjabi, punctuating their fierce, verbal tirades with *fucks* and *cunts* to heighten the realism. Azad was going to indulge in a bit of play-acting, too, groping the floor as Intikhab kicked him. The passengers would feel better they'd been spared such a beating and hand the dosh over. It couldn't fail. And it nearly didn't. Until Intikhab picked on an army of bull queens one night and nearly got them both killed. They just about escaped with their lives.

The days rolled by after that and Azad almost forgot about his 'friend', quite happy to idle away the rest of his life in the bookies with all the other sad Saqibs. Winter beckoned and still no contact. Then, in a flurry of snow and suggestions, Intikhab was back with another idea. They were going to join the sex industry. It all sounded very unlikely.

Azad stared at him. And knew he wasn't joking. But he listened all the same, especially when Intikhab said his brother-in-law had tried it in London, King's Cross or somewhere, and had now given up working. For a small fee they'd convert their cabs into portable brothels, tasteful curtains, that kind of thing. Every rent-boy in Manchester would use them. But, when the Prophet's words

67

came true, his stomach turned. As he watched heads bob up and down on the back seat, buoys tossing on stormy semen seas, he knew he'd entered hell.

Yes, it had all begun then. He'd dropped into the abyss the day he met him. Intikhab Khan was to blame.

Azad looked bleary-eyed into the day, his eyes moist with lack of sleep and tears. Shazia had long gone. He thought he maybe shouldn't have sold her out. Her father had been in touch a few weeks ago. Tempting him again. Always tempting him. He'd pay him if he got hold of her. Pay him a lot. Pay off his debts. He groaned and clutched his head. Poor Shazi. He wasn't in a right state. His gambling was killing him. He shouldn't have done it, he knew, but after last night. God. Last night was the ending of the world.

Intikhab had counted the money out as usual. Well over five hundred between them. Five hundred off what they owed. Azad was all for paying it there and then. He was being leaned on. The other Mr Khan in his life was not known for his patience. But Intikhab told him not to worry. He had good news. He was feeling lucky again. Azad had heard it a million times. And for the millionth time believed him. They drank in Prague Five and watched the world go by. One, two, five rounds. By the end of it, Azad was all for fucking some blonde girl at the end of the bar. Intikhab had his nose in the air, though. The smell of girls and perfume appalled him. They were off to Jezebel's.

Jezebel's casino on Whitworth Street was one small step down from a seaside amusement arcade. It was run by the ubiquitous Mr Saeed Khan, self-styled Bombay mogul and restaurateur, who owned several of the worst eateries on Wilmslow Road. At Jezebel's he held court over every wretched Paddy and Imran in south Manchester. Cheap loans his speciality. It had also been the scene of Intikhab's finest hour. One night he'd swiped ten grand from off the tables. The other Mr Khan was not best pleased.

And here they were again, on a roll like the old days. Azad sensed the evening was going to be very best night of his life. Four thousand and counting. Mr Khan was on hand to see it. Mr Khan, who'd extended his generous palms out to them when they were in need. The Muslim way. His brothers in trouble. He'd lent them the money they didn't have, befriended them, warned them against the dangers of gambling. Then came down on them like a tiger.

Dressed in white suit and tie, he flashed diamantine smiles at the charivari of cocktail guests. The wild Irish losers, the English gentlemen with their frosty smiles and equally unlovely wives, the Asian businessmen in their immaculately contoured suits, the casually vacuous waitresses and prostitutes draped feline over their strong arms. Mr Khan always got his money back.

At five thousand he smiled politely and shrugged his shoulders. They were almost quits. Azad looked at Intikhab who looked at Mr Khan and hoped they'd leave it there. But Mr Khan waved his arms over the table like a genie, indulgently.

'Here's your chance, boys,' he said. 'You can wipe me out.'

And Intikhab grinned.

Azad closed his eyes. And prayed.

Intikhab played.

And lost.

All their credit and more. The hand of God had dealt him an awful one. Azad couldn't believe it. Wouldn't believe it. Intikhab was on a roll. He never lost like that. Where were they going to get the money? Mr Fucking Khan's lips curled cruelly. Allah could only be so merciful.

Intikhab was apoplectic with shock.

They had nothing.

A few brutish-looking Sikhs, gangsters all, approached the table. Mr Khan asked them to escort his friends to the bank. But Intikhab held his hand up. He hadn't finished. Another idea. Azad groaned. He raised his eyes upwards in prayer. It was getting worse. He knew what was coming.

Mr Khan was delighted with it. Azad's stomach churned.

'Trust me,' said Intikhab.

In truth, Azad had no alternative. He couldn't repay the original loan. He looked round the room for sympathetic faces. Fat chance. Every gambler hates a gambler. Every loser thinks the same. He carefully balanced the scales in his mind. What he could lose, what he could gain. He thought briefly of his wife and children at home. Very briefly. Then he thought of a brand-new house and a brand-new life. And a dozen *ghori* doing his bidding on Persian rugs.

The fans above whirred vainly against the summer heat. Sweat broadcast itself on every forehead. Mr Khan continued to smile. His friends continued to stare impassively. Intikhab had his eyes closed. He was surely on a roll.

'Okay,' Azad said, 'the house.'

On the stroke of one, the world ended.

Mr Khan insisted they gamble separately. He liked his odds. They'd do it the Asian way. Highest card takes all.

'Let's trust to Allah,' he said.

And drew the Ten of Spades. He grinned.

Intikhab pulled. The Ace of Hearts! His luck *was* in. There were gasps all round.

Azad's fingers were podgy with sweat. He cut. And drew.

Intikhab covered his eyes.

There were titters.

The Four of Clubs. He hung his head. Every loser thinks the same.

Azad had hanged himself.

Mr Khan wished them a cordial evening. It was nice doing business. Intikhab put his arm on

71

Azad's shoulder and said they'd think of something but Azad wasn't listening. He was thinking whereabouts on God's Earth he was going to hide. He watched Intikhab get back into his taxi and drive off up Canal Street. The Ace of fucking Hearts. What magic was that? Unholy man. He looked up at the stars and predicted a bleak day to come. Hard times and all that.

Azad Riaz put his head in his hands and glowered wretchedly. Last night was the end of everything. And Shazia had just paid for it.

CHAPTER 9

The moment Shazia heard her mother sobbing on the other end of the phone, she knew she'd end up going back. For peace of mind, if nothing else. Damon was right, of course. It would be a dangerous waste of time.

She hailed a black cab on Wilmslow Road and thought just that. She watched as it sped down Wilbraham Road, past a long, dreary line of council houses and over the Parkway to the detached Edwardian mansions of Whalley Range. Iron gates and paved forecourts addressed six-bedroomed affairs occupied by Rusholme restaurateurs and rag-trade millionaires. Lawyers, accountants, doctors, Asians on the up. All very respectable. Unlike waitresses. Shazia took her last stick of gum out. She knew their type. The toil of past generations, pulling family and friends together in a Longsight corner shop, didn't always figure in the calculations of these aspiring, young entrepreneurs. The new Jacuzzi upstairs was as likely the result of drug-dealing, tax evasion, and fraudulent insurance claims, as it was the sweat of a thousand underpaid factory workers. She'd seen it all herself. Shady Paki couriers in silver convertibles making a beeline to Rusholme straight from Manchester Airport. Suitcases full of Afghan horse. The restaurants provided them very good cover.

She found it hard to believe that any of her father's generation, her uncles in tank tops and sideburns, the aunts with their thick-rimmed spectacles and whitened faces, would have considered such a living. Apart from Mamoo Azad, maybe. They were too intent on maintaining the frayed ends of their lives. She remembered how shocked she'd been, playing in the garden long ago, when uniformed officers had taken Johnny Singh away next door. He'd attacked a woman at a bus shelter one night, and never come back.

How different now. All the Asian boys were like that. Acting like badass, gangsta rappers, shuffling their shoulders, mumbling to themselves in Tyson incomprehensibility. Their parents bridled, of course, taut with fear of the new, but the old dispensations had gone. *Respect*, not respectability, was the guideline from above. Shazia had seen it all. The new breed.

The taxi hurtled into the blue. Shazia blinked and felt the caress of the warm air on her arms. They were nearly there. A row of run-down Victorian terraces on the Chorlton border. She told the driver to pull up. A dozen or so Pakistani kids were playing cricket between the parked cars. Up and down, chasing like dervishes the fugitive ball, chasing it to the gates of a nearby house. Shazia looked at it from beneath her black fringe. Her parents' house. An apple tree stood silently in the small front garden. It was now or never.

She thought for a second.

It was now. She got out.

The cricket game started anew. Doubt assailed her at every step. The taxi was pulling away. She should go back. Back to Damon. But fate intervened. As she was about to turn, the ball landed at her feet and a girl of about ten appeared before her. Grinning broadly.

It was Yasmin. Her sister. There was no going back. The stylus of her thoughts jumped on the words and kept repeating them.

'Come home,' her mother had said, 'before it's too late, *beti. Come home.*'

The porch door was half open. Shazia's head brushed against a Medusa-like hanging basket of vines and creepers. Yasmin peeped through the letter box for signs of life. Shazia heard whispers and giggles behind it.

'*Bhai*, let us in. *Bhaji*'s here.'

The door was flung wide and two boys gaped silently at her. The elder, in his early twenties, had a thick shock of unruly hair and the fugitive beginnings of a beard. He had dark, discoloured eyes with thick, exotic lashes. Hard to penetrate. Harder to fathom. Adnan had always been like that. The younger boy, Anjum, was different; he could hardly contain his excitement and appeared on the point of crying.

'You're back then, *bhaji*,' Adnan said, finally. '*Abu*'s been dying to see you.'

Stung and hurt, his tone was defensive. And the stress on the word *dying*, did she imagine that?

She percolated with self-doubt.

'Where's Mum?'

Anjum raced to the back of the house from where the familiar aroma of *methi* and *keema* clipped her nostrils. Adnan invited her into the living room. Formally, like a bloody waiter. She was greeted by her own reflection. A huge, gold-framed mirror hung on the far wall. There was a solitary, wooden coffee table in the middle, covered with that protective plastic sheeting her mother was so fond of. Murals on either side of her, woven with quotations from the Qur'an, hung like angel's wings over her. She felt she was being sentenced.

She looked out the window. The sun was trying to penetrate the apple tree's broad leaf gown. There were whispered voices outside the living-room door. Speaking in tongues. She turned as it opened. And was shocked. It was her mother. Or used to be. She looked like a ghost, the last, faint echoes of beauty long erased from her face, the white plastered make-up streaked with tears.

'*Beti*,' she said. 'You've come.'

She held out her hands for Shazia to take.

Shazia stared at them, the long tapering fingers encircled with gold and diamond. Cold hands, she thought. No.

Rejected, her mother's arms folded gracefully to her sides like wings closing on air. She pursed her lips.

'Adnan, tell your father his daughter is here. She has returned. And bring us some drinks, too, *beta*.'

Adnan left carefully, all the while staring at Shazia.

Her mother sat down, a burning orchid framed by the high-backed sofa, and invited her to sit beside her.

'You broke your father's heart, *beti*, you know that?'

Shazia remained standing. *That didn't take long.* She moved to the mirror, half expecting to see a witch in her mother's place. Mirrors didn't lie.

'He broke mine, *ami*. He threw me out. And worse.'

Her mother paused.

'But he invited you back, *beti*. Twice. No-one asked you to live on your own. No-one wanted you to, either. You could have stayed with your uncles, or Aunt Saima in Blackburn. We all wanted what was best for you.'

Best? Shazia felt her indignation grow, flaming to anger. She counted the seconds of frustration out.

'You wanted to get rid of me, mother, marry me off at sixteen to cousins I'd never even seen. Specky Teps in need of a visa. Bloody hell! How could that be best for me?'

Her mother bolted upright. Fire meeting fire.

'Don't dare speak like that, Shazia. What are you saying? Your cousins are all good men. You know that.'

Shazia scoffed.

'They're all bloody Teps, *ami*. Typical Pakis. Expecting some quiet little girl who'll cook for them all day and bring up their fifteen children. Why would I want that?'

'Why?' her mother echoed incredulously. 'Why? For a home, *beti*, for your happiness. What else do you want?'

To get away, Shazia thought. *Now*. To London.

There was a pause. Her mother was shaking still.

'And what about us, Shazi? Your parents. What are we to do in all this? Do we not count?'

Shazia stared at her hard. No.

'We hear terrible things, Shazi. People look at us in the street and the shame it brings, the shame on me and your father. What do we say to them?'

Shazia felt her anger blaze again.

'Tell them to fuck off,' she said.

The air went dead. Her mother blanched in horror, unbelieving.

'What language is that?' she whispered. 'Have you no shame, *beti*? Have we failed you so utterly?'

And the tears swelled in her eyes, the lips quivering in well-rehearsed union. Then, more calmly, and strangely, she collected herself.

'Yet I still hope,' she said. 'You've come here today, haven't you, Shazi? That's what counts.'

But before Shazia could interject, Adnan came in with a silver tray, piled high with glasses and juice, a bowl of almonds, and a plate of neatly sliced fruit. He placed it on the wooden table.

'Shall I pour, *ami*?' he asked.

'No, thank you, *beta*. Have you told your father?'

'Yes,' he said. 'He's sitting up now.'

'Then you know what to do?'

'Yes, *ami*.'

Adnan looked quizzically at her for a moment and seemed about to say something.

'Go now, *beta*,' his mother urged.

She poured two glasses out, her right hand gesturing to the nearer. Then silence, the ominous calm before a storm. Upstairs, in her father's room, grey clouds were gathering. Behind her, the blue of freedom. Out there beyond the apple tree were the open spaces of the sky. Just a few more minutes.

'What happened?'

Her mother looked at her.

'To your father, *beti*? It's his heart. The strain of the last few years and you living away, it's been too much for him.'

Pursing her lips for dramatic effect, Mrs Ahmed took the stage like a seasoned professional. The Bollywood spotlight. *Dil Se*. The closing number.

'He had an attack, Shazi. It's left him very weak.'

Though the words exploded into Shazia's mind with the fury of her father's fists, the expected pain didn't materialise. Just numbness. A strange amniotic calm. Her body was still again and she bathed once more in the broken waters of terrible memories. Hospitals, chloroform, pain, death. Her pain, his anger. Her loss. The pain she should have felt, the immense sadness, these were set beside it. She remembered it all and was quiet.

'Have you nothing to say?' her mother said finally. 'No words of comfort?'

Uttered like a challenge.

Shazia thought very carefully for two seconds. She hadn't. Ruefully, she remembered the knock on the back of her head the last time she'd been here. Mother had been peacemaker, then. Just that once. She'd probably saved her life. Her father would have dragged her into hell if he'd been able, burnt the demons out of her, swaddled her in cloths of black and kept her locked in some dank room till she came to her senses. *Shame*, he'd cried. His own daughter. *Izzet*, no more. The police had to restrain him physically. No mean feat. He had the authority of Allah.

'Mother, do you want me to see him? That's what I came for.'

Mrs Ahmed looked at her. The way Adnan had looked at her. And nodded.

'Just once, Shazi, it's for the best.'

And they left the faded front room and went into the hall where Yasmin, Anjum and Adnan were gathered. Shazia noticed the smiles were gone. Even Anjum's. A terrible sense of foreboding gripped her. You'd have thought they were here for the funeral.

CHAPTER 10

Dru Round was watching Great Morning TV when the call came. He'd been expecting it. A small, white card had been left in his dressing room last night. Nothing fancy. Just a name: Reg Naylor. And a logo: Granada Media. And three words: 'I'll call you.' Dru turned the card over in his hands and examined it more carefully. He'd been working for this moment for as long as he could remember. Blagging, bragging, digging, shafting. How else does a boy get on?

Reg Naylor. Dru knew him well. He was a permanent fixture on the cardigan gay scene, settling into middle-age waste and greying at the temples. Friday or Saturday night, he'd be at the New Union or upstairs at the Rembrandt, eyeing up the teeny-fags and pretty boys. Knowing, tragically, that this was as close as he'd get to them. Dru had seen the type a thousand times before. After a few months, a year maybe, they disappeared for good, back to their families, back to their hobbies, back to work, dousing the flames they knew would never go out. Dru liked them a lot. Their conversation was always refined, intelligent, cultured; adjectives he'd never use to describe the screaming vacuity of TV leather boys and peanut-brained queens. They were commentators, just like him, sadly reflecting on a world that had long deserted them.

He stared mutely at the television. There was one of those screaming types on Great Morning TV right now. Blonde wig, innuendo, and triple entendres. All Dru could do was grimace. He imagined all the boys in India House wetting themselves over this kind of thing, their critical faculties suspended. The Gay Lobotomy, he called it. The day, usually round their sixteenth birthday, when they stopped thinking for themselves and started listening to every new pop sensation with the cringing adoration of a ten year-old-girl, the day they developed gay sign language and high-pitched squeals as a means of communication, the day they stopped reading and fighting and joined the masses on Gay Pride marches. Out and Proud. Sing it loud.

Dru felt like throwing up. Partly because of the excitement, and partly because of the uneasy mixture of booze, spliffs and cum in his gut. He opened the French windows and walked on to the balcony. The spires and roofs of Didsbury bathed in the most glorious blue June day he could remember. Trees were alive with the chatter of birds, gardens rich in the folds of green earth. And the sky limitless overhead, promising everything.

Dru felt the sickness subside. He had only just sat down again when the call came.

'Dru, dear, is that you?'

It was Reg. Polite. Articulate.

High up in his office at Granada Media, he, too, was watching the company's flagship programme. He viewed the inane frivolity with a slightly patronising air. And despaired. Great Morning TV? The best the network could offer? It was unspeakable. As was the rest of the station. He'd had ten emails just yesterday from the men at the top congratulating him, and everybody else in the Granada group, on the success of all their latest programmes. Viewing figures, marketing share, were all up by 1%. And don't forget to click on and watch Davina Bland present a special World in Need tonight. Loads of special guests were popping in. They'd be pledging to charity.

1%? Reg knew exactly what that meant. It meant they were all in trouble. It meant a lot of focus meetings and an increase of 100% in the horse-shit department. He sighed. He'd been on the way out for ten years. How he kept his job was a mystery even to himself. He was one of the old breed and he knew it. Young London media darlings had swept through every corridor with their focus groups and market-response tables. Brand marketing. Television, they told him, was no longer about programmes. It was about commodities. Computer screens appeared overnight. The world went on-line. Reg switched off.

He hated it all. The one comfort was that it would soon all be over. He would go out with a bang. Which is where Dru came in.

'Now, listen, Dru,' he said, 'I think we've got a slot for you. But they need to see you tonight. What do you say?'

Dru gulped. What did he say? What could he say? Yes, thank you, I'll take it. I'll be good. I'll do the best fucking show you've ever seen. He didn't need to mull it over. Whether it was grabbing the bull by the horns, or the horn of some fat bull queer, there was no time to waste thinking.

'Is there anything I should leave out?' he said.

'Oh no, dear. I don't think so. Just be yourself. That's what we love about you.'

And just what Reg was banking on. The terribly regimented morality of corporate thinking, 'we cannot offend this or that minority', 'we need to support our sponsors', 'we need to appeal to this or that market', struck him as being so terribly shortsighted. But, not having the cocksure convictions of the recently graduated, and being brought up in a world where grace and humility were still the mark of a man, he'd struggled to get his voice heard. Dru was about his very last shot. He'd been given a remit by one of the governors, a dear old friend from way back at Manchester Grammar School, to produce a short series on the city called Gay Life. He'd already scripted it. Alone. All he needed was the blessing of Rupert

St Clair, the fast-track twenty-something head of Granada Drama Development, to approve the content.

'I'm bringing someone tonight, Dru. He'll want to meet you afterwards, I think. He's a bit green about your kind of thing but he'll probably think it okay. Buy the gay pound and that kind of nonsense. Is that all right?'

Always so polite, always so civil. If only every other fucker he dealt with had Reg's manners, the world would be a finer place, Dru thought. He started playing with himself beneath his dressing gown. Yeah, if only everyone had Reg's manners, his old public-school charm. He circled his right hand round the shaft and gave it a few vigorous pumps.

'There's something else, dear.'

Dru stopped immediately. There was *always* something else.

'I'll need you to go on about ten.'

Dru felt his prick visibly shrink in his hand, retreating into the cave between his thighs.

'What for?' he started. 'No-one's even in at ten.'

'I know, dear,' Reg confided, 'but these Oxbridge types like everything done at a decent hour. They really don't like waiting. Do you think you can manage it?'

'Have I a choice?' Dru asked.

There was a slight pause at the other end. Dru thought it might have been irritation.

'No, dear, I'm afraid not. Be good now.'

Reg hung up and looked out over the tops of the city, the way he'd looked out over them every day for the past twenty years. Everything had changed. Hardly any of his old haunts remained. The world had exchanged its pie shops for pretzel bars, its shady Victorian locals for wine bistros. Even the Gay Village had moved on. Ghosts of friends and seldom lovers now walked the lamp-lit canal paths, the forlorn majesty of Victorian façades sadly reflected in the dizzy glass exteriors of Clubland. Now it was his turn. He'd soon be on his way, too, down Peter Street, down Memory Lane, till the world forgot about him.

Dru put the phone down and thought he might need some coke, fast. It was not the prospect of performing that worried him, but the fact that nobody would be there to see him. What point was there in being an artist if you had no audience?

He took his dressing gown off and weighed himself up in the large mirror along the far wall. The shimmer of the curtains sent gentle waves rippling across the tanned beach of his body. Spot-check at near thirty. Still chiselled perfection and square jaw. He'd be like this for another thirty. The simpering fag-boys would still want him, want to suck his dick. Not for him the graceless slide into oblivion. He switched the television off. Great Morning TV had finished. He had the rest of the day to think about.

Still naked, he went out on to the balcony once more and fought the glare of the sun. Millions of miles away, giant nuclear explosions ripped through its sunken belly and sent cosmic flickers of radiation towards him, but all Dru could feel was its warmth, waiting for new birth. The birth of a new star, here on earth.

He stared at the gardens down below, at their beautiful green serenity.

I wonder what it would be like to die, he thought.

CHAPTER 11

Mrs Ahmed led them upstairs, the floor-boards underneath her buckling and creaking alarmingly. Shazia watched the soft pad of her feet, her heart beating quickly. She was taken past the open bathroom door and saw the usual tangled mass of bed linen hanging over the shower rails. At least that hadn't changed. Then, turning, she was led to the end of the landing. Her parents' room.

'Come, *beti*,' her mother said, and led the way in.

It was a twilit world. Huge and heavy grey curtains hung like darkened shrouds across the window. The room was unadorned save for a single photograph, massively enlarged on one wall. Shazi struggled to make it out. Her father, his finely tuned moustache curling apologetically, his face dark and sombre. His wedding day. And beside him, her mother, improbably veiled in red silks, her lustrous eyes burning somewhere in the midst of oblivion.

For Shazia, it was like walking into a picture postcard, one of those black and white ones they sold in old bookshops on Shudehill, depicting scenes of Victorian Manchester. Nothing had changed and she was a little girl again, tiptoeing into her parents' room and hearing her father's snores in the dead of night, hearing her mother moan and talk to herself in a strange tongue, then fleeing back into her own room, vaulting over her sleeping sister lest the ghosts under the bed get her. The present was gone. Here dwelt only the past, memories upon memories piled on top of one another in every shadowy corner and, in the midst of it all, like some old and patient spider caught in the folds of its own web, was their archivist. Her father. He was propped up in bed, his hands resting on the folded sheets. In the gloom it was hard to tell whether he was awake or not. The craters of his eyes were filled with the deeper shadows of night. His head was turned towards her, rigid, like a beheaded Red Indian totem warning her away. The silence was disturbed by the rustling of cloth. Shazia's mother ghosted past her like the *Marie Celeste* and took up moorings on her husband's left side. She kissed his forehead and held his hand, passing her other one over his eyes. She whispered some words into his ear and he craned his neck to the light, slowly and purposefully, straining every muscle to meet the music of its sound. His lips peeled back and repeated the words, the words that had woken the sleeper from his dark.

'Shazi's home?'

Tears welled in Shazia's eyes. Defiance replaced by confusion and duty.

'Come to me, Shazi,' her father pleaded, and held his bony fingers out longingly.

She retraced the steps to his bedside, this time to his right.

'You're really here, *beti*? You've come home to save me?'

Silence. Her eyes were resting on his prostrate form.

He gasped for breath.

'You should never have left me, *beti*. Not the way you did.'

And despite herself, Shazia couldn't stop them, the tears coursing down her cheeks. Her mother motioned to her to take her father's hands. They were clammy, excited things. And strong, too. Feverishly strong. Hands didn't lie.

'You left me, Daddy, left me when I needed you most. What was I meant to do?'

He looked at her.

'Meant, Shazi?' he said. 'I think you know that.'

And he grimaced, rolling his eyes upwards. Sighing deeply.

'But I'm paying for it now. I can't change things, *beti*, can I? Nobody can.'

And he coughed and spluttered slightly, eyeing her under the dark compass of his lids. He gestured to his wife and she helped him upright, fluffing several pillows behind him. He lay there and studied the walls of the room, waving vaguely at the children in the doorway. Adnan nodded and took Yasmin by the hand. Anjum followed meekly, staring.

In the opaque half-light it was hard to be sure of anything but it seemed to Shazia he was more animated now. She found herself listening carefully, as she had as a child, the words flitting like bats in some forgotten antechamber of her mind.

'I know I've done wrong, Shazi. I know I've done things a father shouldn't. But I want to be friends again. Please. Before it's too late.'

He paused.

'I don't have much time, Shazi. I wanted to say sorry.'

Sorry?

His wife stroked his temple, grown feverish in anticipation. Shazia's throat clenched at the unexpectedness of the transformation. Now, more than ever, she wished for some gum. Her mouth was parched, like burning papyrus.

'I want you to do something for me, *beti*,' he said, 'just a little something. It isn't much, I think, and I'll *leave* happier if you agree to it.'

The lump in Shazia's throat dropped into her stomach, made inroads on her bowels. Leave?

'I want you to live a respectable life again, Shazi. If not at home, here with your family, then at least with a good man who'll look after you.'

He anticipated the revolt in her eyes and held his arm aloft.

'Yes, *beti*, I know, but I won't interfere this time. You can choose.'

Shazia looked at her father fading into the darkness. His features blurred till she was staring at a hole, and from that hole was replayed endlessly the echo of that last word: interfere. A cold certainty gripped her, a feeling of déjà vu a million times over. All he'd ever done was interfere. This was no parley or peace talk. She looked at the ghostly outline of her mother, her pursed lips all serious and trembling and expectant, and knew she'd done the wrong thing.

'You don't understand, Dad,' she whispered, perilously close. 'I'm not coming back. I can't. I'm sorry.'

And she gathered her thoughts quickly and made ready to leave. Then realised she couldn't. Her hands were being held back. Tightly. Cold hands were encircling her. Reeling her in. Bait on a line.

'You're not, *beti*?' her father said. 'I'm sorry to hear that.'

And his eyes flickered.

'Come, then, Shazi, you and I, before you go, come and tell me. Tell me what you're going to do with yourself? Will you continue to bring shame on us?'

And his words were dark. No longer a frail, old man, he was coming to life before her eyes. Shazia struggled to pull away. He was going to kill himself, have another seizure. The gravestone covers were thrown back, the pillows removed from behind him, his voice firmer and more measured, as if rousing itself from some great sleep.

'Is that what you want?' he went on, raising it in the first squalls of anger.

Shazia tugged as hard as she could, panic setting in. But met iron. Like trying to pull a ship. Then looked at her mother for help. Like staring into steel. And then, worse. Her father was getting up. And walking. Dead man walking. Dead man rising. Her own heart nearly gave out.

'You'll drag me into the gutter, won't you?' he said. 'Do you think I'm blind to what you get up to, Shazia Ahmed? We have eyes, you know. And ears. You're still my daughter, not some white boy's whore. You're dancing on your father's grave, treading my name into the dust. Now tell me, what will bring you back to us?'

The weight of Islam was in every word. She threw all her weight against it, panic rising all the time.

'Let me go, Dad,' she said. 'You'll end up back in hospital.'

But he smiled, and it was like a sickle being drawn across the sky, slicing the heavens open. Realisation hit like a dead weight in the stomach. It was so obvious.

'You're kidding,' she said, 'tell me you're kidding!' How could she be so stupid? 'Tell me you're really ill. Tell me you haven't set me up again. What the hell do you want? Don't you understand? I'm *never* coming home. Now let go of me.'

But the arms held her fast. She was too slight, too weak, powerless in their grip.

'Don't fight me, Shazia Ahmed, it's for the best. Let me finish this.'

But Shazia was going mad, squirming like an eel. Desperate for life.

'Finish? What are you talking about, finish? Just let me, will you? *Ami*, tell him. Tell him he can't do this,' but her mother's lips were shut tight, a veil of denial drawn up over them. There was now naked fear in Shazia's voice for the second time that day. Why the hell had she come? Oh, Damon, why?

But she was too late.

The slap came out of the blue, like a whale fin smacking against the waves. For a second she just stared. Then the smarting pain, and the rush of electric sparks in her cheeks, hit her. Stunned with shock, the world spun before her.

Smack! Another blow. Smack! And another. Her assailant was behind her. She raised her arms to defend herself and then realised she couldn't. They were no longer attached. Nothing seemed attached. The last blow sent her spinning to the ground. Down and down into the inferno. But, as she fell, her eyes caught those of her attacker. And they could hardly believe it. Between the fast-closing lids, her brother's face was framed, tearful and pained. Adnan. His mouth was moving, silently so, whispering, did she imagine the words?

'*Bhaji*, it's for the best.'

CHAPTER 12

Ashraf Ahmed had had enough. All his long life it seemed he'd had enough. He'd spent every one of his years from ten to thirty working in dingy, old factories in Ardwick Green, sweeping floors, cleaning toilets, and making coffee and tea for a shop floor full of racist bastards who thought he'd swung from a tree. And all the years since working the same shifts for Paki bastards who paid him half as much again. The bosses must have thought they were back in Lahore, paying in rupees. Not that anyone complained. You couldn't. Low wages, high output. No strikes, massive profits. For years it was like that. Plenty of work. Till every other ruthless Asian entrepreneur dipped his hand in the Ras Malai and left them all fighting over the milk. The monopoly broken, Ashraf didn't even get past Go.

Every Friday and Saturday night he'd console himself by heading down to Rusholme for a fish and chip supper. They showed Indian films at the cinema on the corner of Dickenson Road. The wind and rain blew them all into a huddle, looking up at the billboards. Amitabh Bachchan in *Zanjeer*.

Special double-bill *Tonight*. In those days there was no cross-community nonsense. Everyone seemed happy. East really was East. Each picture brought the old country back home.

Ashraf married when he was twenty-eight, a good age for a man, but not when you were broke, a fact not lost on his father, who couldn't find anybody for him. It was left to Auntie Preveen to sort him out. And she'd done so the only way a woman knows how: by some creative manipulation of the figures. His bride to be, a great local beauty, was only fifteen and doing her O levels. Just the kind of girl that would cause him trouble. Trouble because she had brains, and brains in a woman was one sure quality he'd end up hating her for. Especially if she had to set them aside to marry a loser like him.

God, he'd had enough all right, but then, out of the ether one day, he found the answer to all his problems. He'd split open a pomegranate over the dinner table and seen a holy Koranic letter in the squelch of pith and pip. The local malvi confirmed it; it had divine nature. Ashraf turned to Islam with the zeal of the newly converted. It answered his every need. It forced his new wife Mina to stop answering him back, and excused his poverty and ignorance as an act of Allah. Indeed, he began to feel it might have made him closer to Allah than if he'd been a rich and successful businessman like Mr Naveed, the gold-encrusted monster who owned the fabrics factory where he worked. Allah and the mosque gave him purpose, and he burned with a self-righteous fire ever after, forgetting the billboards and fish and chips, and forgetting he was ever in England at all.

He thought his children would do him justice, would respect the Qur'an that he habitually held, and would follow him into adulthood as good Muslims. His eldest, Adnan, was growing into a fine man, respected by all the elders at the mosque. When, as a little boy, he'd joined him at prayers in the living room, facing the wall that pointed to Mecca, his heart had swelled with pride, secure in the knowledge that he was walking down the righteous path. And when his son erred, Ashraf stood over him like a prophet of steel and disciplined him with iron blows while Mina, face pained and tearful, wept behind her veil and prayed that Allah would be merciful.

But Allah was not merciful. Not for Ashraf. While his first child was a stone he could wield and hew with military precision, his second was an uncut diamond, impervious to all his sledge-hammer brutality. His daughter, Shazia, had always been trouble. And he remembered when it all started.

The cold, wintry blasts had sent sheets of snow and hail across the world, carpeting the roads with a film of down. Shazia was across the road, staring at the purple and red Christmas decorations in the windows of the houses opposite, peering through the glass at pointed Christmas trees glowing in the midwinter grey. One of the old ladies had come out and given her something. He watched her race back across the road, clutching it tightly to her chest, and run indoors.

And when he came up at bedtime, his thoughts grew darker still. In the quiet, cold grey of her room, beside the bottom bunk where she slept, Shazia had placed a miniature Christmas tree. She'd put some sweets around it, delicate wrappings for a delicate girl. Ashraf looked at it, horrified. His faith tested. The barbarians were at the gates. What was his daughter thinking? He picked the tree up and examined it closely. The smell of pine made him choke. *Haram* Christian nonsense. He had to show them. Show them the will of Allah. The tree was crushed in his mighty hands. Yes, he thought, it had begun then.

And it didn't stop there. Shazia was trouble thereafter, a permanent distraction at the local mosque. Never sitting still. More interested in chatting to her friends than saying her *namaz*. When asked to recite passages of the Qur'an back to the malvi she'd blow bubble gum behind her veil. She didn't understand Arabic, didn't want to understand it. And when she grew into a teenager, God forbid, she seemed keener on that horrible pop music than on prayer. His house of the Lord was being undermined by his own flesh and blood.

And then, one day, all hell broke loose. Satan's winged minions plunged their claws into his heart.

His daughter, his *beti*, was pregnant. *Pregnant?* At first he thought it was some divine conception like those Christian Infidel talked about (how else could it have happened?), but Mina, rational and studious to the last, showed him how it couldn't be; if he really believed that, it would make him more than half a Christian himself. Besides, she said, Shazia probably became pregnant the way girls always became pregnant. She'd had sex with a boy. Stunned by her words, Ashraf gave her a blow to the head. Allah was certainly not merciful with her this time. Nor with him.

When the outrage and disgrace had simmered for a day, the official inquiry was launched and a tearful, though still defiant Shazia, was hauled up before her father's court. To face his decidedly *un*popular music.

Ashraf remembered it now as he stared at his daughter's prostrate form, lying there in her shalwar kameez, with a veil over her face to disguise the wounds. He once more felt the shock of that fearful blow, the words which tore at his faith and made him sick to the core.

'Who was it, Shazia?' he'd said, with thunder in his eyes. 'Who made you do this?'

But Shazia's eyes glazed over. Her mother's haughty beauty seemed etched in every line of her face until it was no longer a shape he recognised.

'He didn't make me, father. I wanted to.'

Wanted to? Shame and hate ate him up. The *jinn* were out. The blow smote her like the arm of God

101

and she crumpled to earth. The madness took him. Mina tried to intervene but he threw her away.

'*Kaun tha?*' he screamed, blind to everything else. 'Who?'

And, as she was knocked headlong into hell, the name tripped out. Paul.

Paul?

Ashraf stood dumbstruck, heaving from the unequal struggle and the guilt of his violence. He felt sick to his very soul. *Paul?* A *ghora* with his daughter? He needed to wash, to cleanse himself from the calumny and disgrace. He needed Allah to guide him through it. He left to pray, leaving Mina to console his now defiled daughter.

Yes, he remembered where it all began. Only too clearly.

Bright sunlight cascaded into the room and lit Shazia's face, or at least that part not now disguised by the black dupatta. Mina had dressed her the way she should always have been, covered from the eyes of men, the Islamic way, away from the foul and corrupting influences that had brought her here in the first place. And here he was, with his daughter finally at rest before him, finally able to put the whole thing to one side, able at last to escape the ridicule of the community, to walk down the street again and imagine the last few years were but a long and bad dream.

He was going to send her away. He should have done it years ago. Mina was on the far side of the room and her veil barely disguised her tears.

'Be strong,' he warned her. 'Be strong, *begum*.'

When Ashraf opened the door to the living room, he knew he was playing out the endgame. Two men, their eyes screened by sunglasses, their hair slicked back, sat still on the sofa like storefront mannequins. They rose in unison to meet him and snaked out their hands with uniform precision. Both wore gloves but made no attempt to remove them. Ashraf knew their names and type, and that the rest of his carefully laid plan depended upon their discretion. He also knew that discretion was an expensive commodity in the community and was as likely to turn around and bite you. Money always did that.

'*Salaam alaykum*, Mr Ahmed,' said the taller. 'You called us.'

'*Han-ji*,' he replied, nervously. 'Which one of you is Aftab?'

He looked from one to the other, trying to make them out.

One of the men took off his glasses, revealing the remains of a broad and handsome face. He'd been through a lot. Ashraf recognised in it the face of his cousin in Lahore.

'I knew your father,' he said confidentially, hoping to calm himself.

Aftab nodded. Then pointed to his companion.

'This is Tariq,' he said. 'He'll make sure she gets through if something happens to me.' He paused.

103

'Are you *sure* this is what you want, Mr Ahmed? There's no going back from here.'

Ashraf swallowed despite himself. It was strange to find himself answerable again. He'd forgotten what it was like to be frightened.

'You understand, Mr Ahmed,' the man continued, 'that if anything should go wrong, things could get nasty. The trail will lead back to you and we can't help you there, unfortunately.'

Ashraf stared long and hard at him.

'Yes, but nothing will go wrong, will it? That's why I hired you. Why I spoke to your father. He said I could trust you boys. "They've done this before," he said. "Many times."'

Indeed they had. Aftab Akhtar and Tariq Ali were seasoned runners with long acquaintance of the import/export game: in heroin and bodies. They had 'political' backing. A litany of shootings and stabbings in Karachi and Lahore had been conveniently overlooked by more than one circuit judge there, despite the trail not so much leading to them as shaking them by the hand. Many of the retail factories in south Manchester were set up as legitimate cover for the games they played. It didn't matter to them that the legal side of the business was haemorrhaging debt; that made it more convincing. The real power brokers in the area were the drug-mullahs, the Mercedes-driven nawabs from Leicester, Bradford and Cheshire, who rolled into the factories once a month to order a consignment or two. The latest designs were always popular. The restaurants, too, proved most useful; distribution was so much easier over coffee than some lockup in Longsight. Public places were much harder to police.

Ashraf knew what he was letting himself in for before he'd even rung his cousin. He wouldn't have got that idiot brother-in-law Azad involved otherwise. Shazia needed a husband. And fast. He was being made a laughing stock. There'd recently been some bastard cock-ups both in Pakistan and England, cases where the girl had managed to escape, or got to the press, or alerted the airport security. He couldn't have that. All very embarrassing. Made the community look like a bunch of militant savages, selling their daughters off into slavery.

'Professionals, you must use professionals, I know just the men,' his cousin had said. 'I know just the husband for her, too. A good man, well connected. An old business partner of mine. He'll look after her.'

Ashraf, whose religious convictions consumed him utterly, and whose desperation for acceptance in the community dwarfed his regard for his family, assented with barely a word of protest. Nothing could oppose the will of Allah; though it was doubtful even Allah would have chosen the man his cousin had lined up.

A fat, balding forty-six-year-old 'businessman', Khalid Ahmed had been married three times already, all of them to much younger women. He had his podgy fingers in dozens of political pies, running for office some years ago, before his unsavoury involvement in the rape and murder of a young village girl had embarrassed even the male judiciary in Rawalpindi. For Ashraf's cousin, however, the provision of a young and nubile wife to a man of Khalid Ahmed's standing could only strengthen his own political hand.

'We'll all be winners, Ashraf, just wait and see,' he'd urged. 'Khalid doesn't even want a dowry . . . he's not that kind of man.'

They were looking at him. Waiting. Looking down on him. He deserved it. What was he, after all, other than another underpaid factory worker trading his daughter for nothing more than pride? Allah would not protect him from their eyes, would not spare him from their justice. But they hadn't seen what he'd seen, had they? He was doing the work of Allah.

'Shall we get going, Mr Ahmed? Time is short.'

Aftab and Tariq accompanied him up the stairs and into the master bedroom. Mina was already there, kneeling beside her daughter, holding her hand.

'You've given her the tablets, Mr Ahmed?' Aftab said. 'The Morphazine and Rohypnol.'

Ashraf looked at Mina.

'Yes, my wife did, before you came.'

Aftab signalled to Tariq and, with a wave of Mr Ahmed's arm, he approached the bedside.

He lifted Shazia's hand and felt the pulse.

'Fast,' he observed.

But Mina's eyes were averted. Ashraf noticed that her tears were now stanched. She seemed strangely calm.

'It'll have to do,' Aftab said finally. 'We've got to get going. She won't feel a thing, Mr Ahmed. The drug is purely for her convenience, you understand. Not ours. It makes the journey so much more comfortable.'

He said it across the room as if it was the most routine thing in the world. In many ways it was. He'd done it so many times before. Through Shazia's improperly fastened veil he stared at her face and thought it very beautiful. Bodies were so much more interesting than suitcases of smack. He thought it completely wasted on the likes of Khalid Ahmed.

'Pick her up, Tariq. Let's get her into the car.'

He helped lift her from the bed.

'Mr Ahmed? Mrs Ahmed?'

He addressed them both.

'This is your last chance. You can still say no.'

Ashraf shook his head slowly and looked to his wife. But Mina was looking away. She was thinking of all the things she'd never said in her life, of all the sacrifices she'd made, and was secretly glad that here, here at the death, she may have done something good, something which may, in one small way, have made up for the injustices they'd heaped upon their poor, misguided daughter. And, as she thought this, she wished secretly that it was her husband who was being carried out unceremoniously across the shoulders of another man, and that *he* was never coming back.

Ashraf followed the two men down and out into the blazing sunlight. Mina followed silently behind them, her eyes downcast. She didn't want to see the silver Mercedes drive off, nor say one last public farewell to her daughter. She'd done that already. Secretly. A mother's farewell.

Within her diaphanous drapes her hand clutched a small bottle.

A bottle full of pills.

CHAPTER 13

Jamie Farrell was back on Northmoor Road, back on the old hunting ground, with the familiar faces, with the fire and madness in his belly. He sucked on a couple of ice pops, the quicker to get his sugar levels up. Thoughts of his mother and Patrick were all but obliterated. The craving was too great. The red brick houses that tapered off the main road looked half benign in the swamping afternoon heat; Pakistani kids were playing cricket and tag on the narrow roads. It was easy to do, nobody kept a car round here. No fucking point. By evening it wasn't worth scrap.

Jamie knocked at the barricaded door of a boarded-up property on Proud Street, somewhere in the middle of a long line of terraces. A face appeared where an upstairs window used to be, jug eared and toothless.

'Round the back.'

Jamie shot a glance down the road and made his way to the nearest ginnel. These houses would be easy, he thought, too bloody easy. Longsight's army of thieves had already cleared them out of house insurance. At the moment, though, he didn't feel much like a thief. He felt agitated. Big-time agitated. He circuited the backs of the houses and measured himself against the eight-foot-high walls the desperate owners had raised to keep the likes of him out. The extra provision of broken glass and barbed wire was a nice touch, too. It gave the alley the Strangeways look. Jamie hadn't been inside yet, save to see his old man, but, like his peers, he was working on it. One day, he'd get there.

He came to a green and rotten back gate and pushed it open. This was Billy's place, or one of them, anyway. He'd never stayed long enough to call it home. Jamie gave three knocks at the back door, a grey metal sheet locked and bolted from the inside. You could never be too careful. There was more than enough shit in the place to keep a street of smackheads stoned for a month.

The door was unbolted by the jug-eared kid. Billy's boy. Jamie picked his way through the rubble of bricks and spliff ends and smelt the sweet air of their smoke. This place would have housed a working man's family a hundred years ago, fifty years ago, even. Now it had been left to the mice and cockroaches and thieves. Everything had gone, back-boiler, water tank, copper pipe. All that was left was the crumbling brick and timber, and the dust from century-old plaster settling on the floor like a coating of Big C.

Jamie made his way up a flight of rickety stairs and saw six or seven smackheads gouching in corners, bent like old women, their bodies at peace. Jesus, he thought, you don't get worse than a smackhead. One was crying out for saviour, an empty needle stuck in his groin, begging for release. Two other men were crouching over a low wooden table, playing blow football with their nostrils. Snow lay on the pitch, a sheet of shiny foil, in neat tram lines. Jamie looked over. Rocks of crack lay in the middle, brown footballs waiting to be kicked. The two men looked up, their nostrils dilating and red, their eyes streaming.

'Jamie-boy? Is that you, pal?'

A pimple-faced man of no fixed age stood up and faced him. His head was completely shaven, marks and cuts tattooing his neck and arms like blotched constellations. An army of studs and rings chained his left ear to his head. In the dusty afternoon heat you could easily have mistaken him for an old ancestor on the African plains. He'd even branded himself for easy identification. There it was, stamped on the back of his skull: BILLY.

'What canna do for ya, Jamie?' he said. 'I got a lickie bird from ya, pal.'

Broad Scouse.

Jamie was on edge. Though he'd driven with Billy many times, knocked off a few petrol stations and supermarkets with him, he knew he wasn't all there. Not the kind of lunatic you went looking for. *He'd* find *you*. As far as being on friendly terms with him, Jamie wasn't doing too badly. Billy thought he was 'all right'. He didn't owe him anything.

Jamie told him about the events of the morning, the cleaver nearly hacking his head off. Billy was miles away, his eyes bouncing off their sockets like billiard balls. When he finished speaking, Billy was quiet. Swaying.

'Not good, Jamie,' he said, 'but what canna do? Those Pakis are a bit tricky now. It's not all corner shops like it used to be. They've got serious people now. They're not going to stand for their mothers-in-law being held up.'

He looked at his companion, still snorting at the table.

'What d'ya think, Errol?'

A tall, black man stood up. His designer shirt, *Piasso Del Misso*, clung like cling film to his cavernous chest. The black dealers always dressed well. The white ones looked like they'd been kitted up by *George* at Asda. Billy, in his vest and jeans, would have been thrown off a building site for looking slovenly.

'Easy, man,' he growled.

Billy raised what was left of his eyebrows and waited for explanation. Errol's eyes were streaming with joy.

'What's easy, Errol?' Billy said.

But Errol wasn't listening. He was staring at Jamie, or staring right through him, his eyes wide as saucers.

'What's the food like there, man?' he asked.

Jamie shrugged, baffled. Food? The darky was giving him the eye. Who the fuck did he think he was? Jamie hated niggers the way he hated Pakis, the way he hated faggots, the way he hated most nearly everything in his sorry life. But he respected them, too. A black guy was somebody you listened to. Those birdboys on Claremont Road, with their black Mercedes and Uzis, they were well worth listening to, unless you wanted your legs capped, or your head banged up the way Terence's was last year. He'd come that close to getting his head blown off. Black boys didn't mince off like those student faggots he'd knifed, or run like those soft Paki lads back to their stinking streets. No. You listened to niggers, watched them like you watched a snake, warily, knowing their bite would be quick and deadly.

'I like my Indian hot,' Errol said, 'Red-hot. Do those Pakis do that?'

Jamie shrugged. He'd had no time to try, had he? The fucking cleaver was out before he'd had time to tuck in.

'Cos if it's not,' Errol said, 'I think you should waste them, Billy boy. You always remember when a curry's hot. It's like good lines. The pure stuff puts you here,' and he raised one muscled arm above his head, 'the bad stuff . . .' he drew his fat index finger across his throat, '. . . you kill the motherfucker who sold it you. "Da chillies what makes it, boss."'

And Errol should know. He spent most of his life on Wilmslow Road. He'd got good credit in all the curry houses. When his party entered a restaurant, they were always treated well. Black boys and white slags, well, you didn't need to ask. Ali, at the Al-Biswan, had served them a few times himself, and groaned inwardly every time they staked a claim for the window table. It just didn't go down well. Who was going to wander into his lovely place when a bunch of gangsters were cutting deals in the windows? It was lucky the food was so poor. Errol hadn't remembered it, for sure.

In fact, Errol barely remembered anything, unless it was the mobile number of his latest mistress or the amount of money he was due from his protection rackets. He had four kids to four different women in four different parts of the city. North, South, West, and West again. He hated the East. Who didn't? It was just so full of trash. Nobody respected you over there. What do you do when eight-year-olds are eyeing up your Mercedes? Shoot them, or give them lollipops? No, he'd stick to the South and his flat in Didsbury. His two ex-wives (blondes, naturally) were being seen by a couple of his brothers in the posse. Members of his posse with their members in his pussy, that always killed him. Killed him laughing. He'd had two black ho's when he was younger, too, seventeen, eighteen, it was hard to tell. They were more of a problem.

Always shooting their mouths off when he brought candy rocks back for the kids. What was wrong with black girls, these days? They got no respect for ya, that's what.

Billy stared, trying to fathom the logic of Errol's reptilian brain. He was right. You couldn't let people rip you off like that. It sent out a very bad signal, made you look weak. He looked wildly round the room at the pathetic smackheads. It was like an alchemist's store. Pans and plastic bags lay on the floor beside a score of swollen gas burners. Tubes of every shape and size lay scattered like snakes. Reaching behind an outcrop of brickwork that once housed a hot-water boiler, Billy brought out something black and shining. He waved it in front of Errol, who smiled beatifically and insanely at its barrel.

'Is this what you fuckin' mean, Errol? A taste of black steel?'

Errol grinned. His ho's often asked for that.

Billy fired a shot into the air, his eyes flaring wildly. Jamie was expecting a mad deluge of timbers and a shock of blast, but there was just a dull thud in the air above them. Errol looked unimpressed. He was unimpressed. Shooting a gun was always dangerous. When you shot you shot to kill, not play around. That spent cartridge was a piece of evidence you had to get rid of. The Black Posse never missed a trick like that.

Jamie was unimpressed, too. A strange thing was happening to him. He was beginning to zone out.

His body was waking up to some kind of normality. Looking at the infested dump in front of him, the packets of drugs and razor blades and needles on the floor, he was no longer excited about anything. The thrill of running and thieving was all gone. A dangerous time. He thought about those flats in India House, those big, sprawling things in the city centre. That was where he wanted to be, not in some cheap crack-house like this, scoring drugs with a psycho and a professional hit-man. The uncomfortable sensation grew as Billy raved like a monkey about setting somebody or something alight. Jamie was no longer listening, no longer watching. Billy and Errol could have been on the far side of the moon for all he was concerned.

The monkey gibbering stopped. Billy put his arm round his shoulders and invited him to smoke a little crack with them. Errol was going soon. He may as well wait a bit. Jamie declined. He'd end up dead if he stayed too long. This wasn't the Craze. Billy was still Billy. Billy Fuck.

'I need to see someone, Billy. I'll catch you later.'

Billy called him again as he was about to leave.

'Jamie,' he said, his pimples glowing bright red in the fumes around him. 'We'll need a car.'

No need to explain. Jamie understood. He passed Jug Ears on the stairs and slipped out, down the alley and back on to Proud Street. The furnace that was the day blasted the toxic fumes from his body. The plaster and coke flecked the air and settled gently to earth. If there were any plants round there, they'd be buzzing. Stamen City Walkers.

It was as easy as picking candy from a shelf, easy as stoning a baby in its pram. The black saloon had just parked up opposite Crowcroft Park. Jamie saw the lady get out. Forty-something, she looked quite respectable. That nagging feeling was still with him. This was something he'd rather not do. Not today. The Craze had taken every one of his friends, every one of the kids on the estate where he lived. It was taking him, too, little by little, had even taken his father. He thought he should walk away from all this, but how could he now that Billy Whizz was involved?

Jamie was beside her before she had time to cross the road. He laid a hand on her shoulder and twisted her round. Fear ripped across her like a tsunami. No need for hard stuff here. Just the dead-eyed stare. She looked like a teacher, like Mrs Smart, his old English teacher, in fact. She didn't struggle, didn't scream, Jamie's quick-fire 'Give us your keys, bitch' drained every last drop of spirit out of her. Easier than candy. He took the keys from out her handbag, then locked her with those hooded cobra eyes, eyes she'd seen on street corners from the comfort of her car and with her husband beside her, eyes she'd seen in mug shots printed by the *Metro News*. She felt her bladder loosening and her world crumbling.

Jamie got in the car, started her up, and drove off in less than thirty seconds. Yes, the Craze was taking him, was taking every last one of them. It was in him forever now. The car was hot from the merciless sun, his brain frying.

CHAPTER 14

From high above the city the car could easily be seen. Through Chorlton, past the afternoon shoppers, it wound its way down to Princess Parkway. The great south road. Rays of the afternoon sun caught its silver metallic paint, radiating needlepoint slivers of light into the sky. Collapsed on the back seat, eyes closed, all hope extinguished, Shazia Ahmed struggled desperately against her rising panic. Her hands tied under her, all she could do was listen and wait. Listen to the two men talking. Wait for rescue. Time was running out.

'Still out, is she? Check her again.'

Aftab. She recognised the voice. Oily. Seedy. Like syrup.

Shazia felt a hand come snaking out and touch her. Her heart thundered. She sensed a face looking through her veil, breathing hard upon her cheeks, its warm perfume irritating her nostrils. She was sure she would sneeze.

'She is,' said the other. Tariq. More excitable. She felt her face pinioned in massive hands.

'She's wasted on Khalid, you know,' he said matter of factly.

Aftab looked in his rear-view mirror.

'Stop pawing her, you *gunda*. She's not for him, anyway.'

Tariq looked puzzled.

'What do you mean? I thought she was getting married?'

Aftab grinned, cruelly.

'No, you idiot, that's what they told her father. She's going to work for Khalid. In the *nach ghar*. One of his girls. For business use only.'

Tariq stared out of the window and thought what a sick world it was. What father would send his daughter away like that? What crazy bastard Paki would sell his own fucking daughter? He sniffed the air contemptuously and stole another glance at his companion.

Finally, he asked the question he'd been longing to ask. The one that had been eating him up ever since he'd first seen the girl.

'How long does it last? The Rohypnol.'

Aftab's lip curled. He understood.

'She won't remember the next twenty-four hours. We'll slip another one to her on the plane. It's all been taken care of. A room in the Skyway Hotel. No harm in checking the goods, is there?'

Tariq laughed nervously. There certainly wasn't.

Shazia felt her bowels churning. Trussed up like an animal, caged in the dark, she listened to the animals in front. Desperate and frightened. Why *had* she come back? She really should have known. Poor Damon. Poor her. She tried to imagine she was some place else. Like Dorothy in *The Wizard of Oz*. There was no place like . . .home? Hardly. She'd tap her shoes and be at Piccadilly Station. Time to go. Damon would be there. The evening would be bright and they'd leave Manchester forever.

Behind her veil, she began to cry. The car was greenhouse close, suffocating her. All hope wilting in it. She'd never see him again. But, as suddenly as she thought this, she stopped. There *was* still hope. Just one fine strand of hope in a fibrous knot of despair. Her bonds were not as tight as they should have been. Her mother had seen to that. Finally, at the bitter end, she'd come good.

She remembered her kissing her to wakefulness.

'*Beti*,' she whispered, 'listen to me. These pills. They were meant for you. They would've made you very sleepy. You must act like I've given them to you. Do you understand, *beti*? It's your only chance.'

Lying on the bed, with her head pounding, Shazia had been too stunned to realise. To realise that here, here at the death, her mother was making up for all the years she'd done nothing.

'I've brought you some money, too,' she went on. 'It's all I could afford, *beti*. I'm sorry,' and forced a bundle of notes into her pockets.

'And this, too,' she said. 'I took it off. I didn't want your father to see it.'

121

She pressed something into her palm. Cold. Metal. Round. A ring. Damon's ring! Life returned to her sleeping form. The Prince's kiss. She fingered it now, in her pockets, tried to slip it on. All hope centred on Damon Ruff. But, as she did so, the car shuddered to a deadening halt, and the screech of brakes brought her lurching to the present. There was the wild blaring of a horn and she flew off the back seat and on to the floor, letting out a barely stifled cry. The two men looked back, alarmed. She knew they were looking at her. She kept her lids tightly closed.

Heart pounding.

'Is she awake?'

Aftab. Murderous. The car had stalled. He brought it to a grass verge where a group of teenagers circled on darkening bikes.

'Fucking bastard motherfucker.'

Aimed at the driver in front. The driver who'd cut him up.

His rich, fruity Indo-English had the ring of public schools.

'The idiot's getting out. Watch the girl, Tariq.'

Two bloated white boys with Manchester City shirts banged on the door of the Mercedes. Looking for trouble. Shazia hoped for succour. But Tariq lay a muscular arm heavily on her. He was taking no chances.

Aftab wound his window down. Looked at the white boys through his dark Gucci sunglasses. And yawned. He was used to this type. In Lahore, in

122

Karachi, in Faisalabad. Bully boys. Out of shape, out of their depth.

'Oi, Paki, who you fuckin' horning at? Get out your fuckin' car!'

The customary English greeting. The taller and fatter of the two men broke the aerial of the Mercedes and threw it on to the road. Aftab quietly obliged. He stood all the way up, looking slightly incongruous beside them, in his polo neck and pressed black trousers.

'Gentlemen,' he said, pointing to his car.

But, before they'd a chance to look, he'd grabbed the nearest one by his bald pate and brought it down to the level of his midriff. The man was staring down the barrel of a large black gun, something you didn't often see, even at Maine Road. His face paled, and paled further when the gun was pressed against his temple.

'You English bastard,' Aftab said coldly. 'I'll blow your fucking face away.'

His fat friend, with a stomach not so much a washboard as a washing-up bowl, tried to scramble back to his car, but Aftab's words froze him.

'I wouldn't, white boy. Your friend won't thank you.'

Frozen in the back of the car, Shazia stared through her veil at the passenger side door. This was surely her chance. Aftab was out. Tariq distracted. Her hands twitched.

Aftab looked at the man kneeling before him. He thought about blowing his brains out, the way he'd blown away that bastard Sonny Khan in Jhelum last year. No-one gave two rupees about him, either. Looking round with practised indifference, he noticed the kids on the bikes for the first time. They were already sniffing out the situation, their skeletal hardnosed faces obscured by hoods even on this flower-compassed day. They were circling closer and closer.

'Tariq!' he called, and pushed the gun into the City fan's mouth. 'Ask that lot if they want a car for the afternoon.'

Tariq wound the window down, keeping an eye on Shazia. He put his hands to the door.

Please, she urged, *please*. His fingers felt for the lock and fumbled at the handle. *Please just open the door.*

There was a bold tap on the driver's window.

'Don't be an idiot, Tariq. Call them.'

His fingers faltered. Shazia's heart sank. Tariq leaned out and shouted. The kids approached the car like zombies. Tariq smiled to himself. Whatever happened to 'Don't talk to strangers'? He wondered whether all English kids looked like this. Blotchy skin and scars running down their cheeks. Shaven skulls.

He peered warily at them from behind his shades.

'What d'ya want, mister?'

Mancunian grey. Council-estate delivery.

'Thought you'd like a ride,' Tariq said, wondering why the hell every Paki he knew wanted an English education. He nodded at the car in front.

'We ain't sellin' ourselves.'

While they spoke, Aftab kept his eyes on the two City fans. A growing pool of piss threatened to spoil his shoes. The fat one saw it and felt his own bowels shake to jelly the Rusholme fry-up he'd half digested. It was worse than watching City, this. Much worse.

'Who's got the keys, boys?' Aftab asked.

Fat Boy lifted his replica shirt. Slovenly jeans hung half-mast at his hips. The tinkling of metal on metal was clearly audible.

'Hand them over,' Aftab said.

The vultures left their stolen bikes on the verge. No need to worry about them. They frisked the City fans the way they'd seen their brothers do, frisking drunken students down Fallowfield's dark Victorian streets. Straight for the neck and throat. Aftab had to admit they did a good job. Very professional.

One of the boys looked back at him. He appeared on the point of asking something but then retreated into the cowl of his hood. In a minute the car was gone, shooting down the Parkway like a sliver of white steel, joining the fleet of cars arrowing homeward and away.

Fat Boy and friend were left to walk off the beer. Though the sorry affair had taken less than a minute, it seemed like forever. It was etched into their drink-addled brains like a bad dream. They thought they'd seen it all: knives and chains at home to Millwall, black boys in drag on Claremont Road, but not this. Sometime next Saturday they hoped it'd all be over. They'd be back in the Albert with the Maine Road posse. City'd lose again, of course, but they'd be back in the thick of it, telling tales. Tales of how they tripped two Pakis on Princess Parkway and showed them a bit of England's glory. Now, however, they were swimming in their own piss. Their money was gone and their car forgotten. It could have been any bender of a night at the Palace in Levenshulme. Almost.

The Mercedes resumed its journey under the red-hot sky. A line of blue was just visible where Tariq had wound one of the windows down. Shazia saw it through her veil. And reflected. The moment had passed. There might never be another. And yet there may. There was always time. Time to live and time to die. She still had the ring. Every so often Tariq would look round and she'd have to close her eyes again. But she still imagined it. A small strip of blue sky, a letter-box view of freedom. And she imagined it was how prisoners must see the world, as a distant roar somewhere far over the horizon.

CHAPTER 15

The silver Mercedes pulled up to the Skyway Hotel. Two men got out of the car and escorted a young woman into the foyer. The keys of the car were given to a porter who thanked the men for the tip and drove it away. The men were tall, and wore dark sunglasses, the woman between them wearing a cream shalwar kameez and a veil. Mubasher Khan eyed the party on his monitor and took a large chunk out of his kebab. He zeroed in as they crossed to the information desk to try to get a closer look at their faces; the picture was hazy. He'd been asking for it to be fixed for a month now. The men were certainly Asian, though.

He looked down the long list of names and descriptions on his computer printout and fingered the radio controls. He brought out a pencil and circled a couple, putting a question mark beside each. But, as he tried the radio, he was met with a crunch of static. He'd asked for that to be looked at, too.

He drummed his fingers on the desk and tried the radio again. The signal was dead. He was

127

about to ring the front desk and ask them to get security for him when Sandra came in. Mubasher liked Sandra a lot. She was blonde and had big breasts. His fiancée Noreen, brown, flat-chested, glasses and nascent beard, wasn't in the same league. He began to resent his mother more and more for foisting her on him. Where Sandra always spoke about sex, a subject he was seriously interested in, all Noreen would talk about was her job at the Science Park. Her lab was making tomatoes redder, riper, and richer. Like Sandra's lips.

Sandra's perfume was not so much the scent of wild orchid as a whole forest of them. Fresh and clean. Intoxicating. He thought about Noreen's hairy armpits, 'Hairy, Bashy, because I'm certainly not a man's play-thing!' Sandra leant over to look at the monitor, dangling her breasts in front of him. She liked to keep them there for a few minutes so that Bashy could think about them. Weigh them up invisibly with his big, brown hands. It never took him long. His Kashmir Kid stood to immediate attention in his pants, seeking to break cover and shoot.

'Let's play horsey!' she said. The Wythenshawe way.

Their uniforms despatched, the static crackling like uranium ore, Bashy and Sandra played leap-fuck round the room. All parts in working order, after all. Meanwhile, the figures on the monitor had disappeared from view. The computer sheet, knocked by Sandra's feet, fell faintly to earth, dropping like a leaf. As Mubasher ploughed Sandra from behind, the names AFTAB AKHTAR and TARIQ ALI meant no more to him than Noreen and tomatoes.

In the foyer, one of the airport security staff banged his earpiece with his hand. The crackling stopped. He grinned. Handing it to the girl he fancied at reception, the two smirked at each other.

'They've left the fucking radio on,' he said.

When the Mercedes pulled up, Shazia already knew what was in store for her. She was to be taken up to an eighth-floor room and there wait for her flight. Tariq was taking her to Pakistan. She had till six o'clock. Aftab needed to stay. A large consignment of heroin was coming in. They didn't trust the courier.

'Don't worry,' he told Tariq. Who was going to stop them? The girl was easy. The Rohypnol had seen to that. He'd used it many times on them before. She'd be light-headed and compliant. And would forget absolutely everything. *Everything.* He smiled. And if she didn't? Well, goods damaged in transit happened all the time.

They gagged her tightly before pulling the veil back over her face. Then straightened her dupatta. Just in case. They ironed the creases of her kameez out with firm hands. A lady going to get married needs to look her best. Shazia was awake. Wide awake. Desperate. Her mind blazing with retorts. But calm, too. Now was not the time. Tariq's nerves eased and he began to think of the journey home. There'd be no trouble. He'd be sipping champagne on the balcony of the Shalimar Gardens tomorrow. *Insh'Allah.*

The three of them entered the hotel lobby. Shazia felt their hands on her arms. She doubted she'd have the strength to break them. The lobby was almost empty, too. Just a couple of suits on their mobile phones. No, she said to herself, this wasn't the time. She waited while Aftab spoke to the girl at reception and thought how ridiculous she must look, like one of those pillar-boxed-looking Arabic women she used to mock at school; strange, exotic eyes peering out of a black tent. As the three of them made their way to the lift, Shazia made careful note of the time. Four o'clock. She had two hours left.

The room, tastefully decorated in maritime blue, overlooked the runway of Terminal One. Shazia saw one of the planes skate down it and blast off into oblivion. She moved slowly, careful not to tense up, careful to nod her head when the two men asked her to do things. Aftab invited her to sit down beside him. Tariq brought a decanter of whisky and poured two glasses out. His earlier tenseness, with the kids on the Parkway, with the walk through the lobby, had been replaced by a gauche exuberance Aftab had not seen before.

Tariq was too amateurish, he thought, and reminded himself to tell Khalid when next they met.

Tariq's eyes bored into Shazia with scarcely concealed hunger, and she felt the pit of her stomach gripped with fear. Not for the first time she wished for Damon to be there beside her.

'She won't remember anything, no?'

Tariq's words were more a statement than a question.

Aftab looked at him with disgust. Taking off his glasses he took his right hand and fondled Shazia's right breast, squeezing it, pulling at the nipple beneath her cotton kameez. Shazia bridled with revolt. Drug or no drug she'd have spat full in his face. But the gag saved her.

'No, Tariq,' he said. 'She won't remember a thing. Luckily for her.'

He tipped back the whisky with practised ease.

'And to think her parents put her up to this.'

There was an uncomfortable moment in which both men didn't quite know what to do. Waiting for the other to make the first move. When Aftab finally got up from beside her, however, it proved an unexpected one.

'I need to see someone,' he declared with some exasperation, 'I'll pick the tickets up myself.'

And made for the door.

'I'll be back soon, Tariq. Don't let her out of your sight . . . and don't take too long! We haven't much time.'

He left the room.

Just one chance she'd asked for, just one.

Tariq Ali looked at Shazia and tried hard not to think of his mother. He liked to think of himself as one of those tough-guy Mafia types he saw in American films. De Niro, Pesci, Ali. Back home in Pakistan, he drove a great big, white Pontiac Firebird with the Pakistani flag emblazoned on the engine. He loved cruising in the hills with girls in the back, past the white terraces of the far pavilions and the croquet lawns. In fact, he loved cruising more than he loved anything. Even girls. It took his mind off the awful tedium of his work. For that's what it had become. The habitual beatings, the slashings, the money laundering and drug trafficking, it had all become one grisly routine. Which is why he'd offered to do this job. An escort service, they told him.

He looked at the girl. *She* was far from routine. Girls like this drove him mad. He couldn't get enough of them. City girls with purple lipsticks, fucked in Daddy's car. Pretty girls who loved the feel of his leather seats almost as much as he did. Just like those in the De Niro films. People got the wrong idea about his country, he thought. They wanted the same things.

All the while he stared at her through those impenetrable glasses, Shazia was counting the seconds down in her mind, the seconds she had left between now and Aftab's return. She eyed the corkscrew on the coffee table, drowsily and sultry.

132

She dreaded Tariq's first move yet pleaded for it as well. He needed to move, get up, do something. She'd never reach the corkscrew, otherwise. Never.

The minutes dragged by. She waited. And waited. Finally, Tariq got up, took off his jacket and sat next to her. She started to sweat, felt the cold fear grip her. And anticipation, too. He moved. And touched her hair. Her fists clenched into little balls of steel. Shazia could punch, knew she could punch, felt her control breaking and the fury wildly surfacing. But a voice whispered to her, in vesper-hushed tones: *Pray, Shazia Ahmed, pray for your soul*. And she remembered, as a little girl, sneaking into the church off Plymouth Grove, the one the kids on the estate burnt down, and seeing the pretty mirrored glass and the strange angel at the front telling the people to pray. Pray for their souls. And she closed her eyes now the way she'd done then, fighting the dark. *Pray, Shazia Ahmed, pray for your soul*. Tariq's hands grabbed her breasts and rotated them in great circles. She felt nothing. Words of comfort repeated like a mantra in her mind.

The hands were at her neck, pawing at it clumsily. Her veil was lifted. She felt the air become cooler as she breathed more easily. The gag that had been forcing her to gulp so long was removed from her mouth. Pray. Air, at last. Her eyes were focused on the door of the hotel room. She was sure Aftab hadn't locked it. Tariq was whispering.

'Are you going to be good, lady?' he asked.

She turned her eyes dutifully towards him, sensing the moment was coming. He helped her up, clumsily grabbing her breasts again. She eyed the distance between herself and the corkscrew, between herself and the door. A few feet. Not long, surely. *Please, don't let him come back*, she thought. *Not now.*

Tariq sat back in the chair and decided the day hadn't turned out too badly, after all. He invited Shazia to kneel in front of him, then deftly undid the top button of his pressed trousers. Down came the zip. Although he really wanted to have sex with her, he was concerned that Aftab would return too soon and spoil it. He didn't want him to come back, either. He brought out his member, already erect and gorged at its tip with white mucous.

'*Mera lund chuso, kutya,*' he whispered.

Pray, Shazia, pray for your soul.

She stared at the awful appendage in front of her and at the expectant face of her captor. His eyes were closed, waiting for the sultry mouth to close upon it. Thoughts of his mother were long gone. Buried deep and dying. The moment had arrived. Her hands felt behind her as she opened her mouth. Felt for the cold steel of the corkscrew. There. He hadn't seen.

'Go on, baby, Suck it.' Tariq De Niro's pleasure.

Shazia smelt the putrid fumes of the unwashed vagrant, miserly weeping in front of her. Caustic with fear and rage, the hand that gripped the steel made its way up her body. Shazia knew what to do with corkscrews. She hadn't worked at the Al-Biswan all that time for nothing. Tariq felt warm breath tickle the cut meat. He was going to enjoy this. His member bobbed. Once. Twice. Then, the halal slice!

His scream blasted from his throat like the roar of a bull, the searing pain in his groin inuring him to the volley of fists in his face and the gob of spit landing full in his eye. Looking down at his groin, the corkscrew lay embedded in his exposed scrotum. Fear, panic, and rage consumed him. But mainly pain. He reached for a non-existent gun. His fucking jacket was gone.

Shazia had buried the hilt of her anger in that too sorry flesh. The blows to his head were fuelled by revenge, sweet revenge, and desperation. The blood didn't spurt, it poured out like a molten lava flow, smearing the right side of her kameez.

'Now, Shazia Ahmed. Now.'

She vaulted to the door and prayed one last time.

'Turn and open. Please. Turn and open.'

Her hands, clammy and wet with fear, grasped the handle.

It wouldn't move!

The other way?

Still nothing.

Please, she thought, looking back at Tariq. He was rolling on the floor, bellowing and waving wildly, trying to get to her, yet falling over himself in agony.

Please! She banged on the door and screamed herself hoarse.

'Help!' Thunderous, drowning Tariq's screams.

Her fingers pressed and pulled, squirming all over the place. Then she noticed it. The bobble in the middle. She hadn't released the catch! She depressed it immediately, moved it to the right. The handle turned. Freedom. She looked back again at Tariq. He was rummaging one-handed through the crumpled jacket he'd discarded. The other was pressed to his groin. Now the moment had truly arrived. She skipped into the corridor as a gunshot blasted the air behind her.

It was deserted. She thought the noise would have alerted somebody, anybody, but, no, there was nothing. Lifts lay at either end. The room she'd emerged from was perhaps halfway between them. Remembering that it was the right one she'd been taken up, she ran straight for it. She pressed the elevator switch and it lit up pale and yellow. She banged on the doors of the closest rooms. Nobody answered. Like Longsight in the dead of night. She dared not look back. Any second she expected the door in the middle of the corridor to open and Tariq to come out, fully recovered.

She watched the progress of the lift, ticked off the floors one by one as they lit up. It was approaching the eighth. But, without knowing why, a deep unease grew in her, deepening as the lift ascended. The doors she'd desperately wanted to open were now home to her worst fears. What

136

if it was Aftab? The bell rang. It was almost here. They began to open. Shazia pushed through the fire escape just in time, down and down the long flights of stairs, haring into the unknown. She felt her clothes billow around her, alive to the sensation of cool cotton on her skin, blowing the fear and loathing from her body.

The lift opened far above her. For seconds the doors remained ajar. Then closed again. Nothing stirred. Nobody got on, nobody got off. The corridor was empty. Silence returned to the eighth floor of the Skyway Hotel.

Pray, Shazia Ahmed, pray for your soul.

CHAPTER 16

Sweet sensation, Jamie Farrell. The Cresta Run. 2 a.m. on a Manchester morning. The stars are out, a canopy of velvet night over an unquiet world. As the VW Golf revs up, wary householders peer through netted curtains. They're used to it. Used to the screech of tyres down Slade Lane, the smell of rubber burning acrid in the charcoal air. Every joy-ride in South Manchester ends here. Kingsway. It's the golden age. Their time has come. White-powder cokeheads snorting white-powder lines. Time for the coronation.

Billy Whizz is beside him, stoned oblivious. His face is bloodied from where he nutted the previous owner of the car. Some coconut-brown jungle boy looking for love in Longsight. Or at least a kebab. Silly boy. The alarm had warned him, of course, then the glass breaking. He'd rushed out, all suited and incandescent, flaming anger. Billy enjoyed mangling his face. Felt the darkies were taking too many liberties with his kind, pimping them, turning them into a nation of smackheads. Time for a little payback. Jamie looked on and hot-wired. The easiest thing in the world.

The Golf pulled in just before the Kingsway roundabout and revved louder. Jamie looked over at Billy. He was nodding his head insanely, grinning insatiably back at him.

'It's your time, Jamie-boy. It's your time.'

Ready. Steady. Dream.

The car shot off, wound itself round the roundabout, once, twice, three times, then slingshot to the stars, launched on petroleum and coke. Up the hill, not a car in sight. The pedestrian-crossing on green. The Golf accelerated to seventy, eighty, ninety. It arrowed to the south, lunatic fast. Jamie felt the first stirring of star lust. The shock of freedom, of escaping his earthly orbit, catapulted him upwards. Flying to the moon.

Down the long slope, past the railway line, towards Grangethorpe Drive. Green was still for go. Billy was beside him hollering like an ape. Go, Jamie-boy, go. 100. Dream time. Jamie's stomach imploded. His brain fried. He'd entered the twilight zone. Gone. Winked into nothingness. The Craze was upon him and life was sweet again.

Billy banged on the top of the car, stuck his head out, felt the chill air blast holes through his demented skull. Jamie's eyes were fixed on oblivion. Riding the chariot of the gods. There was nothing on the roads. He couldn't believe his luck. The lights of a car passing the other way funeral slow. The Golf thundered by. Then Mauldeth Road. Going amber. The red mist was descending.

'Jump it, Jamie-boy, jump it!' screamed Billy, though the voice was lost in the tumult of engine and piston. Petroleum high.

RED. 100 mph They had a good vantage. Nothing coming. And he hadn't touched the brakes. *He hadn't touched the fuckin' brakes!* A white transit, parked up by Vittoria's, made as if to turn into the road. Jamie blew by it, sending waves of shocked air rippling across its bows. The Greek driver lost sight of his pizza dribbling down his chin.

And there it was. The halfway point. Green End. Towards the old supermarket his mates once firebombed, some grisly reprisal for a robbery in Gorton. Tit-for-tat shit-bags. It's not all about drugs. He'd nearly killed himself that night. The trees on the central verge saved him. He'd scraped the roof off the fuckin' car. Others hadn't been so lucky. Helium balloons decorated every bloody street light on Kingsway. In Memoriam, Arseholes. They were better off dead, anyway. Saved them from far worse. Manchester took no prisoners.

Green End. Green lights. If only they'd stay that way. The car was shuddering with the stress and strain, its wheels spitting sparks on the tarmac below. Burning fire across the city. The young buried themselves in night fears, women rolled across their snoring husbands, fat Patricks crawled home from every squalid drinking den in Longsight. And Jamie bestrode the kingdoms of the world. He was the fastest thing on the planet.

Sweat broke out across his face, emerging from wide canyon pores. His luck was ebbing away. The lights were going red. And worse. A couple of cars were pulling out. His foot hovered over the brake pedal, then back to the accelerator. He was seconds from contact. Seconds from oblivion. The lead car was out in the road. He glanced at Billy and the split-second look told him all he needed to know. He closed his eyes and aimed the missile. The accelerator hit the floor. 110 degrees. He was going to die. Billy and he were going to die! There was going to be one fireball of a conflagration along the Kingsway, brighter and more brilliant than the plumes over the supermarket had been. This would be a real inferno.

Seconds.

The first car, seeing the danger, accelerated clear away, its horn frightening the air. But the second was caught in no-man's land. Its female occupant, heading home, stalled in the headlights of the oncoming car. No chance to scream. She closed he eyes. The last thing she thought of as the car approached was her husband. And her poor children.

Jamie Farrell thought nothing of children. He was still one himself. The orange Datsun clogging his artery was a more pressing concern. Be bold, Jamie Farrell, or you'll take your fucking head off. Billy closed his eyes beside him, waiting for impact. His stomach clenched its teeth just as he felt the swerve to the right. What the hell happened? He went wild.

Jamie had driven through the junction and done the only thing possible. They were in the wrong lane. Cars were flaring up Kingsway, klaxon loud, their lights on full beam in warning. But Jamie paid no heed, his ears stopped by the pressure of speed. He kept his foot to the floor. In the distance, a police siren, rover hot, wailed against the night. The careering cars zooming past his open window appeared like shooting stars, blazing full and fast disappearing in cosmic vapour trails.

Just two to go. Two lights left. Fog Lane and Didsbury Road. Then they were clear to Cheadle. A place no-one had ever reached. Not even Mark D, the biggest dragster of them all. Blown his fucking car up and taken three pedestrians with him. Nice going. His old mother had four funerals to attend. All for the price of one. Life's cheaper up north.

The oncoming traffic broke up. Still alive. Fog Lane approached. Billy *was* impressed. That manic grin was set in stone, a grisly, comic mask. He was witnessing a bit of history. The Golf swung back into lane. The last bit to go. Jamie'd been lucky. No drunken pedestrians bent double in gutters, no other joy-riders screaming across the heavens. He'd been left alone. All set fair for England entranced. And then, out of nowhere, it came.

The sinking feeling. The crack in the hold. Waters of doubt rising up from his belly. There was no stopping them. His foot hovered over the brake pedal, caressing it gently. He had to stop. The Craze had to stop. Put the demons to bed. The way it was meant to. FEAR.

The Golf shot over the rise so quickly that Jamie thought his stomach would lift off. Only a few hundred yards to go. Didsbury Road. Tesco's. The Big One. Through this and they were clear. But their speed had dropped. 110. 100. 90. Billy sensed it. He'd stuck his head back in.

'No slacking, Jamie-boy. Get your fucking foot down. I can see the stars!'

And so could Jamie. Bright ones in the heavens. And two great luminous green ones before him. Green for go. He couldn't stop now. But the voice was getting louder inside him. Urging him on, revolted. Stop.

Bang. First light. Bang. Second light. They were coming thick and fast. Then red. This time a large articulated lorry pulled out on to the road, its mass of steel immovable. Billy hollered louder.

'You can do it, Jamie-boy!'

And he grabbed the steering wheel with one hand and aimed it at the shrinking gap between the kerb and the turning lorry. No going back.

Jamie smashed his hand down on the horn. No sound. Only the voice in his head. Stop the fucking car. Here, on the very edge of everything, with the end of the world in sight. He tried to wrestle the wheel from Billy's hands but Billy was demented with righteous ire. There was only one way through this.

The lorry stopped turning. The Golf threaded the eye of the needle and shaved a few coats of paint in the process. Metal on steel. Metal on concrete. Knives grating. Jamie could think of 110 reasons why they should be dead but not one why they were still alive. And alive they were. Driving into the night.

The car juddered on, past Parrswood School, towards Cheadle. One hundred and counting down. The brakes sickened to the contact of rubber, appalled. Jamie was appalled, too. He tried to toast himself but knew it rang hollow. So did Billy. He'd seen enough.

The Craze was over. The demons put to bed. For this night only.

The car ground to a halt, shattered and spent. Jamie and Billy got the rags out and lit. The easy part.

They ran.

In a few seconds there was an almighty bang. One, two, three gunshots in the darkness. The petrol tank exploded. The awful stench of black acrid smoke. They fled down the path to Broad Oak Lane, unlit, hidden.

The doubt subsided.

'It's over,' Jamie said.

Billy scrutinised him through narrowing eyes.

'It's never over, Jamie-boy. Never.'

And shook his head.

CHAPTER 17

Down and down Shazia plunged, her heart pounding with jackhammer ferocity. She half imagined the rush of feet above her, dreaded looking round lest she see Aftab or Tariq. Through a gap in the railings she looked up. No-one. Nor did she meet anyone coming up. Eventually, she emerged on the third floor, flustered and aching from the flight. The foyer was beneath her. She recognised the marble flooring, the fountain falling to the first floor. Behind her the lifts to the upper floors were closed. A Saudi businessman waited for one, briefcase in hand. He glanced at her. Behind him were four clock faces, set above the lift doors. London, New York, Paris, Manchester? It was after half past four. Tick Tock.

She slowed down, tried to calm herself as she walked past the hotel bar. She prayed she wouldn't be stopped, yet felt the clothes she wore made her stand out horribly. Rather than taking the main stairs down to the ground floor, and passing through the crowded hotel reception area, she decided to keep to the deserted stairwells on the far side of the lobby. The thought that she should just stop now, and call for airport security, slipped further and further from her mind. These people couldn't help. She'd be held and detained while her story was checked. Tariq and Aftab would be found. They'd deny everything. Her parents would be called. Who was going to believe her? And she'd be handed over like a package marked 'return to sender'. No, she needed to get far away.

She left the hotel on the second floor, where it fed directly into one of the airport's space-age Skylinks, giant aluminium tubes that ferried passengers along slow-moving ramps towards Terminals One and Two. She had no idea which way she should be going so she went left on a whim, trusting to instinct, trying to look like she was any other holidaymaker. She couldn't help but notice that every other person around her was Asian: Sikhs, Hindus, Muslims; couldn't help but notice that they were all heading in the same direction. She wasn't used to swimming with the tide. She soon found out why. TERMINAL 2. PIA. Pakistan International Airlines. The gateway to Paradise. This would've been the way they'd have taken her. So much for instinct. She was staring down the corridors like she half expected the devil to come riding down them. Oblivious to all else. The terminal was alive with the sound of the subcontinent. Maybe here, she thought, she'd be invisible.

She emerged into the giant aircraft hangar of the central departure lounge and caught her reflection in one of the many metallic mirrors. She crouched to catch a better look. The sides of her mouth were red where the gag had bitten into her skin. Bastards. But her clothes weren't so bad. Tariq's blood had dried and turned an ochre brown. Behind her, she felt the milling crowds passing like blurs of colour. Her fingers fumbled in her pockets and felt cold metal. She drew it out. The ring. Her engagement ring. She examined it carefully. Thoughts of Damon saying goodbye to her on Wilmslow Road, and all her foolishness saying she'd be all right, flooded into her mind. Of course she wasn't all right. She needed him here. Or better still, she needed to be *there*. And the thought slowly crystallised in her mind. She had to get to Piccadilly.

She stood up, all the way up, and turned to face the crowds. And, as she did so, her heart nearly burst. Standing not twenty yards from her, shaking hands across the cruel white tiles, were two men wearing dark leather jackets. One of them was Aftab. She steadied herself and quickly turned her head away, gazing at the floor. Oh God. Had he seen her? Please no. She tiptoed away round the huddled families, keeping her head down. Just a few steps, she said to herself. A few steps. He must be on his way back. Please don't look up. Please. And she felt her nape hairs prickle dreadfully, at any moment imagined the terrible shout from across the hall. *Please*, she urged.

Suddenly, passing a last group of passengers, she felt a hand come to rest on her right shoulder. Mild panic gave way to absolute terror and, lashing out behind her, she screamed. Not loud, but loud enough. The crowd parted around her, leaving her exposed. In that terrible moment, it seemed that everyone in the whole departure area had their eyes on her. She turned to look at her assailant. It was *not* Aftab. An elderly English gentleman was holding a small bundle of ten-pound notes in his hand. It was the money her mother had given her.

'I do beg your pardon, miss,' he said, 'but these fell out of your pocket. I'm so sorry to startle you.'

She looked at him wanly, on the point of murmuring an apology. Then her eyes took in the sea of faces behind him and fear gripped her again. For looking right across the circle of people towards her *was* Aftab. Once more she was a caged animal.

'I'm so sorry,' Shazia said, 'I really am.'

Then, snatching the notes from his bewildered hands, she turned tail and ran, ran like a storm out of the departure lounge and back down the Skylink. This time she was sure he'd seen her, sure that she'd been recognised. Beneath her feet, cat's-eye floor lights gleamed white and pink as she hurtled over them. Planes took off and landed in slow motion, distant blurs shimmering in the summer's heat. She swept under the security cameras like an Indian typhoon, oblivious to the fact that half of them weren't working, and that high up in the control room, Mubasher Khan was more interested in straddling Sandra for a second time than checking those that were. Shazia knew that the throbbing sound in her head was not the blood coursing through her ears but the very real approach of catching footsteps.

Boom. Boom.

As she passed the entrance to the Skyway Hotel, a sign leapt out at her: Rail Station. She braced herself to look over her shoulder, but fear drove her onwards, past bewildered lines of dawdling holidaymakers, strung out like refugees with their bags before them. There was hope for this lot, at least. Get out of Manchester. Fast. The Skyway forked to the right and suddenly she was there. The Rail Station. Down the escalators.

The station at Manchester Airport lay beneath a space-age canopy like a giant spider. Funnels and tubes of alien architecture spun out like arachnid legs. Weird Easter Island pillars stood silent sentry on its platform. A glass buffet lay like a cocoon upon it, simmering in the baking June heat. There were plenty of people around. Shazia ducked behind one of the pillars, hoping against hope that her sprint had bought her enough time. She dared not look round, dared not break cover lest terrible hands strangle and grasp hold of her.

In truth Shazia had run faster than she'd thought. When Aftab Akhtar had recovered from the shock of seeing her at liberty in the concourse

of Terminal 2, he'd had to give chase with a suitcase full of heroin. Not the ideal companion for
a sprint. And, as he closed on her, the prospect
of some terrible calamity befalling the case
prevented him from going any faster. Airport security had undoubtedly picked his movements up
already. And that ignored lesson number one:
don't attract attention to yourself. The money he
was being paid for delivering the girl to Khalid
Ahmed paled into insignificance beside the
commission he'd get delivering this to Wilmslow
Road. He did, however, wonder how the fuck the
girl had got away from that dog Tariq. She was a
feisty one, that was for sure. Khalid would enjoy
that. If he ever got to see her.

By the time he'd got to the station, Shazia was
about fifty yards in front of him. He'd seen her
break her run to the right and followed her down
the escalator. There were, unfortunately, people
everywhere; white girls with tops hanging lower
than bras, sporting skirts no wider than belts, and
pot-bellied heathens with United caps protecting
their Spanish-bronzed skulls. Absolutely no class,
he thought, as he mingled amongst them. The
English had no idea. He fingered the gun in his
jacket pocket. He'd be doing the world a favour.

The train to Manchester Piccadilly was about
to leave. He jumped on and looked down the aisles
of the carriages, looking left to right, and right to
left. No-one. The girl was nowhere to be seen. He
looked out of the carriages and up the escalators.

He looked down again on the platform from above. Where the fuck was she? She hadn't passed him that way, that was for sure.

Though he couldn't see her, however, she'd seen him. His black coat had passed within three yards of her. Yet she'd remained hidden, hidden as if a veil of invisible air had been drawn silently over her. He was there, on the platform. A terrible, dark shape. She watched him go into the train, watched the seconds count down on the station clock. It was crawling past five. She tried to hold back time. Then, as suddenly as he'd appeared, he was out, racing back up the escalators. She circled the pillar, stowed on to the train, waited. Tick Tock.

The doors closed. The whistle blew. Relief broke around her like a river. She looked around her. And froze.

He was there in front of her.

CHAPTER 18

The moment Shazia Ahmed's eyes met the shades of Aftab Akhtar, a brief solar flare flickered into life along the corona of the sun and was as quickly extinguished. Hope replaced by despair, life engulfed by death. Shazia's fate seemed utterly sealed as she watched the merciless grin curl dangerously across his face. She saw his lips move, snarling, yet couldn't understand why she couldn't hear him. Then she felt the grating of wheels beneath her and saw that the train was moving, pulling away. He was still there, following her, banging his fists right into her face, banging his fists but not connecting. And then she realised. He was still on the platform. She'd been staring at him through the glass of the train. His blows and fury were useless. As futile as the solar flare. The train picked up speed till the blows rained and flailed over sullen air and the livid visage was no more.

It took Shazia a few seconds to realise she'd escaped. She ached with exhaustion and fear, her mind whirring continually like helicopter blades, her eyes staring dimly out of the window at the steep, golden cuttings and barbed-wire fences. She was breaking out. Slowly, second by second, as the train passed by the quiet lawns of Cheadle and sped into the city, she was making her way to freedom. Manchester was calling her home. She let the chatter of returning holidaymakers in the carriage behind wash over her, comforted by the continual whine of tired children. The train hurtled through the huddle of sleepy stations along the Kingsway. Shazia could barely make out their names. She scarcely recognised Manchester from this elevated position. It looked positively benign. The streets were alive with families, revelling in the baking heat.

Then the train joined the West Coast mainline and the vista changed. Miles and miles of terraced streets, boarded-up shops, steel grates, iron shutters. The world she recognised. Past Longsight Depot, past the rail workers on the Up Roads, teeming like flies on diesel engines, stripped to the waist, oil and grease smeared across their faces. Past the old factories in Ardwick and Ancoats where her father used to work, now all closed.

The train crept into the station. The platforms were thronged with humanity of every creed and colour, of every race and hue. Shazia was the first to get off, leaping over cracks in the paving stones. Without the dupatta and the burka to keep it in place, her hair flowed freely off her shoulders, cascading round her like a black waterfall. The crowds parted as she ran, as if news of her coming had been long foretold. She skipped off the platform like some wild gypsy girl. High above her, high above the concourse, a vast and newly appointed sign read: PICCADILLY STATION WELCOME TO MANCHESTER.

Shazia made straight for the bank of pay phones, surprised that none of them were taken. No multimedia text messager for her. Dredging into the deep pockets of her shalwar, she ferreted out the notes and change her mother had left her. She caught the gleam of a ten pence piece, then stuck it in the slot. A cautionary reminder came up when she started dialling. MINIMUM CHARGE 20p. She fished another one out and stuck it in.

The phone rang. Once. Twice. Three times. Fifteen times it rang and she counted every one. No-one answered. She pleaded with it. Please. Pick up the phone. There was a little click and a pause.

'Damon?' she said. 'Damon, are you there?'

The whirr of the answer machine was no consolation. Nor the sound of his voice.

'I'm not in right now,' it said. 'Please leave a message.'

Silence. Shazia poured forth her grief as if to an invisible confessor.

'Damon,' she said, 'I'm in trouble. Desperate trouble.' Pause. 'I don't know what to do. I'm at Piccadilly. I can't stay here.' Another pause. 'Please, Damon. Come quickly.'

She hung up. And considered what she'd just said. The idea that she was still being pursued hadn't really entered her head. Yet those trains from the airport left every fifteen minutes. If Aftab caught the next one? God. She thought of taking the bus to Longsight, of trying to find Damon herself, but the prospect of not doing so, of having to make her way back here, was too much. She needed help now. A change of clothes would be useful, too. She'd be harder to recognise out of these rags.

She looked up and down the concourse. But who to ring? When the problems with her family blew up into open war, friends deserted her in droves, month by month, abandoning her like a sinking ship. She was greeted with waves of indifference and the community's hostility. But she learned to live with it, learned to live with everything life had thrown at her. Almost. Not the child. She'd never forgotten *that*, never forgotten her father's granite insistence, nor the scornful stares of the neighbours, their sons calling her *kunjaree* while knocking themselves off the wrist every night thinking about her. The life had been sucked out of her, sucked out like her baby had. Her beautiful baby. Sucked straight out of her womb. She'd been left to bleed, a martyr to intolerance and bigotry. If the boyfriend had been some thick villager from Baluchistan, the family would have closed ranks, and prayed. But a child that was half an infidel? That was too much. For her father especially. The ridicule, the taunts, the bleached skin of sin.

God. Who to ring? Everyone had gone. Fading numbers in a faded diary. New boyfriends discarded her like storm-tossed flotsam, new girlfriends kept iceberg cool. There was no other option then. The last and only possible person to ring. Amina Aslam.

She rang her flat. Then rang again. No reply. She left a brief message, then tried her at her parents'. Probably stuck watching Zee TV, dreaming of kisses from Shah Rukh Khan and doing her hair up like Madhuri, or Sonali, or Ashwarya. *Dil To Pagl Hai*, indeed. Shazia let it ring.

A man answered. Curt. Tired. Aggressive.

'*Salaam Alaykum*,' he said, in an hilarious Teppy drawl.

Oh no, thought Shazia, her father.

'Is Amina there, please?' she said.

TP paused and seemed to clear his throat.

'*Kaun hai*?'

Shazia's turn to pause. She had the terrible feeling everybody knew her business and that revealing her name would bring Aftab, Tariq, her father, Fat Umer even, lurching to her side.

'It's an old school friend of hers. Uzma. Uzma Ali.'

It was the only name she could think of. She couldn't even recall if there was any such girl. It seemed to satisfy TP, though. He bawled Amina's name out, momentarily drowning out the sound of Bollywood. Shazia waited.

And quickly rewound the tape. It hadn't been that long since they'd shared a flat together, a little place off Dickenson Road. Amina had to move out when her parents got wind: Shazia was a bad girl. And besides, they had other plans for her. They had someone lined up. Poor Amina. Mo was good for freebies, but he was no Brad Pitt. Amina spent most of her time longing to get out. Then she went cool and quiet and, after Shazia's engagement, silent.

'Hello.'

The voice was quiet and distant, a bit Teppy itself. She was putting it on for her father's benefit.

'Amina?' Shazia whispered. 'Is that you?'

Amina recognised the voice immediately. Alarm bells ringing in her head. There was a few seconds' silence before she said anything. Then Shazia was off. Launching into sonic Armageddon, breathless with fear about being chased and needing help fast. Like *now* fast. Amina could hardly take it all in.

'Please, Amina, I haven't got much time. I'll be on Canal Street, outside the Rembrandt. You know it?'

She did. Pause. Before the phone went dead Shazia shot out a last SOS.

'Bring some clothes. Jeans and T-shirt, if you can, and a pair of shoes. I'll explain later.'

Whirr.

Clothes?

Amina Aslam was left holding dead air. She could hear the high-pitched singing on the television, the sound of string and sitar. It all seemed overfamiliar. Like the map of a young Asian girl's life, it followed a predictable pattern. There was harmony at the end of every reel. Maybe the world was changing but the old dispensations died hard. Tragedy waited in the wings for those who strayed from the path. You only had to know Shazia to realise this. The path of Islam ran straight and true. All the other ways were unclear.

She put the phone down, said goodbye to her family, and to the movies, and made her way back to her flat. The crooked way.

In a train carriage four miles away, two men sat grimly on, staring into the distance. For them the path was straight and clear. Revenge was etched on to their brows, tattooed across their minds. Aftab Akhtar could think of nothing else except nailing that girl across the tracks. Tariq Ali, nothing short of skewering her. The way she'd skewered him. Every time he moved, a searing pain shot through his groin and he winced horribly, impaled on some invisible spear. Every time it did so, the froth and spatter of vengeance raged like the maelstrom deeps.

The moment the girl had got away from him, Aftab Akhtar realised he only had two options left. To let her go and lose the bounty, or delay the delivery of his suitcase and go after her. Each one carried its own risk. That prick Tariq. How had he fucked up like this? He had no choice. He had to go after her. And silence her. Khalid Ahmed would have to keep porking the local *haram*.

So he ran, ran back to the Skyway Hotel, knowing that he could afford to give her no more than fifteen minutes' start on him. It was a remote chance. But he'd always been lucky. Before shacking up with that idiot Tariq, anyway.

He burst into the hotel room, preparing to castrate him. And stood still. Someone had done the job for him. The sight of Tariq on the hotel floor, holding his testicles, left him speechless. Could it be all that bad? Probably what he deserved anyway, the dirty sod. But then he saw the steel and blood, and his own balls shrank in fear and sympathy.

But time was pressing. They needed to get the next train. He removed the corkscrew with a sharp tug, like a nurse removing an old man's catheter. He wasn't going to start examining Tariq's balls. The scream rent the air, a volley of abuse despatched into the ether louder than any cannon fire. It wasn't fatal, Aftab decided, and gave Tariq two choices. Patch yourself up now and run or try explaining it away to the airport authorities.

'And remember,' he warned, 'you don't know me.'

Some choice.

CHAPTER 19

Amina Aslam wrapped her black dupatta round her head and gritted her teeth. She hated cutting through the back alleys to Naz's take-away. It was like walking through a war zone. Not a place for the faint-hearted. But she was in a hurry. And it was the quick way home. Shazia, who she hadn't heard from in months, had blown right back into her life, breathless amidst the machine-gun delivery. And she was asking for help. Desperate help. She couldn't ignore her. Not now. But, even as she thought it, storm clouds of suspicion gathered, blown in by winds of doubt, and her mood darkened. Maybe she'd found out. Maybe Shazia had finally found out.

Amina Aslam was not the jealous type; she'd never needed to be. The boys had always come running to her. At school, at the library, at college. No need to chase anything, even if she could. Her Backstage Pass to life had already been signed: pretty. But what good was that to her when she was chained to a mirror every evening, waiting for Mo to ring, and dreaming of someone else? No, she wasn't the jealous type. But she was of Shazia

161

Ahmed. Shazia had something she desperately wanted.

She made her way up the hill and hoped nobody was about. She hated passing people in this maze. Hands could come out of any doorway and drag you in. If only she wasn't in such a hurry. She rounded a narrow corner and groaned. A group of white boys were up ahead, perhaps a dozen of them, not much younger than she was. Her stomach churned. She hoped her purple shalwar kameez would protect her. It had in the past. She held her breath as she ap proached them and wished she was more like Shazia. Shazia would have walked through them with her head held high, threatening fire and brimstone if they so much as looked at her. She'd have fought them, too. Fists and all. Amina had seen her do it. But the boys were stoned, main-lining on indifference and dope. They left her alone.

She came to the top of the incline, behind some flats and a few old lock-ups. More barbed wire here than in those pictures of the First World War she'd seen at school. Just over the ridge was a parked-up black saloon. The windows dimmed. Her heart beat faster. Before and behind her, the narrow road was deserted. What to do? She couldn't go back. Just one more corner and she'd be there. Naz's takeaway was just round that corner. She bit her lip and continued. One. Two. But when she heard the pounding of feet and the shouts coming her way, she realised that not even her scarf might save her this time.

Jamie Farrell sat in the back of the black saloon, staring at nothing in particular. Terence was in the passenger seat, sunglasses on, eating a kebab. Jamie was undecided on which was the more revolting. The smell of grease and pickle, or the dreadful slurping noises accompanying Terry's every bite. Things like that irritated the hell out of him. Would have irritated him even if he wasn't so preoccupied. He hadn't eaten properly all day and felt weaker than ever. More awake than ever, too. Thoughts of his dad kept surfacing, urging him to see him, tell him what was going on with his mam. But then, what the fuck point was there? He couldn't do anything now, could he?

The thick chocolate smell from the McVitie's factory was still cloying the air. Jamie could have drowned in it. Wanted to drown in it. In front of him Terence tore into his meat like a jackal. Next to him, Billy sat silently behind the wheel. Stoned. Jamie thought they stuck out a mile, maybe two. Three men in a black saloon on what felt like the hottest day of the century, you could overlook that. Three men in a black saloon car in The Palace Nightclub car park, all wearing sunglasses, all with shaved heads, one with the unmistakable word BILLY stamped on him, all looking at nothing in particular, that was the darker part of shady. It was lucky Errol hadn't come for the ride. That would have sealed it. But Errol had had an itch in his pants and wanted one of his ho's to take the sauce. Lucky bastard.

The late-afternoon sun burnt the car like a giant magnifying glass, threatening to fry its occupants. Billy was feeling it badly. Muttering to himself like one of those retards Jamie always saw on Albert Road. Muttering about nothing at all. He turned to face Jamie in the back of the car. Jamie stared back. Billy was further down the ladder than he was. On the very bottom rung. Not all there. Never had been. Billy lived on the other side of the world. The Craze had eaten him whole.

'I'm gonna kill for ya, Jamie. You's mi mate.'

Jamie studied that terrible face, that Neanderthal backwater, and realised horribly that it was not the face of a stranger at all. It was something much more familiar. He was looking at himself in five years, three years, one year from now. He was going to end up inside. For good. He'd be seeing his dad for all the wrong reasons.

Terence threw the remains of his kebab out of the window. A host of flies greeted its arrival with holy fervour, gorging on its flesh made fat. A blonde girl like a stick insect, perhaps fifteen years old, pushed a pram round it, her legs white as Christmas. She stared at the black saloon with complete lack of dread, her eyes caustic with anger that she had to push a baby around at her age when she could be out in town with her mates. Dumb bitch.

'Watch where you're throwing things, you!' she said.

There it was again, Jamie thought. That look, that fucking look. He stared at the girl as she passed. And images of the middle-aged lady, frozen in fear, handing her keys over to him, surfaced unexpectedly. He shook his head. What the hell was wrong with him?

'Go fuck yourself, you tart!' shouted Terence.

That's right. Nice and quiet, thought Jamie.

Billy had woken up. His timing was perfect. It needed to be. One false move and he'd be the one lying in a pool of piss in some dark alley in Longsight, a small hole in his head. Late afternoon was always a good time. Nobody expects it then. Before the streets darken and the creatures of the night emerge.

He drove the car into the corridor of heat that was Stockport Road and parked the stolen black saloon in a narrow street behind Naz's take-away, a network of side-streets where petty thieves and hoods hung out, where joy-riders left the burnt-out carcasses of GTIs to the Gods of Crime. They'd all done it. He handed out black balaclavas as if it was a military exercise.

'Don't put them on till you're in there,' he said. 'Don't take them off till we're back.'

They waited. Waited for Billy to get out and lead. Terence picked at his teeth. Jamie wished he was anywhere else on earth but there. Terence, the fuckwit, was getting off on it, the unbearable

165

expectation of violence. He felt his own throat tighten horribly, though. The heat was suffocating him. He thought he'd pass out if he didn't get air soon.

Then it was over. Billy was out of the car and heading down the hill, the smell of grease and curry assaulting the senses. That feeling was growing in him, and yet so was the memory of the morning. Fresh on the menu once again. Stockport Road was aflame, simmering, the air shimmering like a mirage before him.

The three men had no need to push through the glass doors, they were open sesame already. Their lucky day. No queue. Jamie noticed acne boy had a friend working with him, a strange leering man with whipcord muscle and a goatee beard. They hadn't been recognised. They pulled on their balaclavas.

Acne boy was the first to turn. His eyes widened like moons when he saw the hooded Klansmen looking at him.

'*Abu!*' he shouted. '*Abu! Chor yahan hain!*'

The man with the cleaver appeared again, weapon in hand, grimacing and charging like a bull. Goatee was there, too, springing up and over the counter to join him. The response was blinding quick, quicker than Jamie, or Terence, or even Billy expected. Meeting fire with fire. No time for thinking. Hardly time even to act. Acne boy was almost on him, his skin erupting once more.

Fucking Paki, Jamie thought, and brought his knuckleduster into the flight path of the meteor that was the boy's head. The crunch of bone on steel sickened him, yet he rained in blow after blow.

Two other men, great hulking Pakistanis with arms like tractors, and wearing bloodied aprons, came charging into the fray. One of them grabbed Terence, whose arms were being chopped and torn by the machete man. Bloody hell, this would be a proper fight. Then, as suddenly as it began, it ended. An unholy blast rent the air. Terence's arms hung limply at his sides and the man was left holding a limp rag doll. Jamie couldn't quite grasp what had happened. He'd let go the crumpled form of acne boy and was struggling with someone else. And then his eyes, wild with panic, and sweating beneath his balaclava, came to rest on Goatee. He was grinning from ear to ear and, in his hand, he was carrying a dark .22.

Oh, fuckin' hell. Fuckin', fuckin' hell! screamed Jamie's brain, *the Paki bastard's shot him. He's fuckin' shot Terence!*

He drew his flick-knife from out his pocket and let it slide, watching it carve through the open air. The madness was growing again. A scream welcomed it in. A crumpled figure dropped beside him, clutching its arm. A cool incision in his muscle, a surgeon's stroke compared to the savage halal butchery of the machete. Then there was a dull thud, and another. Almost inaudible in the madness that was his brain. Thud. Thud. As if in slow-motion, Jamie turned round and saw Billy, standing there as cool as drawn steel, gun extending from his hand like a metallic claw. Thud. Thud.

The machete man, with his drooping moustache, seemed to float in the air for a few seconds, hovering like a giant mushroom cloud above doomed Nagasaki. Then, a burst of red exploded from his forehead like one of acne boy's pustules and he sank to his knee, taking one last earthly look at his son, hoping he'd be taken far away from the brutal days and nights of his life. He'd taken his last orders in defence of the right. Whatever that was.

Goatee joined him. Moving to assist his fallen uncle. And paid with his life. There was no time to care in these godless days, not in Manchester, the capital of hell. Billy's bullet caught him squarely in the temple. He keeled over like a skittle at a bowling alley, swaying from side to side before falling backwards into oblivion.

Jamie was nearly sick. Sick with fear. The Craze. He'd never been this far before. Red lights, joy-riding, drug-dealing. This was the work of innocents. He was climbing down that ladder to join Billy. With each successive brutal act, the consequences would recede further into the distance, into the grey matter of the quickly forgotten. For Billy, of course, there was no hope. No reason. Nothing at all to prevent him doing this, day in, day out.

'Run!' he screamed. 'Run!'

And they ran like the Furies were after them, leaving Terence to his fate, like *good* soldiers in danger's hour. Their footsteps reverberated like thunder and their shouts murdered the air with their cruelty.

Up the hill beside the take-away they tore, back to the black saloon. Jamie, flustered and insane, peeled the balaclava from his face.

'Put the fuckin' thing back on!' screamed Billy, but Jamie wasn't listening.

He couldn't breathe in there. He wanted to peel all his skin away, to get out of his body and fly.

They ran, and ran. Bang.

Bang!

Ran straight into Amina Aslam.

Billy waved his gun at her. Revenge for Terence.

'Die, Paki!' he shouted.

But Jamie smacked into them both and saved her life. He landed on top of her.

His inscrutable white face, with its pale lips and half-closed eyes, looked down into her wide, brown eyes, at her lustrous purple lips. East met West, the one passively waiting the savagery of the other. As it always had done. For a few terrible seconds, Jamie marvelled at being this close to something so alien, so utterly foreign. Like the fag's flats in India House where he did his dealing, this Paki girl, whatever she was, had touched the rawest of nerves, had awoken in him the strangest of feelings.

'Jamie-boy, get the fuck out of the way!' Billy shouted.

But Jamie stood his ground. Billy's gun fanned the air and he ran.

Blood on his hands, blood in the air, blood pumping through his veins like a piston, his senses wild and alert, Jamie Farrell felt untouchable. The car wound backwards through the narrow roads like a black phantom, down Chapel Street, up to Mount Road. Billy knew where to bury it. He kept shouting. Shouting at Jamie for being such a fool. But Jamie was miles away. He was amongst the stars again and heard nothing.

'You stupid cunt. You took your fucking mask off. D'ya think she'll forget *your* face?'

Jamie could have wept. The feeling was love.

CHAPTER 20

When Amina Aslam recovered her senses enough to realise what had happened, the car had long gone, and all she could hear were the shouts and screams from the main road. The features of that brutal face staring down at her, promising savagery, burned into her retina. She dusted herself down, tried to blink it away. No luck. She had to go.

Fear and need drove her back the way she'd come, back through the narrow alleys and wasteland, fleeing like a purple gazelle from the massacre on the plains. Until she came to Stockport Road at last, and saw the police cars hurtle down the road, their sirens wailing like harpies in the high heat, swooping like birds over a stricken vessel. Maybe she should tell them. The men. The face. But something stopped her. She had to see Shazia Ahmed. She would come back later, tell the police everything. So she crossed the main road at the lights near the Midway pub and ran as fast as she could, holding on to her scarf. All she could think of was turning the key in the door of her flat, rifling through some clothes and getting out of there.

She was in and out in minutes, frisking wildly through the chaos of her wardrobe, trying to find something that would do. She hardly wore English clothes, and certainly not dresses. Her fiancée Mo didn't like them. And neither did her parents. He was gone now, of course, back to London. A couple of pairs of jeans, bought when she was living with Shazia, were buried at the back. She dug them out, chose the cleanest, and shovelled them into the bottom of a holdall. She picked up a pair of black slip-ons and dropped them in, too. And then wondered what the hell she was doing. All this for Shazia.

As she was about to leave, she suddenly remembered something, and dived underneath what was left of the coffee table. The answer machine was on, winking at her. Twice. She pressed the play button eagerly, and caught her breath. It was *him*.

'Hi, Amina . . . it's me.' Pause. 'Just returning your call.'

The hairs on the back of her neck rose immediately. He'd rung. Summoned by her in a moment of desperation. Summoned by her dark, secret longing. She just hadn't been thinking clearly at all, had she? College had been going badly, she just wanted someone to talk to.

But before the message had even finished she'd replayed it.

'Hi, Amina . . . it's me . . . just returning your call.'

Damon Ruff.

She ran out of the flat, her heart pumping honey. Neanderthal was gone, the face of another Englishman in her mind. The door banged behind her. In the stillness of the room she'd just left, the answer machine beeped and played a second message.

'Amina? Are you there? It's Shazi. If you're there, please pick up.'

Silence. Then the click of a receiver. And silence again.

Amina was gone with her memories.

Late fall in Longsight and the streets were dark and long. Sensible feet scurried for home and shut their doors, waiting. Waiting for morning to bring succour. But for Amina Aslam that hope had come early: she heard footsteps on the stairwell. Shazia had returned. She opened the door to greet her. And opened her mouth wide.

'Oh,' she said.

Damon Ruff flashed one of those smiles and wiped the fringe out of his deep, blue eyes.

'Hi,' he said. 'You look surprised. Have I caught you out?'

Amina stared at him, her heart unexpectedly a-flutter.

'How do you mean?'

'A spy,' he said, 'in the house of love?'

And he grinned at her broadly.

Her skin darkened.

'I was collecting the last of my stuff,' she said. 'Didn't Shazia tell you?'

'Yes,' he said. 'It's a shame.'

And the words settled in the fractious air between them.

'You've got your own place, then?'

'Yes,' she said, and stuffed some more tops into a black bin liner.

Damon took his jacket off and laid it on the settee. Compared to his, it was an opulent chaise-longue. Flowers, cushions, and springs intact. Like the flat, it was beautifully presented. Like the girls in it. You could sink into them, too. No wonder Shazi felt sorry for him. He had nothing. Poor baby. But he played up to it.

He went into the kitchen to make himself a coffee. It was bitter outside, and the rain continued to fall. He looked out over the city blankly, then caught a sight of Amina in the window's reflection, packing her cases. She was rearranging her scarf. She'd taken it off her head and was furling it before her like a black kite. He hadn't seen her like that before. Her hair fell about her shoulders, down to her waist. He stood in the kitchen doorway, cup in hand, and watched her. She was wearing one of those trouser suits he liked, purple and tight. His favourite. She wandered in and out of the room, oblivious. It *was* a shame she was going.

He coughed. Then smiled at her.

'You want a hand?'

She looked at him embarrassedly, her hair asunder, then at the mess on the floor.

'No thanks,' she said. 'I think I'll manage.' Then looking at the coffee in his hand. 'But I wouldn't mind one of them.'

He clasped a hand to his head dramatically.

'God, I'm sorry,' he said. 'I just wasn't thinking.'

Not of that, anyway. He was thinking of her.

When he came back into the lounge, all was changed. Amina was sitting on the settee, her dupatta tight over her head again. Hidden. She'd put his jacket to one side. Carefully. Her fingers had been through him already.

He sat down at the far end and feigned indifference. He was a master of it.

'You should have left it,' he said. 'It looked better.'

He gave her her coffee.

She looked at him quizzically.

'What?' she said. 'The coat?'

'No,' he said. 'Your hair.'

Her skin darkened again. There was something about Damon Ruff she just couldn't explain. It left her breathless just thinking about him. He was dangerous *and* beautiful. How long could you keep hiding those feelings? One day they were all going to spill out and there'd be hell to pay. She'd caught him just now, staring at her. Did he really think a girl didn't see that kind of thing? They sense it. That's why she took the scarf off. He was the opposite of Mo. Mo was parentally approved and had a good cv. His parents, her parents. All the ends tied up. Damon had nothing. Mo was a date on the calendar waiting to be fixed. Damon was an unmarked diary. But he also belonged to Shazia. She sighed. Another good reason for her to be going. To stop thinking about him.

She changed the subject.

'Shazia showed me the ring,' she said. 'Congratulations.'

The reminder choked him mid-sentence. The ring. The engagement ring.

He looked at her curiously.

'Thanks,' he said blandly. If she only knew. Shazia needed something to hold on to.

'She'll be back soon.'

And they both stared at the black bags in front of them and listened to the rain fall, rhythmically and unendingly, and drank their coffee slowly. The parting of the ways. Amina tried to get up but couldn't. Something was stirring in her heart, something she could not put out, and Damon Ruff sensed it. The movement of her breasts beneath the purple, and the memory of her hair hanging over them, roused him to action. Amina the quiet, Amina the forlorn, Amina the fallen. He held his hands to her face. Slowly he pulled the dupatta from her head and let it fall behind her. The still waters of faith were breaking around her, the little faith she still had, and she looked at him from beneath her fringe, frightened. She caught him doing the same thing. He was the handsomest thing she'd ever seen. Beautiful handsome. And untouchable.

He planted his full lips on hers, and hers parted virgin and easily under him. She darkened still further and her lungs burst for lack of air. Then he spoke to her and told her what he wanted to do, and the approach delighted her even as it terrified her. Regret that she'd not left her slippers on was tempered by the thrill of it. And when he bowed his eyes and stretched his porcelain hands to her Arab arches, she thrilled the more. Neither froze nor panicked. She let him caress her gently and felt the first quivering of flesh tingle up her leg, felt the lips of desire part sweetly in anticipation. But Damon remained obeisant before her, and bided his time. And all the while both thought about Shazia and knew she'd soon be there, and neither, in their youthful madness, cared.

How long he sat there, how long she waited, she could not remember. Everything passed by in a dream. Lying there, listening to the rain, while Damon's tongue set fire to her belly. Each flick across each painted toenail sent it burning across her body. The beacons were lit, the Armada approaching. But Damon refused to dock. She wanted him badly, and fearfully so, for this was something she'd never done, and was never likely to do, until Mo got there. If he ever got there. Damon's refusal was a sign of higher things. He wanted her and respected her. *Ghora* weren't all bad. And the more he kept his hands and lips from the rest of her body, the more she wanted him to take hold of her, to fill her up, to plug the gaps. She'd been holed below the water-line without a shot being fired, and was drowning in his attention. Thoughts of Shazia disappeared over the horizon. This was *her* chance, and she savoured each wild and foolish moment as if it would be her last.

Kneeling on the floor, Damon Ruff loosened the fold in his jeans where his cock was straining and tried to buy it a better angle. He didn't want Amina to see. Not now. Maybe not ever. His kisses had unleashed a tidal wave in him, a typhoon tide, and it was unstoppable. Wild as Kashmir he was, and he had power over her. Those purple lips, those Ashwarya eyes, the rise and fall of her hilly mounds, Damon knew his topography, the lay of the land. The jewel in England was brown, and it was there for the taking. And his fingers ran up her valleys and hills till they came to rest on her breasts, and the choice was there for him to take. He could stand up and reveal all, and crush her like more than half of him wanted to do – already he could see the black strap of her bra escape the netting of her kameez, black on purple on brown, like a black narcissus – or he could make good his retreat and beg forgiveness, mumble his way through in coy apology, the way girls had let him a thousand times before. *I'm sorry, you're just so beautiful. I don't normally do this kind of thing. Honestly. I'm so sorry.*

And he was sorry. Sorry that it had gone so far. Not just for Shazia, but for the ammunition he had given Amina. What terrible revenge could she wreak on him? Women were so vengeful. He had compromised himself utterly and realised he was as much in her power as she his. The consequences of everything you do come back to haunt you. He looked at Amina's face, that beautiful face, and tried to work out what to do, but as with most things in his life, he found the answer in his genes. He made to stand up, flagpole stiff, and reached his hands towards her, and she was wide-eyed and waiting and longing.

Then there was a footfall on the stair, and a mad dash of heels on wooden boards. Damon looked at Amina and read in her eyes the afternoon's vale-dictory: she wanted him badly. And she, in turn, stared into those too blue eyes and forgave him his trespass, for her heart was fit to bursting with longing. She had emerged briefly from the shadow of Shazia Ahmed, and the sensation lit her night up like a shooting star. Yet, when Shazia bounced in, gum in mouth, all was lost. It was love. And lust. And over. She watched Damon plant his lips on another's and her spirit died. He turned to face her and – did she imagine it? – he was as crushed as she. But she couldn't tell.

'You're nearly done, then?' Shazia said.

Amina nodded.

'Damon helped me.'

Shazia smiled at her.

'Well, you're doing better than me. I can't get him to do anything.' Then more slowly. 'I'm going to miss you.'

And she came up to Amina and put her arms round her, and hugged her. But Amina didn't feel anything. She was staring over Shazia's shoulder at Damon. Would it always be like this, she wondered, the promise of what could have been? And she stared into the empty space between them, listening to the rain fall outside, rhythmically and unendingly, and hoped it wouldn't.

CHAPTER 21

Shazia Ahmed made her way down to Canal Street and lost herself in the crowd some five minutes before Aftab Akhtar and Tariq Ali walked through the station concourse. They made quick circuits of the area before meeting beside the bank of phones she'd so recently left. Aftab had a feeling about this one. Something he couldn't explain. He was *drawn* to the girl. Finding her here would certainly be easier than in Karachi. People talked openly here. Even without money. Less likely to fear a knife in the gut or a gun in the face. Tariq was complaining bitterly about the pain in his groin, treading carefully. He had to get it seen to. Aftab ignored him. And bandied his wallet round like a game-show host. A starter for ten.

But everyone shook their heads. One Asian girl in all that mass of humanity, well, they really hadn't been looking. Two maybes, though. One a toothless, black cleaner, the other from the man who owned the little bric-a-brac kiosk near the station entrance. It was all Aftab Akhtar wanted to hear. People were most careless when they thought they were safe. Tariq had paid the price already. Something Aftab was keen to remind him.

'You stay here,' he said, 'and keep your fucking eyes open this time.'

He'd give it a couple of hours, while the trail was fresh. If he couldn't find her by then, he'd call it off. They'd cruise down to Wilmslow Road and deliver his bag of goodies, then get Tariq some medical help. The bastard was the least of his worries.

The moment Shazia Ahmed put the receiver down, she felt a weight fall from her shoulders. Help was on its way. Gathering her shalwar kameez about her, she made her way out. All of Manchester lay before her; the tall towers round Piccadilly, the Court House clock, the sky a deep blue behind it. No more derelict wasteland. Just parking lots and plush hotels. So different from the grubby, grey streets there used to be. There was even greenery amidst all that concrete and glass. Shazia marvelled at it all, sometimes running for the thrill of running, most times for the fear of standing still.

In the distance, born on the air like the roar of distant waves, she heard the sound of a large crowd, the screams and shouts of children and the whirr of great machinery. Cardboard signs on every lamppost told her what it was. The fair had come to town. As she drew nearer the desire to see it grew, till it became an insatiable urge. But fear of missing Amina dragged her away. Maybe later, if there was time to do anything.

It was after seven o'clock when she finally got to Canal Street. The place was heaving, alive with pretty boys and louche queens. She wondered where they'd all come from, all these people. And she remembered poor Saqie Khan who used to live on the corner of her street, above the news-agents that seemed to be robbed by machete-wielding black kids every month. Her father said he'd done some terrible thing to another boy. Something unspeakable. Some days later he'd disappeared back to Pakistan. Shazia watched him go. Pakistan would drum it out of him, they said. And the name tolled heavily in her head. That's where they wanted her to go. To sort her out. To keep her quiet. Poor Saqie.

Shazia walked up and down Canal Street, keeping a careful eye on the Rembrandt pub. It wouldn't be too difficult to spot Amina. Not in this sea of men. Amina Aslam. To think it came down to her, after all this. She was the only one she'd ever confided in. About the baby. About the beatings. About the sorcery of her grandmother, mixing potions in Jhelum to frighten the bad spirits out of her, and the imam praying to Allah for guidance on the matter. Amina had listened with awe and wonder. Shazia's story was a salutary reminder to any girl of the power of family and community. For those who turned from East to West, there was only one outcome. She should be treated like one of them. Take not friends from the ranks of the heathen until they flee in the way of Allah. They are enemies of Islam.

The shadows lengthened vaguely on the cobbled stones. Shazia was looking up at the sky. She began to wonder if Amina would turn up at all. Half an hour's waiting had become forty-five minutes and there was still no sign of her. Longsight to Piccadilly, even by bus, didn't take that long. She noticed that the heat was less oppressive than it had been. The evening was cooling off. She wondered if she might just wait here herself, wait till nine o'clock. Would Damon be there then?

Tick Tock. Tick Tock. Then a flood of bodies around her.

And a girl's voice behind them.

'Shazia?'

Breathless and familiar. She turned to face it. And was shocked when she did. Amina looked as distraught as she. Her hair was strewn about her shoulders like a black delta, her eyes swollen like the banks of a river, and fit to break. It should have been the other way round. She should have been asking the questions.

'What happened to you?'

Amina hardly had the strength to respond. What *hadn't* happened? She held the holdall up in front of her and smiled wanly.

'I've brought the stuff you asked for. Not very clean, I'm afraid. But probably cleaner than that.'

She pointed to Shazia's shalwar kameez.

'I hardly recognised you in it.'

Shazia looked down. She hardly recognised herself.

'Amina,' she said. 'You don't know what this means.' And she paused for a second. There were tears in her eyes. 'I had no-one else I could trust.'

Amina stared at her but couldn't speak. Guilt hung over her.

'Come on. I'll tell you all.'

They turned to go. The Rembrandt, with its Victorian splendour lovingly restored, was no more than fifty yards away. And, if the sight of two Pakistani girls walking into a gay S&M bar looked a little strange, no-one let on. Drag artists were more than welcome. Shazia led Amina into the cool darkness of the building and ushered her upstairs to the little-used ladies' toilets. The regular clientele had seen stranger things than that. When the door closed behind them, the girls felt they were the only two people left alive in Manchester. And the past finally caught up with them.

Aftab Akhtar raised his haughty profile to the evening sky and looked at his watch. He'd give it a bit. The girl couldn't have got far. He took off his sunglasses and stared down the road, the air flickering faintly before him. His eyes bore into the billowing crowds and imagined a cream shalwar kameez. It was time to hunt again. He could feel it in his bones the way he had when Sonny Khan walked into that hotel room and he'd blown his fucking brains out. Destiny.

'*Kismet, ma'chod.*'

Righting his glasses across the generous wedge of his nose he moved swiftly down the hill.

Having no other choice than to leave his suitcase full of best Kashmir sherbet with Tariq, he did his best to pre-empt any silly ideas.

'It's wired, Tariq, *samajta*? Try to open it, it'll take your fucking face off.'

No time to worry if he believed him or not. He'd get back to him if there were problems.

So Aftab ran and felt the crowds thicken around him, the noise of rides and thunder in his ears. The sounds of the fair.

What better place to start, he thought.

CHAPTER 22

The clock on the wall had just struck seven when Dru Round walked out. The whirr of overhead fans had forced him back on the streets. Canal Street. The heart of the Gay Village, where old Victorian pubs, now done up in floral splendour, danced cheek by jowl with glass-fronted media bars and sordid Jizz clubs like Shaft, Cum, and DeepDrill. Bum Queens in tight T-shirts catwalked the canal edge, drinking Bacardi, toasting the day and the promise of a golden night to come. Dru eased his way through them, a plain white shirt open to his chest, eyeing them all through reflective sunshades. The faces were alien to him, so different from those he'd seen in the half-light of the early hours, in the vampire squalor of the clubs. Their sunbed bronze was a far cry from the blotchy pallor of their youth, when they'd first been drawn here. Canal Street was always their first taste of excess, lonely queers from brutal, northern towns. The sense of freedom, of belonging to a great queer sea, energised them, gave them strength to withstand the mediocrity, the beatings, the savagery of life at home.

Dru had seen loads of them come and go. The same pattern. Numbing to conformity, washing themselves in the sweat of a thousand amphetamine-inflamed bodies, screaming and snorting, dripping ecstasy, dropping E's with as much reckless abandon as they dropped their flies for any hungry cock. Yes, he'd seen it all. And worse. He'd seen the desperation of the middle-aged, types like Reg, clinging to their youth with as much civility as they could, whilst their body cried out for the kind of mind-bending love their youth had promised them. You hung round for the memories, in the hope they'd sun-kiss your body like the acid lips of some forgotten paramour. Ageing on Canal Street, you may as well throw yourself in the Medlock. Sure, the place was your first taste of excess, but it was your last, too. You faded here, like the old pictures of Manchester on the walls of the Rembrandt and the New Union; faded into obscurity. Your visits were ones of ever diminishing returns.

Dru felt the expectation of the evening on his neck. He'd been snorting since Reg rang him that morning. In and out of the bars, paying lip service to the passing trade. He wasn't going to end up at the end of a line like the old fellas. He'd be where the wild things were: in TV, in Film, in Multimedia Land. Reg would have told him it was all a 'crock of shit, dear', but all Dru could hear at that moment were those voices in his head.

Down a little side alley littered with condoms was the back entrance to the DeepDrill Club. You'd have overlooked it if you weren't looking for a quiet spot to get blown. The building used to be Manchester's Bunny Club. School girls from Central High used to spend their lunch breaks here, trying to peer in past the bouncers, down into those mogadon depths. Now it was Manchester's premier gay club, an intoxicating mix of drag and derring-do, of blond Chinese boys performing unseemly acts with pumpkins while leathered lesbians from Thailand stuck nails in each other's tongues. Or so the literature said. In reality it was like every other club in the area, just happened to be the flavour of the second.

Dru hated it. He made his way down the alleyway and felt immediately the release from the heat. It was cool down here. A large grille had been opened at the back of the building. A flight of white, stone steps led down to the changing rooms. The 'artistes'' quarters, though only an old dressing table and mirror indicated it; otherwise, the seedy air of public toilets hung over the place. Dru looked at himself in the mirror and tried not to think about scoring again. The knots in his stomach were tightening, aggravating his sense of unease. He clenched his fists and held them up to the mirror, shadow boxing. He'd been doing that all his life, making all the right moves, all the right noises, but never landing the telling punch. This show tonight, though, this was going to make all the difference. This Rupert St Clair would see his best ever.

He'd taken his shirt off to admire his chest a little more when Charlie Boy came in. Charlie Boy, the manager's right hand. Dru detested him. Everything sickly, vapid and interminably dull about the scene was crystallised in his limp-wristed affectations. His shorts and Ibiza tan made him want to throw up, his slack-arse simpering servitude made him want to punch the living hell out of him.

'Hi, Dru,' Charlie Boy gushed. 'How are you hanging?'

Dru nodded.

'Charlie,' he said.

A few punches.

'You were good last night,' Charlie said.

A few more. He turned round.

Charlie Boy looked round the room, resting his long eyes on the chest in front of him, creaming at the bit.

'God, it's so dismal in here, isn't it? Shall I brighten things up for you? Some flowers?'

Walking clichés. Dru felt his agitation grow.

'What do you want?' he said.

Charlie flicked the fringe out of his eyes. An awkward silence.

'David rang this afternoon.'

Dru looked at him. News travelled fast. Faster if you were well hung. And fastest if you were well-hung and action man to boot. The kid from last night.

Dru had Charlie Boy twigged in a minute. The fucking queen. Had him clocked in a second. He was after some, too.

'So what do you know, Charlie? I really didn't. You and Steve getting on well?'

'We have our moments,' said Charlie Boy. 'The problem is, well, you know,' and he made a gross display of looking at the baggage in Dru's groin.

The fucking rat, Dru thought.

Charlie smiled in what he thought was a coy and suggestive way. The idea of Dru Round being such a horse had tickled his fondant fancies. The thought of such heterosexual aggression was a definite turn-on. And his body? Well, that was sculpture, Leonardo.

To Dru, the smile on Charlie's face was as sickening a sight as he'd ever seen. The girlish capitulation to anything and everything irritated him to the point of violence. And the news that last night's fuck had broken cover to a rat like him made him want to vomit.

He touched Charlie's chest with his right hand. Charlie, all Greek with the prospect of being taken by an older, more powerful man, felt weak with love. He sincerely hoped Steve was still upstairs. Charlie knew he made lots of noise. It was just one of those things. He closed his eyes.

Dru watched all these preliminaries through glazed eyes, contemptuous. He brought Charlie's hands behind his back and pressed his lips to the boy's neck, watching the nape hairs rise and fall like wheat blown in a gale. And he sensed the storm of hatred brewing in the lining of his gut. Atlantic swells of loneliness washing over him. The madness of desire. Nowhere on earth did he feel as abandoned as he did here. He engaged in sex, that brutal eruption of fear and loathing, with the solemnity of an undertaker. Each time felt like the last time of all.

His strong hands burnt like liquid fire over Charlie's torso, his kisses blew hot blasts of air over his neck and shoulders. Then, it hit him. Tendrils of violence extended out through the tips of his fingers and he felt them turn into claws. The pounding in his brain deafened him. It was not lust, this. It was madness. A terrible, mad epiphany that accompanied his most heated moments. When the consequences of all and everything receded into the black fathoms.

As Charlie first gasped, the lights went out in Dru's mind. A craze had taken hold of him. His right hand grabbed Charlie's throat with iron while his left forced itself into the small of his back. Charlie choked out his surprise. His throat had been relaxed and flaccid. Now he felt the circle of steel around it. His hands grasped vainly at too powerful fingers. No chance of him executing his normal evasive manoeuvre, running and screaming at the top of his voice. Running and screaming the way he'd done last year in Piccadilly Gardens, when some hooded Moss Side cobras chased him to the very doors of the

Rembrandt. Fifty leather boys in weights and chains, all looking like serial killers with their bruising tattoos and Burt Reynolds moustaches, had saved him that day. Black steel was chased out of town. Here he was caught; drowning; intoxication becoming suffocation.

The lights were going out. The pulpy jelly Dru was squeezing the life out of snapped and swayed alarmingly like a ship at sea. In his brain, now given to madness, the mantra of the last few months came Hare Krishna to mind.

'I wonder what it would be like to die.'

And here was that moment, the opportunity to find out. In that very second the whole grisly thought would become reality. How often had he thought it, awake at night, with a sack of flesh beneath him? Crushing the life out of it to see if it would shock him out of himself. In the mirror of the dressing room he caught sight of their reflections, stoned statues locked in some ghastly rite. One figure, eyes closed, his body arched and reeling backwards, was falling into the arms of a muscled Adonis, his eyes boring into him. Could that really be *him*? And, at the very moment he held it in his hands, he felt death slipping through his fingers again. Felt the only thing he ever wanted receding further and further from view.

His hands dropped to his sides like dead things as the body of Charlie Boy crumpled unconscious to the floor. He checked the pulse on the neck. Just. Then turned the body on its side to prevent

any choking, all the things he'd read about, mem-
orised. It was as near as he'd ever got.

He needed help, he knew it. He was too close
to the edge. The next time. Well, there wouldn't
be a next time. He had to make it tonight. That
was his ticket out. Tonight.

Dru left the way he'd come. It was after half
past seven. As he emerged into the alleyway behind
the club, he felt the air prickle his scalp and
realised he was perspiring horribly. He really did
need to score. And he knew just the place to do
it. Candy's. She always had good stuff.

The black cab parked up just off Canal Street.
Going nowhere. Azad Riaz was banging his head
on the dashboard as he had done all day. He still
hadn't been home, the nightmare of the night
before strangling the very life out of him. The Four
of fucking Clubs! What had possessed him? And
that bastard Intikhab Khan swanning off like
Omar Sharif. The rest of his life stretched out
miserably before him. He had precisely *nothing* to
live for. Certainly not his family.

Fucking Intikhab Khan. He'd shafted him good
and proper. He was doomed. Had been doomed
from birth. Everybody looked at him like they
already knew. It was written on his face. His
mother saw it when he was born, his wife when
he groaned lifting the veil from her face. And
Shazia had seen it this morning. Shazia. Poor
Shazia. Of all his crimes and misdemeanours,

that was the worst. Worse than letting his carriage out as a portable sex machine. Worse than mugging his fares. Worse than anything. Shazia was family. If he had to do anything now, it should be to warn her. If Allah would just once look down on him.

Once.

His head was just beginning to hurt when somebody knocked on the window. He kept his head down, pretending he hadn't heard. It came again. He swore under his breath in Punjabi, and wound the window down.

'What?' he said. TP. The English hated that.

Behind his sunshades, Dru Round prepared for Holy War.

'India House,' he said.

And before Azad had a chance to tell him to fuck right off, he'd opened the passenger door.

The English were all like that. Pushy bastards.

'Hold on, friend,' he said. 'I need some air.'

He made his way to the canal edge. Should have dived right in. But, as he drew on the great gulps of thick, summer air and stretched his aching limbs, a peculiar refraction of light from off a glass-fronted bar left him, and him alone, in sunlight. As if Allah had chosen him.

He looked up and down the road. Towards Canal Street. And his jaw dropped like a stone.

Dru looked absently in the same direction, anxious to be off, dreaming of Candy's coke.

'Allah is oft-returning. Most merciful.'

Not fifty yards from the taxi, like furtive nuns, two Pakistani girls came hurrying. It was HER! It really was her. Incredibly. Impossibly. This was his chance. No longer would he be Kaffir. No longer would he skip Friday prayer. Allah had answered him. And he waved his hands frantically above him.

'Shazia!' he called. 'Shazia! It's me. Here!'

But as he did so, the light dimmed around him and she disappeared.

CHAPTER 23

The black saloon tore round the bend of Barlow Road and on to Mount Road. Billy was delirious and incendiary, a bomb waiting to go off, a car crash waiting to happen. He swerved this way and that, trying to right himself, all the while raining curses down on Jamie's head. He'd pay for his softness, would pay for letting the girl go. The Paki should have died. Like the rest of them. Bang. *Bang*! His head nearly went through the windscreen. That bald head, criss-crossed with purple arteries, pumped oil and madness into his burnt-out brain. The conflagration was seconds from igniting. He was going to take the pair of them out in one blitzkrieg strike, right into the Maginot Line of concrete posts that guarded Costcutter. The car mounted the pavement in preparation. Jamie gulped.

Then Billy grinned, his gold tooth gleaming in the blasted heath that was his mouth, and Jamie knew he was playing with him, testing him, waiting for him to scream. To scream, 'Stop, Billy. Fucking stop.' But Jamie knew he couldn't. Not this time. Those pedestrains fleeing for cover, it was part of the game. And Jamie had seen through it. Billy rejoined the road just in time. The bumper grazed the side of a litter bin and jolted them midstream. A fanfare of car horns greeted them, and wheels screeched burning rubber. Billy would have got out and knifed the fuckers, made them crawl on their bellies for that, but the street was alive with menace, and the army of witnesses was growing. Hard boys turning stone faces away from their bikes and trashy girls drawing hard on their cigs. A crash and a killing on Mount Road; the jackals were out. And the police were near.

Billy span the car the other way and shot down the road. First right on to Stanley Grove. Paradise Alley. Jamie was going home. Fuck. Billy hit the floor and sped into the unknown. His madness was growing. The car had to disappear. They had to disappear. They ran over the ramps and Jamie felt the underbelly of the car scrape against the tarmac. The sound of metal being stripped away. He felt his guts peeling in sympathy. Burning from the inside. He needed a place to stop, to throw them up. To get away. To forget. But Billy was unstoppable. While they had the car, they'd use it. Kirkmanshulme Lane, New Bank Street. He had safe houses everywhere. He had friends inside.

And Jamie's thoughts turned to his father and knew his time was fast approaching. Billy had warned him. You'll pay for it, Jamie. You'll pay. And his father's face was clear in front of him, ravaged and drawn in despair, as sad as the day it left him. There's no hope that way, son. I'm not coming back. No-one here gets out alive. He was there to prove it. *Run*. And Jamie realised he had to. Quickly. *Just leave the car. Just get out*. But, even as he thought it, he knew he couldn't. The wheels of his life were being driven by someone else. As they always had been. He was being chauffeured elsewhere. Longsight opened up before him and was going to take him back. The badlands. The car circled, round estates that never ended, through heat that never let up.

'Where are we going?' Jamie murmured, and his voice drifted out lifelessly, wandering nowhere.

'I'm thinking, Jamie-boy. I'm thinking.'

And Billy was. His face screwed up in the afternoon heat and his eyes narrowed to nothing.

Jamie hoped it wouldn't take long. For both their sakes. He was suffocating.

'What about Terence, Billy?'

The image of him floating in the air came billowing back, a reminder of why they were here.

Billy turned his head towards him as if to say *Don't you know, Jamie?*

His voice was dead and cold.

'He'll be alright. Don't get soft again, Jamie. The Pakis will see to him.'

And that was it. Billy was gone again, and the car picked up speed down Pink Bank Lane. Jamie no longer cared. Terence was in front of him and he couldn't see. He felt the car ride the speed ramps along Northmoor Road and the thrill was gone. All that was left was fear. They were going shopping. Asda approaching, and the railway bridge. But they never made it. Billy hit the brakes hard, too hard, and they careered over the verge and on to some waste ground. Some getaway. Every bastard within a mile would have heard that. The saloon crashed into a nearby fence. Day over.

They heard sirens blaring along Stockport Road, swooping down on doomed Levenshulme, inter-city through the traffic. All that noise because of them. And Jamie couldn't move. He was dazed. And confused. And thinking. But Billy shook him roughly, and his eyes were murder, and Jamie knew that things wouldn't end here. There were miles to go before he'd sleep. And he felt Billy's massive hands lift him out of the car and drag him down a steep embankment. The sirens sound-ed nearer, and the voices of people were almost on top of them. But there was method in his madness. They crossed the road to Asda and took the back way, into the shade, into the cavalry charge of approaching trolleys and the crowds of unlovely humanity. And they disappeared, indis-tinguishable from the tattooed army of shoppers in the car park.

A footpath appeared before them, all graffitied and barbed wire, dark and long, funnelling into the unknown. And Billy was holding him, pushing him, and his legs began moving, then opened, jogging and running. Running to get the hell out of there. Towards the rail depot: New Bank Street,

Halsbury Close, Langport Avenue. The shooting gallery.

'Where are we going?'

Billy ignored him. He was eyeing one of the council houses on the opposite side of the road. A black Mercedes was parked outside. Birdboy country. Even Jamie didn't come down here. He watched Billy knock on through the metal grille. He didn't care. A large black man answered the door, in trainers and slacks. Identikit drug-dealer. He looked about him as they spoke, insouciantly, as if discussing the weather, or his garden, or his car. They were chatting. Just *chatting*. But when Billy came away, he was unhappy.

'We can't stay here, Jamie-boy. Police are on an op. Everything's quiet. We've got to move.'

'Where?'

Billy looked around them. They had to go on. It was their only chance to stay alive.

'You got your phone?'

The question hit a brick wall. And hurt.

'Terence had it.'

Billy looked at him and paused. He understood.

'He'll be okay, Jamie-boy. Terence's sound. It ain't all over. Not yet.'

And Jamie was left holding on to the hope. But the sun beat down on his red neck and burned him, and he wasn't so sure. There was always pain to bear, and there was always a mark left. How much more could he take? On any other day but this.

'Well, we need one, Jamie.'

Billy's words broke the spell and his eyes bored into him, daring him.

Jamie's stomach churned. They were heading towards Stockport Road, as casual as they could. A fugitive black girl made her way towards them, all breasts and bottom, and sista attitude, shouting into the air. Her brothers, a call away. She was holding one to her ear. Billy grinned.

But Jamie couldn't move. Not because he didn't want to, but because of what was happening. He couldn't see. The girl was metamorphosing before his very eyes. Her café au lait Caribbean skin was lightening to the colour of the desert, and her rainbow-coloured skirt running into purple. He was behind Naz's takeaway again with the face of the Asian girl in front of him. He could feel her breathing beneath him, could taste her perfume. And she was staring at him, beautiful and distant and untouchable.

'You won't get away, Jamie Farrell. None of you will.' And he realised she was right. His muscles were stone, his fists wouldn't swing, and his mouth couldn't speak. And Billy knew it, too.

He was already too late. Billy had started.

The girl gave him the mobile without a struggle. No fists, no screams, no knives. Nothing. And Billy was smiling, his gold tooth catching her eye. Jamie had never seen that before. He looked almost human. It belonged in a dream. And he began to imagine everything had been a dream, and he was going to wake up. But Billy's voice stopped his heart and he realised he wasn't. Billy's hands were clutching his face and he was staring into those eyes again.

The girl was gone, shouting once more.

'Don't mess with sistas, Jamie. Not round here.'

'I thought,' but the words died, and he hung his hands. 'Who did you call?'

'Errol. Errol's going to get us out of here.'

And the sun burned him, hotter than ever.

CHAPTER 24

When Shazia Ahmed finally finished telling her story, a dark shadow crossed Amina Aslam's heart. She felt she'd been eclipsed again, her own run-in with the thugs at the take-away forgotten. Beside the incendiary heat of Shazia's life, hers still barely flamed at all. Lost in the blaze of a passing comet.

'I'm leaving,' Shazia said.

Dressed in Amina's jeans and T-shirt she felt more herself. She wrapped the bloodstained rags of her shalwar kameez up and stuffed it into a paper-towel basket.

'Where will you go?' Amina asked.

'London,' Shazia said.

Amina thought of Mo. That's where he was. He could stay there for all she cared. What was the point pretending? She was sure he'd found somebody else. London was such a big place. What would he want with Manchester? What would he want with her?

'On your own?'

A seed of hope germinated in the back of her mind. *The answer machine message.*

Shazia looked at her strangely. And had a sudden desire to hide the truth.

'Yes, I think so.'

Amina pursed her lips.

'But you don't know anyone down there, do you?'

Probing.

Shazia shrugged her shoulders. 'No.'

Pause.

'Does Damon know?'

The air thickened. Shazia Ahmed felt troubled again. Not so safe. She looked into Amina's dark eyes, masked by the peacock feathers of her long lashes, and couldn't escape the thought that she, too, may have betrayed her. Was her father, even now, on his way here?

'No,' she said, quietly. 'I haven't told him.'

Amina's heart missed several beats.

Shazia decided they should leave. She had to keep moving. She had to keep Amina moving. Just in case.

But Amina was quiet, struggling to contain her feelings, wishing there was somewhere to hide them. Had she made a mistake? Asking about Damon. It was too obvious. And yet, maybe, it had done some good. It had answered the 64,000-rupee question, the question that had been burning them both up for months now. Shazia *really* didn't know.

And so they left the Rembrandt and made their way down Canal Street, keeping close together, seldom stopping, looking over the quay into the pea-soup sludge at the bottom. Shazia had lost a shoe in there long ago. They'd cleaned all the prams and trolleys out since. Even the sewage looked better these days. And, strangely, it seemed to both girls that they'd reached a crossroads here, as if both their futures began along this cobbled street. But to anyone else, high above Whitworth Street, they were all but invisible, two insignificant specks in a swift-moving stream. Amina's purple shalwar kameez would flicker on the film of an eye and vanish. The noise and bustle of the evening crowds surrounded them. The fair was drawing them in and a great longing overcame them. Shazia, for the rides and the anonymity of the crowd. Amina, for something else. Where she spent the last two hours of Shazia's time in Manchester was an irrelevance. Her thoughts were elsewhere.

They turned down Sackville Street and Amina's eyes were fixed ahead, daydreaming. But Shazia's were darting from side to side, half expecting her father, or Aftab, to emerge. And she found them drawn to a distant, black taxi. Its driver had just got out and was standing by the canal side. As they drew nearer and nearer, a tremor of unease grew in her. There was something familiar about him. His look. His slouch. What was it? Then she noticed the registration plate. And froze. Impossible. It couldn't be. But no. It *was*. He was standing in a field of sunlight, staring right at her. And the penny dropped.

Mamoo Azad! Here at the end as he was at the beginning. What part had he to play in her father's madness? The bastard. He'd sold her out. For a fraction of a second she stopped, her mouth a perfect 'O' of surprise, then felt the tug on her arm and her being pulled away, reeling from shock. The last she saw was his arms waving madly at her, and his face wild and desperate. And born on the summer air, like poison darts, her name came calling.

They turned into Piccadilly Gardens, home of the old city bus station, where the bomb-shelter corrugated-iron sheds used to be; sheds that looked like giant abattoirs, or prison. They'd built it on the grounds of the old Manchester Royal Infirmary. With the number of weekend stabbings, they should have left it there. The gardens, really a few square feet of hawthorn bushes and spring flowers, drowned in the fetid Manchester cocktail of piss, sick and booze. And blood. Now everything was open plan and CCTV. Gangs of youths no longer patrolled the sheds like jackals. But take a wrong turn down Oldham Street into Back Piccadilly and you'd still be skinned for your change. Queue up at any 192 bus stop, and you'd still run the gauntlet of abuse from the new generation of council-estate trash. Or better still, you could go to the fair.

The fair at Piccadilly took place twice a year. During the day, the screams of wayward children and the raucous laughs of adults gave the area a semblance of life. But, during the evening, the screams and shouts of drunken boys, and the gruesome cackles of teenage girls blew in from Collyhurst and Gorton, and the rides crackled with electric menace. The yawning of machinery and the whirr of steel became a Metropolis backdrop to the coming nights of violence.

It was nudging eight o'clock when Shazia and Amina arrived. The evening sun, slicing across the top of the city, threw great shadows across the Gardens. A great Ferris wheel loomed large like a spaceship, its upper hemisphere bathed in golden light, its lower half sinking into shadow. Day and night. On the ground, invisible currents drew the heaving summer crowds past every stall and shy. And where once hot-dog stands stood, with blotchy-looking Englishmen puffing their red cheeks, now there were kebab joints, peopled with swarthy-looking Asians roasting spits. In the balmy air, the smell of flesh was everywhere, from the dead carcasses of cows and sheep to the sweat off a thousand bodies. Shazia and Amina walked through it, distant and distracted. Shazia's mind was full of her uncle, Amina's full of Damon Ruff.
  A small group of Indian girls waited at the foot of the Big Wheel, clutching their mobile phones and paging their boyfriends their secret rendezvous. Shazia and Amina lined up behind them. They were joined by a group of black kids and

white kids, their hands arrowing up to heaven like spears. That's where they wanted to be. Right there, at the very top of everything.

The Big Wheel juddered into life and began to rise. Shazia stared into space. Amina couldn't keep still. Jealousy had wormed its way into her heart.

'You're lucky, you know, Shazi,' she said finally.

Shazia stared at her. That was a word she definitely wouldn't use.

'Why?' she said.

'Because you're getting out. You'll be free. London will be good for you. My parents would never let me.'

In the distance, somewhere over Piccadilly, a crescent moon was faintly visible, hanging from the arbours of the sky. It would be luminous tonight and smile down upon the world. Like the one on the Pakistani flag. But, as the cradle began to descend, the smile turned into a rictus grin, and Shazia wondered whether the moon was not mocking her, mocking them all. *Lucky?*

But Amina was silent, toying with her secret, and wondering how she'd ever keep it quiet. As the giant clock face turned, it wound back again to autumn, to the evening when Damon Ruff appeared. How he held her feet in his hands and caressed her, tracing the contour of instep and ankle, how he fired kisses down on her breathless and open mouth, and how he made her cry out; cry out the way Mo never had. How the guilt flared at each bite he took out of her. And how she'd been in shadow ever since, opportunities waxing and waning with no hint of a hereafter, save maybe in the flicker of an eye. And now her heart beat faster still for Shazia Ahmed was leaving without him.

It was hard to recall how long they'd been up there, maybe six orbits, when Shazia realised that the wheel was slowing down. She felt the machinery crank itself for one final effort, then come to a complete stop. As if by chance, it did so at the apogee, twelve o'clock to the ground. They swayed gently on the roof of the world, waiting for the passengers to alight, cradle by cradle. Shazia vaguely wondered if there was not a quicker way.

As the carriage made its descent, the noise and din of the fair rose to greet them. Minute by minute, the world was spinning into focus. Long, snaking lines of lights drifted like currents in the sand banks of the crowd. Little by little, blurred faces of pink and brown gradually took shape till it was possible to identify them individually. A group of Chinese children huddled close to their parents, pointing upwards, a louche and slender twenty-something girl with red, rich, pre-Raphaelite hair, clutching a mobile phone, a rookery of twelve-year-old boys circling danger-ously round her. The cradle dropped again.

By chance, Shazia's eyes were drawn to one of the kebab stands some sixty yards away and about thirty feet below her. Above it, like a luminous blancmange, shone a ludicrous pink dome. OASIS. And beneath it stood a solitary figure. The passing crowds took no notice of him. But *she* did. And when the aquiline features turned perceptibly in the direction of the Big Wheel, and dark sunglasses appeared to bore right into the cradle, she noticed it more. A terrible paralysis gripped her. Her mouth went dry. *Oh God*. How could it be?

Amina was just about to stand up, so close were they to the ground, but Shazia's hand checked her immediately and she dragged her down. Desperately, hopelessly, she looked at her.

'It's him!' she said. 'I can't believe it. It's him!'

Amina bit her lip. *Damon?*

'Who?' she said.

'The man at the airport. He's here. By the Dome.'

Amina gulped nervously and peerëd over the top.

The wheel turned and dropped the cradle another level.

'Where?' she said. 'I can't see anyone.'

And Shazia looked out again. The Dome winked back at her. Flavours of the East. It bore a picture of a camel and a samosa and a tent pitched on a high desert dune. But there was no-one beneath it, no summer Bedouin camped outside. He'd vanished like a mirage.

'He *was* there, Amina.'

Thoughts of Mamoo Azad, doubts over Amina, were exiled from her mind. Aftab was here, somewhere in this great crowd, and she was descending into it, into the maelstrom of the fiery evening. She felt herself drowning. Piccadilly and London seemed further away than ever.

The long line of ten-pound notes Aftab Akhtar had handed out to those who may or may not have seen Shazia would have stretched from Manchester to Karachi if he'd let it. Not that he'd have got his money's worth. You just didn't know with the English. They were such a shifty lot.

He cut his way through the crowd like a shark in a clear sea, eyeing the shameless white girls with their puffy, pink breasts reddening in the sun. And their vulture-faced boyfriends with their bloated potbellies. Such cruel faces, he thought. Such an unseemly mass of humanity. And to think this lot ruled India. How the hell had they managed that?

For perhaps half an hour, Aftab searched everywhere fruitlessly. Then, at the dodgems, a possible sighting. A girl in a cream suit. He made his way to her right, hidden from view. Stalked her like a leopard till he was close enough to strike. But, as he was about to do so, she turned around. A nose like a parrot's beak protruded from her face. No luck. He shot imaginary bullets at every coconut shy in frustration, and fired poisoned darts at every board. There were no prizes for coming second. Ever.

Eventually, he stopped at a particularly revolting kebab stall called OASIS. Its domed roof glowed in garish pink. He wondered if the English really fell for this kind of thing. Dared not try one of the burgers, even if it was halal. The proprietor looked a real Tep, all bullish insolence like those villagers back home. A group of English lads were sticking into the grease and gherkins. Multi-culturalism, he mused, wryly. The English were getting a taste of their own medicine. Still, they'd only themselves to blame. You bring shit into the house, it'll only stink it out. And now the heathens were doing better than they were. Thank Allah his family hadn't come over.

Aftab stared into the sky. The Big Wheel was directly before him. He wondered whether he shouldn't take a ride. He had that feeling. The view was good up there. He made his way quietly into the queue and ushered aside some Asian lads who seemed to be taking up too much room. Their language was a volley of black and blue. Dirty Punjabi. He grabbed the nearest one by his hand and twisted it horribly. There was a short snap of bone. The others backed off, scared.

Fucking villagers, he thought.

And waited to board.

Amina and Shazia left the safety of the cradle with mixed emotions. The realisation that Shazia had seen one of her kidnappers reawakened all the afternoon's dread. The fact that Aftab was some-how here, at large, and could even now be observing them, gnawed at them from the evening shadows. And the shadows were growing longer. Despite the sun, despite the defiance of a thousand neon lights, grey twilight would soon be upon them. They left while they still could.

Running through the turnstiles, with their heads down, they looked neither right nor left, oblivious to everything. The safety of the crowd beckoned them. But the air behind them moved and a black figure emerged from it. He recognised instantly the fine features of Shazia Ahmed. He could hardly believe his luck. His feelings hadn't let him down, he knew it.

He looked up at the crescent moon, now clearly visible in the evening sky. Like a gibbet, it hung ominously over the fair.

CHAPTER 25

When Mamoo Azad's hands finally dropped to his sides, he realised the end was near. And how stupid he must have looked. Not waving but drowning. The stinging embarrassment of Shazia's rejection left him sweating and fidgety. Dru Round had to cajole him back into the cab with the promise of an extra ten. Twenty, make it. Money always spoke to him.

They left for India House, the drone of the city crackling like radio static in the summer air. Azad tried to block it out. Tried to concentrate on the too familiar streets before him. Manchester A to Z. Tried not to think of Shazia running away from him, nor Intikhab gloating over him, nor his family. He needed to talk. That's why you talked. To keep yourself from going insane. From thinking the guy in the back was going to produce a ligature, or a gun, and send you off into the next life without so much as a *kudafis*.

The panoramic vista of Whitworth Street opened out in wide-angle cinemascope. It wasn't working. A terrible lump was welling up in the back of his throat. He began to think about his poor children falling further behind at school, the eczema round their eyes and ears making them look like plague victims, and his poor wife trying to disguise the dark circles round her own. Why was it so hard? To go home like other men do. To apologise to his wife. To tell her to her frightened face that he loved her. Would that really be so hard? Fucking yes, he decided. She had no money and now no house.

The shadows lengthened. Before he knew it they were there. Dru Round was getting out.

'Look,' he said, 'I won't be that long. Can you come back later?'

He handed Azad the extra twenty. Azad certainly could.

'Quarter past nine.'

The twenty vanished. A conjurer's sleight of hand. Intikhab had taught him that one. Azad watched him go. Idiot, he thought.

He drove back to Canal Street and mildly entertained the thought of suicide. He wondered if there wasn't some simpler way. He put his head on the steering wheel again and began to bash it slowly, trying to force himself into wakefulness. He stared at his cell phone. He should call her. Let her know he was still alive. She'd rung fifteen times. What the hell was the matter with him?

He put the radio on and looked in his rear-view mirror. Shazia had been there only this morning. His thoughts steeled and darkened. Why had she ignored him? He caught the end of a local news bulletin on Piccadilly 102.

'Three people are now confirmed dead after this afternoon's attack on an Indian take-away in south Manchester . . .'

Three dead, he thought, what's the fuckin' world coming to?

When Dru Round got out of the taxi the only thing he could think of was coke. He stood before India House like Hillary before Everest. To get high, he had to climb.

India House had been overrun with gays and dealers from its first erection. It had all the charm and sophistication of a San Francisco gym. But it did have its advantages. It meant sprawling back home from the Village at three in the morning was no longer the terrible struggle it had been. The often nauseous taxi rides home to Didsbury and Chorlton, your cock at half-mast, guilt-ridden that you didn't really fancy the shaven-headed student beside you, all that was a thing of the past. Home was now a wankable two minutes away. What matter if you didn't like them? Time for both of you to return to the bull market at New York New York or for some brAss rubbing at the DeepDrill.

Taking the lift up to the top floor, Dru took a long look at himself in the darkened mirror. He scowled. This'd be the last time he'd be tooting with Candy. If Reg had all the clout he said he had, and Rupert St Clair could get him the TV slot, then the sky was the limit. He'd have them wheeled in on trays, along with contracts thicker

217

than telephone directories; all the numbers of the rich and famous who wanted to work with him. It'd be that easy. In less than two hours all that could be his, the difference between scratching round in perpetual obscurity and being recognised on every billboard in the land. No wonder he felt so tense.

When the lift doors opened, Dru emerged into a twilit corridor. Two narrow slits high up in the roof admitted narrow beams of sunlight. They were not enough to dispel the shadows. You could turn right or left. Right to Candy's, left to the emergency stairs and the maintenance shaft. The corridor was deserted. And stifling. All the heat of the day seemed to have been locked up here. It felt like the tropics.

No wonder his flowers do so well, he thought.

It had been months since he last visited Candy. He wasn't too fond of him, either. He found his 'too chic to smile' media persona slightly colder than a snake's, a real 'puff adder'. But his fingers *were* in a lot of fruit pies. And he was the queen's queen. He made cushions and furry slippers seem dangerous. Just the kind of vacuous type who'd do well presenting Great Morning TV, in fact. He was one of those bloody awful theatrical types Dru felt like squeezing the life out of. But needs must, and Candy was the very best person you went to if you wanted to score high-grade cocaine. He'd been weaned on the stuff. And, strangely, he liked Dru, too.

A strange sense of foreboding crept over him. The air was so heavy he thought he'd choke. And he remembered the voices on the intercom. Candy had company. Not one of his fairies, either. The voices were altogether rougher. Too Mancunian. Who the hell was he mixing with these days? You'd have thought he'd learned his lesson after those rent-boys he'd invited back last year turned out to be police officers. Candy had thought it was all part of the act, of course, and couldn't wait for them to strip off – till a burly sergeant burst in and cuffed him. Even so, it took a deal convincing him that it was all for real.

As he turned and walked down the corridor, Dru began to feel uneasy. A tight knot of fear began to harden in the pit of his stomach. He flexed his gym-pumped biceps and rolled his head across his shoulders. The nape hairs on the back of his neck were sticking up like porcupine quills.

Must be the show getting to me, he thought.

He stood before the door.

And knocked.

A faint shuffling was heard behind it. Candy, a long, black wig torn from the side of his head, poked his head round. He was sporting two large panda eyes and a cut lip. Funny makeup.

'Oh, hello, Dru,' he said. 'Come in.' Dazed and drugged. 'I've got guests, unfortunately. Hope you don't mind.'

The door opened.

Dru drank in the coke-perfumed air, which the scent of wild orchids failed to mask. Pulling aside some drapes and beads which hung from the ceiling, he appeared to have walked on to a film set. Candy's flat was a picture of Hollywood opulence. Lavish wild vines snaked up stucco walls, flowers cloistered together in every sheltered arbour. Wooden latticework carved intricately with various friezes of young boys fucking each other, classical style. A host of sherbet silks and cushions scattered across the mosaic floor like jaded houris. Candy played the Sheikh here, Rudolph Nureyev for the dancing boys he brought back. Or Yvonne de Carlo for everyone else. At the far end of the suite a marble staircase led up to a wide, wooden balcony. The whole of it was decorated with trailing hanging baskets, flowers of every hue and type, and fronded leaves of every length and shape. It was one of the seven wonders of the Gay Village, the hanging gardens of Hollywood Babylon.

Yet it was not this which attracted Dru's gaze so much as the two shaven-headed men standing beneath it. He didn't think they were there to sniff sherbet with Candy. He vaguely remembered seeing one of them before, hanging round in Whitworth Street, but couldn't be sure.

As Candy shut the door behind him, alarm bells pealed closer to hand.

One of the men shouted across the room.

'Who the fuck is it?'

Nasal, whining, dark, threatening. No need for introductions, then.

'It's a dear friend of mine, Billy,' Candy said. 'Please be calm.'

Candy seemed to have taken strength from Dru's arrival. There was a slightly patronising air in his reply. But in his wild eyes there was desperation, the desperation of a man in trouble. The bags around them were weeping.

Friendly spoke again.

'Join the party, motherfucker.'

Dru's muscles tensed. Gay steel. He was no wall-flower to be menaced by Mancunian grey. 'Fuck you, too, ugly,' he said, his eyes squinting.

Silence descending, the scented air seemed to be sucked from the room. Candy held his breath. But Dru didn't move. He stared with those dead-ening eyes on the two men. And their own dead eyes stared back.

Tick Tock. Then the quiet was broken. Friendly's companion was laughing. The shock of hearing someone insult Billy was just too priceless. The puzzled look on his face only made it funnier. Billy was gnashing his teeth in fury, his grizzled stubble glazed with perspiration. It was about the funniest thing Jamie Farrell had ever heard. All the tension of the day was released: the fight with Patrick, the gunshots at Naz's take-away, the unbearable aftermath with Billy going crazier than ever, crashing the car on Stanley Grove, and haring off down Kirky Lane.

221

And suddenly, Billy seemed to find it funny, too. He creased up and coughed and began laughing out loud. Candy watched him stumble round his apartment with barely contained fear. He'd felt the power and unpredictability of the man already. Jamie, he could handle, but this Billy, he was different. He should never have let them in. The idiot was choking with laughter and repeating the word 'ugly' over and over again, finally coming up to Dru, standing there taut and motionless, gold-tooth grin slicing open his face, doing his best to smile.

'Ugly?' he said.

Then exploded. A fist shot out that would have punctured a lung. Billy was a champion bare-knuckle fighter. He'd downed many a Paddy in Levenshulme with that one. And straight for the tender spot under Dru's ribs he aimed.

And missed.

Instead, his own face exploded with pain. *Real* pain. Dru hadn't spent all those years in the gym for nothing. His fist connected with the force of cruel steel. Billy was thrown to the floor. Jamie looked at the sodden figure and wished he'd had the nerve to do that. Imagine it, a faggot burning Billy's behind like that. He *was* impressed.

Dru anticipated the punch well before it came. These car thieves and petty hoods were all the same. Show them a bit of muscle and they buckle. They prey on fear. Dru had none of that. The fist to his midriff was slow and predictable, as easy to dodge as one of Manchester's trams. Time to strike.

But as Dru knelt over Billy for a second blow, twisting him round to give his face another pasting, he found Billy's face as composed as a corpse's. The grey eyes were leaking, a sure sign he'd just inhaled, but were calmly focused, too. Dru wondered what he had to be composed about, then felt something hard pushing into his stomach. He looked down.

Fuck, he thought. A gun.

CHAPTER 26

When Jamie Farrell, holed up in Errol's garret in Moss Side, heard that Terence had died on the way to Manchester Royal, a terrible sadness filtered through his body. The high water-table of drugs in his system was washed away, and memories of his father in Strangeways surfaced, like the flailing arms of a drowning man. That's where he was going to end up. He could hardly blame his mother for leaving him there. He *was* no good. Even shacking up with a pimp like Irish Patrick was preferable to another life sentence with Dad.

Billy, however, took the news on his granite chin like it was an everyday occurrence, which, in Manchester, it was. People got killed all the time.

'We all die, Jamie-boy. People like us. We deserve it. Think a' the ones who don't. That should cut you up. Terence was a fucker. He would a' gone soon, any road.'

But Jamie wasn't listening. From far away, a whisper of a memory reached him. School days at Stanley Grove. Fifty-a-side football in the play-ground. Terence had his own friends, then. Who knows where he'd have got to if he'd stuck with them? College, maybe. Or a job. But no, one summer he ended up in Jamie's class. And another summer, ten years later, he ended up dead. All he'd done was cross a playground. You wouldn't think it mattered, but here it meant the world.

He'd known something was wrong the moment Terence's body crumpled to the floor. And they'd left him to die. As the car screeched away from Naz's take-away, he was lying there with a bullet in his chest. Poor Terence. For him it was all over. Billy was wrong about him. But he had got them clear away. Black Errol had picked them up in his BMW. He hadn't liked getting his fingers dirty at all, his type never do. His fingers had been knuckle deep in his white slut's pussy when Billy rang.

'You can't stay here, man,' Errol told them, 'I don't want no smack coming down on my head coz of this. You gotta go.'

'Well, where the fuck where?' shouted Billy.

Just as Errol was warming up to sound Billy off, girlfriend number four came in, her silk dressing gown lashed round her like cling film, emphasising rather too well her generous disposition. Blonde, naturally, with her hair a sea of kiss curls. Errol told her to park her white ass back on the bed.

'I'm bored,' she said.

Errol thought very carefully about what he was going to say next. If he hadn't had company, he'd have cuffed her a few times and told her to shut the fuck up. The boredom of women was endless. Like a life sentence. He'd watched his poor dad suffer the same way, doing the right thing by his mother till she fucked off with a cook from a catering college. It was women that handed on misery to man. Marrying his mother, his dad disappeared into an abyss of longing. He died of neglect.

'Sugar,' he said. 'I'm busy.'

And he wagged his finger like a cobra before her eyes. Keeping up appearances. Didn't want these whities thinking the boyz had no class. Not that it would have made any difference. The only women Billy and Jamie had seen in the past six months were skinny crack whores from Longsight, the kind of paleface who'd go down on you for a drag of draw. He'd get no lectures from them.

Jamie stared at the girl as she swung her hips and left. Then he had a sudden thought. Sugar. Candy! The queen with the penthouse suite. That was well out of the way. She owed him quite a bit, too. On the tick. He'd muscled in on her last year, knocking off a few flats in India House. The place was a mine. Poor stuff, though. He ended up supplying the whole block. Those girls had *serious* money.

Errol and Billy were deep in what looked like thought.

'I've got it,' he said. 'I know where we can go.'

In the lexicon of Billy's mind, the word *gay* did not get a single entry; it was just not part of the

226

vocabulary. It hovered somewhere beneath the horizon along with words like *library* and *theatre*, just words that he'd heard about somewhere down the line.

In the landscape of Errol's mind, the word *gay* only meant one thing: Rodney. His nonce of a brother, Rodney, who fucked off to London to become a dancer and ended up working the streets off All Saints Road. It was very lucky for him the boyz never found out about that. Those stains were the hardest to wash out.

So, when Jamie mentioned Candy and his penthouse suite, there were two quite different reactions from the two men. Errol began to murmur dark and dreadful things about batty boys while Billy was stupefied, trying to fathom it all.

'Whatever you say, Jamie-boy,' he said, and stared at him. 'We'll pay him a visit.'

So Errol dropped them off in his BMW, its black lacquer swallowing the sun's rays like a tar pit. It was a glorious early evening. He'd have had the windows right down if he'd been on his own. Still, favours were favours. Billy had saved his ass a couple of times, too. That time he drew a gun on an IRA man at the Midway Pub. A touch of the blarney stone. Billy had dug him out of that one. His five hundred pounds had bought his life. And it was a good investment. Billy had made contact. Contact with the blackest dealers in Moss Side.

Cruising down Wilmslow Road, Errol felt good about himself. He knew the polished jet cutting through the tide of traffic got him noticed. It was what he wanted. A great fuck-off to authority. And a great fucking turn-on for the girls. He could park up in front of any police car these days and they wouldn't touch him. He'd have to shoot someone in broad daylight before they did that. PC Whitey had his orders. Political Correctness. And he'd probably only do that if he had some coconut with him. The trees in Whitworth Park ruffled their leaves in indignation at his passing, the girls in skimpy tops ate their ice creams, oblivious to his eyes boring holes between their thighs. High summer, a sweltering June night, he'd go back to the flat and take girlfriend number four out.

In the back, Billy was too stoned to think anything. He took his top off and flexed his muscles, admiring the tattoos over the taut skin. Sweat was glistening over his bald pate. Beside him, Jamie sat and stared into the middle distance and thought about Terence and about what Billy had said, that he would have died anyway. Billy Fuck. Billy Whizz. He probably had Terence's number already. He decided that, after today, after the next few days, he'd leave Billy for good. The next bullet could be for him. The Craze. It had to stop somewhere.

The BMW pulled up on Whitworth Street beside India House. Billy staggered out. Jamie followed. Billy was thinking of drugs, Jamie of a door marked EXIT. Yet, every time he tried to open it, he found himself staring at a brick wall. That girl was right. He wouldn't get away. She stared back without fear, as poised and serene as Holy Mary, her brown eyes like sunken pools.

Errol watched them go, pleased to be washing his hands of them. That Billy was a menace. He watched them disappear in the rear-view mirror till they were no more than a blip on his horizon. Now the evening belonged to him. He decided he *would* take number four out tonight, despite her insolence. He'd take her to the Al-Biswan in Rusholme. There was a gorgeous Asian girl who worked behind the bar there. He'd see if his Mercedes smile and BMW charm would work on her. She might have a taste for the dark side. Just like these white bitches. The prospect stiffened his trousers. Yeah, he'd do all that, but not before he cuffed number four. The dumb bitch did have to learn some manners.

Up till the moment Jamie and Billy broke into his flat, Candy's day was going just perfectly. Like everyone else in India House, he holed himself up in curlers during the daylight hours, watching all of Great Morning TV and every soap opera going. He'd made himself beautiful by bathing in coconut and amber extract from The Body Shop, and spent an hour or so on his hair, fixing the hair extensions just so. Just like Yvonne de Carlo. Time was a beautiful thing and Candy liked nothing more than languishing in it, keeping those wretched wrinkles at bay with extract of hedgehog saliva and cucumber, letting the milk and honey unclog every pore of his whiter than white flesh.

In dressing gown and slippers, he'd made his way on to the balcony of his suite and marvelled at the heat of the sun. Though he hated to be in it, he knew that it was good for the flowers, and what was good for them was good for him. In the absence of anything more meaningful than watching boys have sex in front of him, and fearing to bruise his purity, he turned to flowers as if they were his surrogate children, minding and tending them indulgently.

Dru had rung earlier, too, saying he might come round. Candy wished he would. That was one lusty boy there. He could only imagine the terrible damage Dru might wreak over his defenceless body. And should he give in to awful temptation? The flowers would look away.

Yes, it had been a lovely day. Till the knock came.

Candy answered it half expecting any number of people. Friends and queens. Lovers and draw. What he wasn't expecting was Jamie Farrell and a man with the word BILLY tattooed on his head. Now Candy knew that Jamie was only there for one thing, but what his friend was there for he could hardly guess. He didn't think he wanted to know. So when Jamie told him that they wanted to stay for a few days, it was quite a surprise. It was also out of the question. Better to sleep on the streets than have those two in your house. The protest had barely died on his lips, however, when Billy sent his right fist into his face. For a second, Candy imagined himself standing up to it, behaving like a man, but his true nature got the better of him and he crumpled like a tissue. He desperately wanted to fall unconscious but all he could manage was a swoon. It was only when he heard the buzzer from the lobby that he woke from it. Saved by the bell.

Billy didn't want him to answer it but he begged and implored him that he must. The person was expected. If he didn't, they'd know something was wrong. Billy stared at him, stoned immaculate, and Candy quaked. There was no mistaking the consequences.

He answered the intercom.

And his heart soared. It was Dru Round. His knight in shining armour!

Five minutes later, his knight in shining armour was on the floor with a gun pointing at his belly. The last reel was going badly for the hero. He wondered what Yvonne de Carlo would do at that moment.

CHAPTER 27

Aftab Akhtar stalked the two girls like a Bengal tiger. He hung back from them just enough to keep them in range, but near enough to pounce. The jungle of the fair was no different from Katchi Abadis or the squalid slums of Karachi. He'd bide his time. He had plenty of it. Although vaguely irritated that the girl now had company – it was always more difficult to make two people disappear – he was enjoying himself. The kill was in sight. And he was sure she hadn't seen him. The will of Allah was at work. They'd make a mistake soon; be swept apart, or slip down some dark road. And then he'd be on them.

'Why are we still running, Shazi?' Amina said, between deep breaths. Exercise was quite beyond her.

Shazia looked back.

'We've got to.'

'You can't be sure it was him, you know. You were a long way away. There's thousands of people here. He could be anywhere.'

Shazia looked round her madly. All the screams and rides and people made her dizzy. It should

232

be simple. All she had to do was keep out of trouble for an hour and a half. And she smiled ruefully to herself. As if that had ever been easy for her.

'We have to get back to Canal Street.'

Amina agreed. Shazia's paranoia had her looking into every glowing shadow, every hidden corner, every stall and shy. They pushed through the crowd again, wading into danger, and were met with a wave of tuts and curses, deaf to the chorus of insults.

Then they were out. On Portland Street. Past the hotels that reared high over Piccadilly Gardens. Down Aytoun Street. At any moment Shazia expected to see the black figure emerging from the crowd. But there was no-one. Only a few businessmen in shirt sleeves, balding and sweating, having a last one for the road before leaving for home. And hoping to catch a few more at the golf-club before closing time.

As Amina and Shazia turned down a side road before the newly built courthouse, all the crowds suddenly vanished. A dozen or so cars were sprawled along it, CCTV cameras peering down on them from the concrete sky. In the distance, they could make out the lights of the Gay Village, and hear the steady fours to the floor disco beat pumping out of every bar. Just a few hundred yards and not a soul in sight. Like furtive children they made their way down it, winding through the parked cars carefully. Trees passed, pillars passed, and still nothing emerged from the shadows. Half the distance gone and half the distance home.

When Aftab Akhtar saw the girls leave the fair, he knew his time had come. They were in the open. Exposed. Looking wildly about. They'd made the mistake. Too frightened to go to ground. He flagged down the nearest taxi.

'Shazi, I've got to stop, my slipper has split. It's all the running.'

Amina was hobbling on one foot. Shazia groaned.

'We've only got a little bit to go, Amina. Can't it wait?'

Amina grimaced. She felt as weak and stupid as all the pathetic women she'd seen in old films, fainting and swooning and getting caught, the kind you felt the hero should leave behind. But her feet really were killing her. Two huge blisters had broken out on her right foot, the foot Damon had long ago held in his hand. It could have done with his touch right now.

Shazia looked at her, not with hate and desperation, but with pity. What kind of hell had she dragged her into? A little more than three hours ago, she was safely at home. Now she was being chased by gangsters and getting run down by maniacs. And it was all because of her. Her bloody phone call. Trouble followed her wherever she went. There was no escaping it. She *was* doomed.

A black taxi turned into the road in front of them and pulled up on the corner. In the shadows. Shazia looked behind but there was still no sign of pursuit. She helped Amina along, allowing her to put most of her weight on her shoulder. In that way they made good speed.

The music was getting louder. The safety of Canal Street beckoned. Just a little bit further. The door of the cab opened. Slowly. Amina was too busy wincing to notice. Shazia, too busy helping. It was only when they heard the voice that they stopped. And the demons returned.

'Excuse me, ladies.'

Talking to them. It came from inside.

'Leave it,' urged Amina. 'I can hardly walk.'

Shazia needed no reminding. She wasn't about to stop. It was probably one of those seedy bastards her friend Noreen used to tell her about at school. The kind that offered you money for a twisted-wrister and a gulp of cum. No-one could work out how she knew. Or what she even meant.

They walked on. Pretending they hadn't heard. But the voice came again, louder this time, the slam of a door echoing behind it. And Shazia recognised it.

'Going somewhere, Shazia Ahmed?'

The sun stopped shining. Dark shadows unfurled. The sky went out.

The second her name was spoken, Shazia's heart stopped beating. She didn't need to look round to know who it was. The pungent, subcontinental

English was hard to forget. It rang down the nose. She swivelled quickly, backing off. Amina was too frightened to move. Aftab.

'I've brought you something, Shazia,' he said, and put his hand into his jacket pocket.

She backed off further. A gun? He was going to bring out a gun? But, no, it was worse. Much worse. In his hands he held the metal corkscrew.

'I've washed the blood off, Shazia. Tariq sends his regards. He's looking forward to seeing you again.'

Shazia blanched. Beside her, Amina was quaking. She'd quite forgotten the blisters on her feet. Naked fear kept her rooted to the ground. All she could see was the point of metal gleaming in the man's gloved hand. Seconds now lay between them. Seconds left to run. Why had she stopped? What a bloody fool. They were snakebitten. The second's delay was all Aftab needed. He launched himself at Shazia and grabbed her by the arm. Pulled her viciously towards him. He'd leave the other till later. She was petrified. Easy. Shazia screamed. But as he clasped one huge fist over her mouth a searing pain tore across the left side of his face, and he felt the blood coursing down his cheek. His eye began watering profusely, welling up like a geyser. The girls fizzled from view.

Blind to anything but Shazia, he'd overlooked the shoe Amina carried in her hand. Big mistake. Desperation guided it whipping across his face.

The needle-sharp heel caught the lower lid of his eye. Everyone makes mistakes. Everyone. Just as Tariq had done. He should have talked later. You don't survive in every crack-pit in Lahore by talking first.

Now he'd been stung. And it was about to get worse. Shazia had broken free of his grip and buried her teeth in the fleshy part of his arm. Bit him to the bone. The moment she did so, his hand let go. Agony exploded through it. Crippling agony. He couldn't feel it any more. Shouting with rage, he heard them go, helplessly watching them disappear through the watery haze.

Sackville Street opened up before the girls like a jungle sea. They didn't need to look back to know they were still being chased. The blare of horns told them. Amina lost her other shoe in the flight. She ran barefoot along the cobbles, heedless of the glass and stone beneath her. Down narrow streets, through lines of fairy queens, they ran, each face a gargoyle mask of rouge, or laced with lipstick smiles.

There was no time to think. No time to shout. Delay meant only one thing: the end. Shazia prayed for someone to stop and help. Not likely in these days of robbery and forgetting. The poor man on the road to Longsight had planned it, and the Good Samaritan was beaten and mugged for his clothes. No-one gets involved in Manchester. Look away and live. Yet, in their mad flight, as they crossed into Canal Street, Shazia knew shouting was their only chance. She ran right into a large group of middle-aged men with cropped hair and burly moustaches. Construction workers.

Apologising profusely, she pointed out behind her and yelled.

'Please help, we've been attacked!'

And she couldn't believe how close Aftab actually was. What madness drove him on? He was almost upon them. Seeing the men block his path, he hammered the first one to the ground with a giant sledging blow. But the weight of several others knocked him over, and then one of them sat on him. Aftab lay there helpless. And he wasn't used to that. Each second lost was buying those bitches their freedom. There was nothing else for it. He drew out his gun. The man recoiled and scrambled off, terrified.

A very few seconds later, Aftab was up. But the girls had vanished. The drums beat the floor in the distance and he beat his fists uselessly in echo. He groaned inwardly. Stung twice by a couple of girls and a party of *gaandu*. Some feeling he'd had that evening. He should have shot the fucking lot of them.

Shazia and Amina doubled back on themselves, snaked down one of the alleys behind Clone Zone, and ended up back at the Rembrandt, back in the toilets on the second floor. Amina was crying pitifully, her feet all cut up, her mascara smeared panda-eyed, and her hair falling wildly. Not so

Shazia. She was looking at herself in the mirror. Tears wouldn't flow. She'd shed too many already. The awful prediction of doom was welling up inside her. A thought she couldn't shake. She had to get to Piccadilly.

She knelt down beside Amina and touched her hair.

'I'm sorry, Amina, I really am. I should never have called you.'

Amina murmured faintly. At the very edge of exhaustion.

'It's right what they say about you, isn't it, Shazi?' she said.

Shazia looked stunned.

'I'm sorry for you. Bad things happen to you.'

Shazia paused. 'That's why I'm going, Amina. I have nothing here.'

Amina stared back at her. To think she'd spent so long wanting to be more like her. And for what?

'I need you to do one more thing for me, Amina. Please.' Shazia looked at her. 'I need you to go to the station.'

The words fell dead on empty air.

Amina mumbled. 'Why?'

Shazia paused.

'Because Damon's there.'

Amina's heart was being cut up thicker than the soles of her feet.

'I thought you said . . .'

'I lied. He's waiting for me.'

Another pause. Amina thought. The answer machine message: *'Hi, Amina . . . it's me . . . just returning your call.'*

What was this madness? She must be kidding. She was going straight home. Or better still, getting the bloody police.

'Please, Amina.'

Then, brain whirring, Amina softened. Thinking.

'I don't understand, Shazi, why not go yourself?'

Time to come clean.

'Because they're watching for me, Amina. Waiting. No-one's after you. It's me they want. You'll be okay.'

Amina doubted it. The heel had seen to that.

'And suppose your friend finds me and asks me where you are? Do you think I'm going to keep quiet? You're crazy, Shazi.'

Shazia looked at her and realised she was right. She *was* crazy. Crazy for dreaming too hard. Crazy for believing her parents. Crazy for thinking she'd ever get away. Everything they said would happen, had happened. Could she really blame her father for trying to drag her back? Could she blame her mother for her blank obedience to him?

And while she thought this, a demon of a thought was growing horns in the back of Amina's head, too. This was *her* chance. *Her* chance to escape. Damon, if he was there, would be on his own. And she could lie to save herself. That ticket to London could be hers.

'Please, Amina.'

She took off the shoes Amina had given her and handed them back. Then, reaching into her jeans she took out the money her mother had given her.

'Here,' she said, 'take this. It's for you, for helping. I don't think I'll need it.'

Amina looked down at it sadly and waved it away.

'What if he doesn't believe me, Shazi? How will he know I'm not part of all this? He hasn't seen me for ages.'

Shazia looked at her. She was right. He may think it a ruse to get him away. She needed something. But what? She paused, then held her hand up. The only thing she could think of. The ring. She'd never lightly give that up. Never. Damon would know.

'Give him this, Amina. He'll know you've seen me.'

Amina watched her, halfway between madness and desire. Poor Shazia. The cream shalwar kameez they'd stuffed into the paper-towel basket was still there, all tears and blood and sweat. Shazia looked down at it. Painful memories circled like dark crows. The image of blood on crisp, linen sheets and the slow, painful vacuuming of her womb came calling. On its shoulders sat the memory of her father's sledgehammer fists, and behind, the livid visage of Aftab.

'Pray for your soul, Shazia Ahmed.'

Yes, they were to blame. Allah grant her forgiveness. Jesus give her strength. A vengeful fury darkened the room. The dim, electric lights flickered. She suddenly felt liberated from caring, freed from the chain of consequences that had come so close to destroying her. She was past all that.

'Tell him I'll meet him . . .'

She paused and looked at Amina sadly. She still couldn't trust her.

'Where we first went out.'

Amina looked at her silently. Desperation collared by determination. Shazia had changed. Her beauty remained undimmed by darkness and torment but her soul had iced over. And to think of all those days she'd wasted wishing and dreaming she was more like her. All out. All wasted. She had to go.

She put the money on the side where the wash basins were, pulled the shoes over her bleeding feet and took the ring. Realising the pockets of her shalwar were too shallow, she held it over the third finger of her left hand.

'Do you mind?' she asked. 'It'll be safer there. I don't want to lose it.'

Shazia shrugged. What did anything matter?

Amina slipped the ring on. Fatefully, it stuck there, halfway down. It wouldn't budge. Embarrassedly, she held it up. The ring for Damon. He was hers.

'Goodbye, Shazi,' she said.

And so, at the door of the Ladies' in the Rembrandt pub, Amina Aslam looked once more at her friend, but if sadness or relief were best written across her face, you could not tell. She opened it to leave.

And looked back.

'Where we first went out, Amina,' Shazia said.

'Where we *first* went out.'

All out.

CHAPTER 28

She'd have screamed. Yvonne de Carlo would have screamed. Tony Curtis was lying on the floor with ten inches of steel in his belly. The last reel *was* going badly. But Candy fluffed his lines. When Dru knocked Billy sprawling across the Moroccan cushions, Candy's heart had leaped with girlish delight. Dru was like one of those prize fighters in the wild west, Billy the Kid slaying Billy the Whizz. Now it sank. What could he do?

Jamie Farrell was thinking exactly the same thing. Though he knew what he should do: peel Dru off Billy, give him a crunching uppercut and knock his fucking head back. Thicker than thieves and all that. He should stick up for his mates. The one thing he had to stop, though, was that gun going off. Not another body. That gunshot had done for Terence, blown a fucking hole through his chest. Now Billy was going to blow this poor sod away.

On the floor, Billy bored his gun into Dru's belly. There was no give. The idiot on top of him had tightened his muscles and was leaning on it. Billy's hand was taking the strain of the man's weight.

In his present state, with what was left of his mind scattered to the four winds, this behaviour defied comprehension. His eyes narrowed to Hong Kong apertures. When you shoot a man you read his life in his face. You expect the normal things: bafflement, fear, and surprise. But not this. Not dead calm.

Dru lay on top of Billy with the knowledge that this would be his last day on Earth. He looked down at Billy's sweating head with all the antipathy of the criminally insane. He only wished his assailant was more glorious looking, more Olympian, punishing him for his miserable ineptitude. To die at the hands of some scumbag from Longsight was not the finale he was looking for. He was planning that for the TV show.

'I'm going to blow your fucking head off, motherfucker,' Billy said.

Candy closed his eyes. He felt his bladder loosen. Awaited the shudder of artillery like the onset of some fearful storm. But the seconds rolled by like clouds. There was a prolonged and terrible calm. Time for Jamie Farrell. Time for him to save the gay. He launched himself at the stricken pair on the floor, knocking Dru over and into the cushions. Candy vented his alarm by screaming. A gunshot ripped open the air with a shock of blast. Straight into the ceiling and into the sky. Billy thought he'd scored a direct hit.

The moment Dru hit the ground, he was on military alert, half expecting his assailant to be on top of him. But his arms thrashed wildly and he realised that fresh air was filling his lungs again, gallons and gallons of the beautiful stuff. He could have OD'd on it. Jamie was looking at him.

'Sit there,' he said. Mancunian steel.

Billy was waving his gun like a madman, beating his chest like a crazed gorilla, stampeding over the cushions and through the silken drapes like a drunken rhinoceros.

'You stupid cunt, Jamie-boy, I'm going to fuckin' cut you up, too.'

Jamie scowled. Billy meant it. Billy always meant it. But fear of him was ebbing.

'Billy,' he said, knowing he was buying about a second's worth of life before his own head was blown clear from his shoulders, 'now is not the time. They're worth more to us alive.'

Billy pressed his swarthy face right up to Jamie's. And whispered slowly.

'What are you talking about?'

Jamie's mouth went dry.

'Drugs, Billy,' he said. 'Money.'

And flicked his fingers.

'Candy's loaded. We can sort them out later.'

Billy's brain spluttered into life.

'How loaded, Jamie-boy?'

Jamie looked at Candy, who'd finished scream-ing, and was now on all fours, begging for release, crying.

'Oh, take everything you want, please,' she pleaded, lying. 'Please.'

Billy bent down and clasped his palm in Candy's hair. He yanked it back viciously.

'Well, where is it, beautiful?' he said, warming to his task.

The wig came off in his hand. Candy's bald pate glistened nakedly. He groaned.

'I keep it at the club. I'll get it for you if you like?'

Billy kicked him. Hard.

'I don't think so, sweetheart. You'll have to stay here. We'll all have to stay here.'

Dru had shaken himself down and was standing over Candy's sprawling form. He hadn't the slightest doubt that the lunatic with the gun would kill them. For what that was worth. So he had to buy time. Time he knew he didn't have. A stand-up grandfather clock on the far wall, half obscured by the fading sun, confirmed what he already knew. Nine o'clock. He could forget the routine. At this rate he'd be lucky to see the DeepDrill and Reg Naylor ever again. His death wish metamorphosed into self-preservation. If you had anything to live for, it was opportunity. Beyond tonight, there was nothing. Candy had his flowers and boys; he had his career. He had to keep it alive.

'We can't,' he said, finally.

Billy looked at him.

'Shut up, fucker!'

Dru ignored him. Keep calm.

'Look, Billy,' he said, 'you can do what you want – you've got the gun. No-one's arguing with you.

But people know we're here. My agent. Others. Eventually, they'll be round. The longer you leave it, the more difficult it'll get. You can't stay here forever. How many times are you going to ignore the door, or the phone? Somebody will turn up. Think about it.'

Candy didn't think he'd heard anything so beautiful in all his life. He was sure Billy would think so, too. He was wrong.

'So fucking what?'

And he was off like an ape again, discharging his gun into the ceiling. A rain of plaster and wood settled on the blue mosaic floor, flotsam from a passing ship.

'You won't be answering.'

Candy knelt, rooted in fear, but Dru's mind was in performance mode. The stakes couldn't be higher. He had to raise the ante.

'You're a tough man, Billy,' he said, 'hard to miss, I bet. Did you smile on your way up?'

Billy's eyes narrowed.

Dru winked.

'You'll be on the computer database by now, I'm sure. CCTV. Time of entry, that kind of stuff. It's easily checked. Still, we've all got time to walk out of here, haven't we? We can all still win.'

His stomach churned.

Jamie looked at Billy, alive with the idea that there was a way out of it for himself. He watched him sniffing the end of the gun, snorting up the smoking lead.

'He's right, Billy,' he dared. 'We can't stay here.'

Billy was thinking, too, whirring the slow machinery of his brain.

He pointed at Dru. He was used to these last-minute stories. People with things to live for care that way. He'd forgotten what it was like to care about anything. Not that he held any grudges. He'd settle them later. Made in Manchester.

'Do you know the club this ponce is talking about?'

He waved his gun in the direction of Candy's head.

Dru nodded.

'Yes. Scarlet Harlot's.'

Billy walked over to Jamie and stared at him. Deep down he had a soft spot for the kid. The kind you had for a pet Rottweiler. But not if he got this wrong.

'I'm trusting you, Jamie,' he said. 'Don't let me down.'

'He's loaded,' Jamie muttered.

Strangeways, here we come. Billy's eyes glazed over. Another million synapses blinked out of existence. He walked back over to Candy.

'Where do you keep it, sweetheart?'

Candy shivered.

'In a safe.'

He pointed to the kitchen wall.

'The combination's written up there.'

Billy helped him up. Candy took a pen and scrambled some numbers down on a piece of paper. Took a key down. His fingers fumbled terribly. The digits were all lopsided and stricken, like doomed men. Dru looked over at him and knew he was making a terrible mistake. Maybe he was hoping the CCTV really had alerted security, or that somebody had heard the gunshots. He seriously doubted the concierge would get involved, though.

Billy smiled.

And pointed the gun at Dru.

'You're coming with me, fucker. We're going to take a ride together. Jamie, take any cards he's got. And anything the ponce has got, too. We're going shopping.'

More than anything, Jamie wished he was some place else. Paranoia. The feeling was killing him. Frisking Candy, he felt sick to his stomach. Candy wasn't so bad. And his flat was heaven. Something like that was going to be his one day. If he could ever stand up to Billy Whizz. Candy wasn't going to do anything to anyone. He had nothing coming to him.

Dru looked at the clock on the wall and saw it bearing down on a quarter past nine. There was still a chance. Just.

Candy looked after them as they made to the door. His heart burst with hope that they were going, that they'd leave him in peace. He wouldn't say anything, honestly. He really wouldn't. Jamie had enough on him anyway to take him down for a very long time. But Jamie was silent, his eyes on Dru. But Dru didn't look back. It was too painful. At the moment he could have seen for himself, he couldn't bear to look.

Billy took his gun, levelled it at Candy's head and pulled the trigger. Yvonne de Carlo really would have screamed. If she'd had the time. Her brains were blown clean out, making a Jackson Pollock of the drapes and walls. It wasn't quite the ending Candy had envisaged. He had less than a second to consider how it might play on film before the director cried, 'Cut!' And so missed the petals, blown from a hundred orchids, rain down and shroud his slender frame.

The lift plummeted to earth like a fallen angel. Jamie knew where they were going. There was no way out. He felt Billy's hot breath on his ear.

'Don't try that again, Jamie-boy.'

He knew just what he meant.

So did Dru.

'If you speak, shout, or move, you're a dead man.'

Three men emerged into the pale arms of the evening.

Dru breathed more easily. It was there. The black cab was waiting.

CHAPTER 29

The world was coming to an end. No matter which way he looked at it, no matter how hard he smashed his head, Azad Riaz kept coming to the same conclusion. There was no going back. Unless he came up with the money, and fast, he was dead. His wife's brothers would finish the job.

The last time, they'd beaten him senseless, threatened him with broken glass and sticks, told him not to bother their sister again. Proposed a week-long separation to show him what it was like living without a good woman. He'd slept in the back of his cab, on the doorsteps of the Plaza Casino, and loved every minute of it. His wife hadn't. She found herself looking out of the window all night, fearing thieves at the back of the house, wondering whether the razor wire and glass Azad had spiked the wall with would be enough to deter them. Hoping her children could sleep through it. It couldn't last. She begged her brothers to bring him back. But, when Azad returned, unchastened, with a wicked glint in his eye, she knew she'd made a mistake. He knew it, too. The meeting confirmed it. He was an absolute disgrace. And the guilt was killing him.

Now, as Azad struggled to focus through the tears, a vision in purple and black appeared in his rear-view mirror. He peered at it darkly, dimly recognising its shape and face, yet unable to put a name to it. He knew where he'd seen it before, though, and ducked down and waited.

When Amina Aslam left Shazia, the fear of pursuit lay heavy on her. Any one of the million faces that seemed to mill around her could be the face of the killer. Her eyes flitted across the smoky haze of the Rembrandt pub and she prayed no-one was looking. They weren't. She wouldn't look long enough to find out. It was just after nine o'clock. The lanes of boys along Canal Street parted before her, eunuchs to her hourglass form. They drank at the Oasis of Sodom, with no thought of to-morrow. What was an escaping houri to them, a dark Arab girl slipping through their midst? Her feet, already blistered, burnt terribly. They needed water, needed bathing. Needed *his* hands. Soon, maybe.

She rounded a dark corner. A black taxi was parked up. Sirens sounded. She crossed to the other side of the road, wary, attempting to skip past it, but the cobbled street was too narrow. Past this cab, another fifty yards, and she'd be on the main road. Minutes from Piccadilly. She had to try. But, as she approached, her fear grew. The passenger's side was too close to the wall. She'd have to go the driver's side. The red sun shone directly on to its windows, blinding her. She couldn't see a thing. One step, two, slowly, then the windows cleared. And she could see. There was nobody inside. The vague shadows appeared to be just that. She breathed again and ran. But when she was level with the driver's cabin, the door opened in front of her, and she clattered into it.

Caught. A man's voice.

'Amina?'

Asian, too.

She was on the point of screaming when she realised she recognised him. It wasn't the gunman. It was Shazia's uncle. She hadn't seen him for ages. He looked terrible, his eyes covered with a watery film, his head a criss-cross of cuts and puffed-up flesh. She wondered if he'd been beaten up.

'I'm in a hurry,' she said, frightened, yet relieved. 'I'm sorry.'

'So am I,' he said.

He smiled.

'For scaring you.'

Silence.

'Where's Shazia?' A shot in the dark. Getting out the cab.

Amina watched him, a second away from fleeing down the cobbles. Though his face was not unfriendly, his manner was distracted. His smile was crooked, too. She wouldn't be staying long.

'I don't know,' she said. 'Honestly.'

How did he know?

There was an uncomfortable pause but, seeing a group of men heading down the road towards them, Amina took heart.

'I'm sorry,' she said, 'I really must go.'

'Do you need a lift?' he said.

Alarm bells as loud as police sirens began wailing inside her head.

The men were near. Now was the time. Run.

'No th . . .' she said, but before the words died on her lips, he was on her.

She stared at his swarthy face, as manic and brutal as the white boy's had been. His anger was growing in his desperation. And hers, too. She struggled vainly in his grip.

'Just let me go, will you? I don't know, do I!'

Azad measured the distance between themselves and the approaching men. It was too fine. They'd already noticed him pinning her arms back. This would look very bad. A gambler and a rapist. Not bad for one day.

He whispered hoarsely.

'Look, where is she? Where's Shazia? I need to speak to her.'

But Amina spat full in his face. The bitch. If only his wife had as much gumption.

He aimed to strike her, one hand circling her wrists to hold her.

'*Kahan?*'

She screamed, and the men came running.

'Manto, you bastard, outside Manto. Now fuck off!'

Shazia would have been proud. The group of boys, decent student types, swallowed them up, wrestled with Azad, and broke his grip. She pulled herself clear. Free again. Then, resisting their inquiries, she fled, the purple and black trailing behind her like the wings of a bird. She flew across the old London Road and up the hill to Piccadilly. Away to freedom. She gave no further heed to her bleeding feet, nor to the threat of pursuit. In front of her lay hundreds of yards of concrete. The path was clear at last.

Azad Riaz stared after her retreating form. And clutched his head where he'd been punched. One bird flown the nest already. He supposed he might chance the other. That's if he could get it to talk. The possibility that Amina Aslam had lied to him didn't even enter his head. All he could remember was the startled, nonplussed look of his niece. Manto was only just down the road. He still had some explaining to do.

At the top of the hill Piccadilly Station was built on, Amina looked back across the city, desolate. She walked into the cool of the station concourse, still heaving with people. The office firebrands had quaffed their last short, and shirt sleeves rolled up, prepared to read the *Metro News* on their way back to Hazel Grove. Some of them rang their wives to tell them that they loved them, but most were still taking calls from work. The contracts still hadn't been signed.

Underneath Arrivals and Departures, which appeared before her like a giant mechanised blackboard, Amina scoured the aisles of upturned faces, waiting for sign and revelation that their train was on time. *He* was not among them. She tried the corners of the station shops without luck. Perhaps he hadn't arrived? Perhaps he wasn't coming? She looked in the concourse bar. Nothing but a few old men and an Asian man with a large leather briefcase.

He was sprawled backwards on his chair in what appeared to be sleep. One of the bar staff was directing a blonde policewoman towards him.

Amina made her way back to the entrance of the station, forlorn. And it was then that she felt the tap on her shoulder. And heard the voice.

'Amina?' it said. 'Is it you?'

She spun round quickly, her heart splitting in two, her mouth trembling. The brown fringe, the piercing eyes, the curled, attentive smile. It had to be. Damon Ruff was in front of her.

CHAPTER 30

Amina Aslam lost count of the number of times she'd imagined this moment, while Mo for Mohammed ploughed London Fields and gave no thought or feeling for the girl he'd left behind. It always began the same way. She'd take her clothes off and stare at herself in the mirror. This thing, like her emotions, she lived to cover up. And she'd slide between the covers, silken light on her flesh, and dream. Dream that, in the twilight, her door would open softly and admit another. Dream stranger's fingers tiptoeing across the sheets. Dream them drawing them back expertly, with surgical precision, undressing her wounds.

And feel guilty because it wasn't Mohammed.

'This,' he smiled, 'is this what you've been hiding from me?'

Unbelieving.

'It's God's will,' she said. *Believing women should lower their gaze and guard their modesty, display not their beauty and ornaments. Except to their husbands.*

And the glow of the moon, shining through narrow slits in the curtains, fell fully on his face.

It was the face of Damon Ruff. Every night she saw him, and every night he disappeared.

For his own part, Damon Ruff had also thought about the moment, usually when he'd fallen out with Shazia, and generally in the small hours, when he'd had a little too much to drink. Getting Amina's imaginary lips over him, drawing his cum up like it was a straw, that was the easy part, but then it stalled. Guilt turned him flaccid. And it wasn't over Shazia. It was Amina. He'd have felt bad showering her like that.

Now, as she turned to face him, he momentarily reconsidered. Her wide, wild eyes were whirlpools of passion. The pouting purple of her lips, a trepanner at his groin, mining the seams of his dark desires. Fire and storm engulfed him. She *was* beautiful.

'It's been a long time,' he said.

She looked at the bags he was carrying, the dawning of manhood on his golden face, and held her breath. A long time going on never if he boarded that train. She'd already lost one man to London. Another would, indeed, be carelessness. But how could she tell him, here, and at such a time? Shazia needed her, and needed him more.

She stammered.

'It's Shazi, Damon, she's in trouble.'

His stomach tightened. That word again. *Trouble*. It was made for Shazia. Here at the last, things had gone wrong, the way things always went wrong. And, as Amina spoke, he realised more than ever that nothing would ever go right for Shazia Ahmed. The fabulous tale of kidnap and guns was just one more tragedy in a long line of tragedies. How many times had he warned her?

He stared into silence, overwhelmed. And doubtful, too.

'She needs you, Damon,' Amina said. *I need you, Damon.*

She was looking at him. In agony.

Poor Amina, he thought. How simple life would have been if they'd just been bolder, faced what they'd done rather than try to hide it. They could have got on with their lives. Banished the day to the dust and stars. But he couldn't. And she couldn't. They were haunted by it. A moment they'd never forget, a thought to fertilise his barren old age with, trying to resurrect old Lazarus. Poor Amina. How had she got involved in all this? Sucked in like he was.

He turned to look at the station clock: 9:14.

'Listen to me, Amina,' he said.

But he couldn't face her. It was written all over him.

She knew already. She loved him. And he didn't trust her. Not after what had happened. She pulled unsuccessfully at her fingers.

'Look,' she said. 'Shazia gave me this.'

And held up her left hand.

His jaw dropped. The ring. The engagement ring.

'I couldn't get it off,' Amina said, sadly.

Then it sunk in. She *was* telling the truth.

'Forgive me, Amina,' he said.

And he bounded manfully to the left-luggage counter, shouting after him.

'We've got to get going.'

The blisters on her feet had long since burst, the skin shredded. How could she? She watched him deposit the bags and run back to her. In forty-five minutes it would all be over. Did she have the strength to carry on?

'Look,' he said, grasping her arms boldly, she wished *more* boldly. 'You don't have to come, Amina. You've done enough already. Just tell me where she is.'

Amina's lips trembled. Now was the moment. There would be no other. She had to tell him.

I love you, Damon.

But the words came out different.

Damon looked at her, horrified.

'What do you mean?'

'That's what she said. She was worried I'd let her down, I think. I'm sorry.'

He groaned.

Fuck, he thought, *where we first went out?* Where the hell was that?

And he grabbed her hand, all the time trying to remember. Trust a girl to think of that. And all the while Amina imagined she was flying with her angel. Mo had never held her hand the way he held it, had never touched her feet the way he had. She wanted to taste some of the freedom Shazia tasted, if only for a short while. Who would begrudge her that?

CHAPTER 31

The taxi prowled the narrow streets, up and down, evading the octopus tentacles of outstretched arms and the shrieking catcalls of hopeful clubbers. Azad Riaz had other business to attend to. He had to find his niece. And quickly. He wouldn't rest till he'd found her and warned her. And asked her forgiveness. He had to set his house in order before the end. He had to save someone to save himself.

He pulled up outside Manto where that bitch Amina told him to look. A group of bearded women huddled together. He'd seen the type before: short, cropped hair, baggy jeans, dungarees. Paler than milk. About as far from Shazia as you could possibly imagine. He couldn't understand women like that; he couldn't understand women full stop.

It was late evening and verging on twilight. The shadows lengthened across the city. Revellers spilling out on to the cobbled forecourts welcomed the mildest of breezes across their sweat-sodden brows. A flotilla of designer T-shirts miraculously unfurled. But nowhere amongst them could Azad see Shazia. Not a brown face to be seen. It was like those paintings he'd seen at the Lowry Centre, the white stick men in front of factory stacks, furtive figures all. England before the invasion.

For the fifth time he drove past Chorlton Street Coach Station. Nothing. And, as he did so, a man walked right out in front of him, his eyes gleaming in the jungle of pillars. Azad hit the brakes hard, smashed one hand down on the horn, harder.

'Are you blind?' he shouted.

The man looked at him through dark sunglasses, unfazed. He walked round to the driver's side and bent his head to the window. Azad waited, and groaned. Not another meathead. He'd deal with this one the same way. You didn't take the racist gibes; you didn't take people throwing up over your seats.

'*Salaam alaykum,*' the man said.

Pakistani. Ring on every finger. Manicured nails. Leather coat. Azad had seen the type before. Many, many times before. At the casinos where he'd blown away the last of his money, and now his fucking house. Like Mr Khan, Mr Bhutto here smoked fifties for fun. Whisky, cigars, and French tarts. Half the wealth of Pakistan was stashed in his shoes. He hadn't begun life in a corner shop, that was for sure.

'*Salaam,*' Azad answered, all TP. 'You want your eyes tested.'

No response. The man pointed his face further into the cabin. Azad noticed he'd received a nasty laceration to his cheek. Freshly minted, too.

'I need your cab, fucker.'

Allah, he wasn't messing. Azad prepared to drive through him.

But the man didn't move.

'I really wouldn't, brother,' he said.

And, from out of his leather Gucci jacket, he produced a long, black gun.

Azad inhaled sharply. Mr Bhutto was serious. This was one bad day. His foot left the accelerator. Shazia would have to wait.

The man got in the back, his gun never leaving the orbit of Azad's head. It filled the rear-view mirror like a giant telescope. Azad was convinced it was the last thing he was ever going to see. Some old woman was going to find him dumped in a wheelie bin in Longsight or Cheetham Hill.

The man asked him to drive. Drive round. He was looking for someone. All Azad could see was the silent, black eye staring at him. Thoughts of anything other than a bullet going off seemed very distant. He dreaded an emergency stop or a bump on the road.

'Do you have to?' he asked. 'You're putting me off.'

The gun touched the back of his head in answer. Fuck. It was 9:16.

After ten minutes listening to the man barking left and right, Azad began to suffer a bad bout of déjà vu. Someone had been holding a gun to his head all his life. He'd lived his entire life on hire purchase and hadn't made a single payment for it. Well, the creditors were moving in. He didn't think his wife'd have to worry about the bills any more. She'd have more on her plate with the funeral.

In the back of the cab, Aftab Akhtar was also getting tetchy. The thought of being worsted twice by Shazia Ahmed sickened him. He didn't have long left, either. Ten o'clock tops. That case needed to be delivered *tonight*, or he'd be back to Pakistan in a body bag. And that thought he really didn't like. He seriously doubted Khalid Ahmed would lift even one of his podgy fingers to help him if every killer between here and Southall had a bounty on his head. Those Sikh boys didn't hang around.

Minutes passed. The sun shone through the open window. He took out a small slip of paper from his wallet and examined it. In gold ink someone had written two words: Al-Biswan. The prospect of finding the girl all but gone, he turned it in his hands. It was getting dark. He put the gun to one side and studied the bald patch on the back of Azad's head. Time for something else.

'Are you happy, brother?' he asked suddenly.

Azad was taken aback. Taken a long way back. He'd never been happy. He shrugged. What the fuck kind of question was that?

'Do you ever think why?' the man said.

Azad nodded. His wife.

'It's because you've got no balls.'

A passing arm tried to flag the cab down. He ignored it. No balls? It was true.

'Do you ever think about what kind of example you're setting?'

Aftab was almost whispering in his ear now. Whispering venom.

'When I see Teps like you, brother, in taxis, in factories, in restaurants, it sickens me. You're white men's dogs, the lot of you. Is there no life left in you, no fight? Don't you ever think about that?'

Azad stared at him, vexed. He did, indeed. He thought about grabbing that gun and shooting Mr Bhutto between his fucking eyes.

The taxi crept down Canal Street again.

'You know the problem, don't you?' said Aftab. Whispering again. Confidential.

Shadows were thrown across his face.

'You're village stock. A thousand years of inbreeding has brought you to this. You don't have a chance. Thank your grandparents. Poor, uneducated bastards. No wonder the English look down on you. You should have stayed home. The sun always shines in Pakistan. You're too like them. Lazy bastards. You could rule this lot if you cared. They've forgotten themselves, too.'

Azad let the words wash right over him. He kind of hoped there'd be a point to them. Or better still, he kind of hoped the man would just shut up. He was right about one thing, though. The country had become a dumping ground. All those refugees. The Pakistanis were the new English already. Dig the new breed.

'How about you work for me for a while?' Aftab asked suddenly.

Allah, he *was* mad!

Azad shrugged again. It seemed the only safe response. Dumb.

Aftab stared at the back of his head and tried vainly to imagine what it would be like to work for a living. He leaned closer to the glass divide and slid back the partition fully. Azad could feel his breath blowing across his neck.

'Tell me something. What do you do it all for? Is it your wife and your kids? Or the little extras?'

'All of them,' Azad said flatly.

'The little extras, right?' said Aftab.

Azad nodded, then shrugged again.

'You know how it is,' he said, then paused. 'Well, you probably don't, do you?'

He didn't. The cab came to a shuddering halt.

A party of beer boys, half throttled on lager and shorts, steamed across Portland Street in the direction of Yates' wine bar. Azad half expected the gun to go off. He shrank.

'I've got nothing. I'm broke.'

Aftab nodded slowly in what passed for understanding. This was exactly the kind of peasant attitude he despised. No wonder they were so backward in this country.

He aired his wallet once more and drew out a thick wad of English notes.

'I bet you could do with some then, my friend,' he said.

Indeed he could, Azad thought. A lot of it.

'What do you say, then?' Aftab asked. 'You'll work for me tonight. A few extras?'

Azad swallowed hard. Done deal.

Aftab stared out of the window, silently caressing the barrel of his gun. He'd get the poor sod to take him back to the station, get that idiot Tariq, and then off down to Rusholme. They'd be downing shorts at the Al-Biswan before they knew it. *Insh'Allah*.

The girl'd have to wait.

The taxi circled again. Azad Riaz wondered vaguely whether anyone had noticed his continual circuit of the Village. Passion wagons like his were always getting stopped. A convenient shagpit for two horny fags, a wank and blow parlour for any number of skinny, blonde whores.

He muttered to himself, thoughts of Shazia limply hanging on the dead, summer air. And hoped the extras wouldn't take long.

CHAPTER 32

'You don't understand, Reg, that's the way it's going now. We can learn from the Americans.'

Rupert St Clair, Granada head honcho, thirty-something Manchester University graduate, had been on fast track the day his mum bought him his first Ferrari. Never mind that it was stolen from the driveway of his Didsbury maisonette the first week he was here. That red Ferrari signified everything Rupert thought himself to be: sleek, sharp, and sophisticated. And successful.

'The Americans are successful, Reg. And why?'

He raised his eyes quizzically, urging Reg on.

Blank face.

'The right branding, Reg. Marketability. That's where we've been going wrong. Why we don't sell abroad. We're years behind. We need to keep up, Reg. America, Australia. We need to get those boys involved. People want to see programmes like Best Friends. And we can make it for them.'

Rupert St Clair liked the air of finality an *And* gave his sentences. Like the words *product placement* and *America*, it featured prominently in his media lexicon. He'd done the courses, attended the seminars, seen the greats at work.

'But you didn't know who the Marx Brothers were,' Reg rejoined tactfully.

Rupert raised his eyes again. Reg just didn't get it at all.

'Well, who does, Reg? Take a look around you. All these people. How many of them do you think have heard of the Marx Brothers?'

Reg looked round the bar. Media airheads rubbed shoulders with fags in pink dresses. Dippy blonde students screeched their end-of-year flatulence down mobile phones. Depressingly, very depressingly, Reg knew that Rupert was right.

'We're all Best Friends now,' Rupert said. 'And don't forget it.'

Reg groaned inwardly. They'd been drinking here since nine o'clock and already he felt like killing the guy. Rupert said he could only manage an hour the moment he arrived. He'd already fielded six calls. Reg was pretty low in his priorities.

'So what's this guy like, Reg? Tell us a bit about him. No-one sent me a profile.'

Reg hoped he'd be able to do a bit of selling himself, but quickly noticed Rupert's gaze flicker and wander after that important ten-second mark.

'Well, he writes very well, I think,' Reg began.

'Writes?' Rupert looked at him. 'Well, we have writers, Reg. We have teams of writers. Like they have in America. I'm not interested in writers, I'm interested in looks. Will he appeal to his market? What is his market, do you think?'

But, as Reg was about to volunteer his defence, the mobile phone rang again, and Rupert was off. Reg half imagined he was holding court with the other cretins in the bar, shouting into the empty air like he was mentally ill. Looking at all these people, this great variety of life, it was almost impossible to reconcile the Canal Street he used to know. The magic of the place, its seedy allure, had all gone. It had been upgraded to Las Vegas kitsch and London wine bars, nothing more than a tourist attraction now. 'Come and visit the Gay Village', it boldly pronounced in the council's most recent literature. Gay life had become a commodity like everything else.

When Rupert finished shouting they left the bar and emerged squinting into the evening light. Reg was anxious to get to the DeepDrill. He wanted a word with Dru before he went on stage. He was not sure how the rogue elements of his act would play with Rupert. Rupert was looking for audience response. Testing the market, that kind of thing. He sighed. To be reduced to this, at his age, to be fretting over the opinion of some conceited media student who'd never heard of the Marx Brothers.

As they passed Prague Five, a lone Asian girl furtively approached them and asked them for the time. Reg was half expecting her to ask for money. The smile he gave her was as much a smile of relief she hadn't. But he chastised himself for thinking such ungentlemanly thoughts. He felt Rupert looking back after her, and wondered if he'd had other ungentlemanly thoughts.

'A pretty thing,' Reg offered.

'Indeed,' Rupert nodded, 'I think that'll be our next market. One of our new children's projects will have a good few Asian characters in it. It's all changing now, Reg. It's very exciting.'

Married to the job, then.

They wandered down Canal Street to the DeepDrill Club, its metal doors thrown back, the sign above the entrance depicting a rugged road worker, stripped to the waist, getting ready to drill a circle of earth. The doorman, his left ear punched with more studs than you'd find on an average belt, smiled at Reg and waved him in.

Rupert was trying to put two and two together.

'Is this a gay club, Reg?' he asked, as they descended into darkness.

Reg almost choked.

'Depends what night, I think,' he replied tactfully. 'Sometimes it's Lesbian night, sometimes TV, sometimes it's Leather, sometimes it's Bi. They have quite a crowd, usually.'

In the Pit, where sorceress nymph boys juggled their balls, and flaming trannies performed cartwheels in their cages, a crowd was, indeed, gathering. The smell of lacquer and perfume and pot had nicely settled over the whole place. It was just what Reg wanted. Dru had obviously done his homework. They'd be going mad for him within the hour. It would vindicate everything he'd ever said. He'd get no more of those leprous looks they gave him along the corridors at Granada, no more shuffling uncomfortably in meetings about bloody product placements and web presence. He'd have found a star.

The other thing Reg liked about the Pit was that it made Rupert extremely uncomfortable. The music was so loud down there that he couldn't hear his mobile phone. He was looking about him, feverishly checking his watch, trying not to catch the wayward glances of passing strangers. Poor Rupert. He was a very good-looking boy.

'I need to see Dru,' said Reg, suddenly.

A pained look crossed Rupert's face. Reg drank in its sweetness. This'll get the sod for the thousand snide remarks he'd made in those meetings. The 'Reg will know about that kind of thing, he's been here long enough' kind.

'I won't be long,' he said triumphantly. 'I hope.'

Reg pushed through the crowd and smoke, and made his way to the old stairwell behind the stage. A few sound engineers were checking the microphones and patching in numerous leads across an old mixing desk. Boxes and boxes of strobes and spotlights were being hastily erected. Reg was momentarily thrown. He couldn't remember Dru's show requiring so many props.

'A lot of gear for a PA?' he shouted into the thunder of music.

One of the roadies looked at him quizzically.

'PA?' he asked. 'We've got a full show tonight, mate. A Fashion Disco.'

Reg ducked his head down beneath a particularly low awning and made his way to the changing rooms. Must be lined up for after Dru, he thought. It made sense. Probably explained the crowd, too.

It was quiet down there. Very quiet. Reg had been there many times before but could never remember it being so eerily silent. No giggles, no fairy transistors. Just the slow mumble of voices. Like monks at prayer.

The dressing-room door was closed. Reg knocked and put his head round.

His stomach tightened. No Dru. Just Steve and Charlie. Steve raised his eyes but Charlie kept his averted. You didn't need a rocket scientist, or even Rupert St Clair, to realise he'd been crying.

'What's going on, Steve?' he asked, alarmed. 'Where's Dru?'

Steve shrugged his shoulders. Reg had never seen him so resigned. Even through the hardest of times, when the police tried to close his club down after repeated acts of gross lewdness, or when he was being leaned on by Leroy Mikele's Moss Side Yardies, he'd maintained that quiet, purposeful dignity that Reg regarded the mark of a real gentleman. He had time for such men. They were a throwback to better days.

'Who knows,' Steve finally said, 'and to be honest, who cares?'

Reg frowned.

'Well, me, actually. He should be on in twenty minutes. His career's on the line.'

Steve gave a derisory snort.

'I'll say,' he said. 'I don't think he'll have many opportunities where he's going.'

Reg's heart raced.

'What are you talking about?'

Steve gestured him to cross the room.

'Show him your neck, Charlie,' he said.

Charlie complied. A dark cloud of purple ink billowed round his Adam's apple, stretching ominously across his golden, tanned skin. There were a few searing scratches to boot. Reg was stunned.

'The paramedic said he was lucky to be alive,' Steve said. 'Charlie's lost his voice for a good long while.'

It couldn't be.

'Dru?' he asked, appalled at the thought.

'Apparently so,' Steve said. 'Charlie's in shock. Even if he could say anything, I doubt he would.'

Steve traced the bruise on Charlie's neck and ran his hand through his hair.

'He's mad, you know, Reg,' he said, absently. 'Always has been.'

But Reg could hardly string two thoughts together. He stared at Steve like he was mouthing a stream of grunts.

'If you see him, you can tell him from me. He won't play in this city again. I'll stake his life on it. If you know where he's gone, tell him the police have been. They'll be in touch.'

Reg looked from one to the other. The penny, weighed down to an anchor of million-pound television deals, finally dropped. Dru had blown everything. He'd blown every last opportunity right out of the water. And blown him out, too.

He left the back way, out of the dressing room and into the alley behind the club, now murderously dark. The word 'why' futilely echoed from wall to narrow wall. He thought of Rupert St Clair, squirming in the Pit, waiting for him to return. He wouldn't, of course. Better to let him watch the fashion show, and enjoy the beauty pageant. Better to let him live a little outside the media bubble. Reg was leaving, anyway. He'd hoped he'd go out in style, with the plaudits of his peers ringing in his ears, and a Bafta or two on his mantelpiece in recognition of his life on earth. But age had taught him that any kind of exit was preferable to being carried out. No, he wouldn't be going back. And the Pit was some kind of revenge for Harpo, Chico, Zeppo and Groucho.

It was nearly a quarter to ten and Reg Naylor walked down Canal Street for the very last time. All the ghosts of the cobbled streets walked with him, all the lovers and wayward angels who'd fallen here to earth. They followed him invisibly. He looked up into the sky and watched the stars appear miraculously from the edge of oblivion. And there it was, Charles' Wain, as it had been all those years ago. The passage of his life had not affected it at all. Let us go, then, he'd said then, full of hope. Now there was nothing. He sighed, a long, sad sigh, and disappeared into the evening forever.

CHAPTER 33

At the bottom of Sackville Street, bravely resisting time's overtures, stands Manchester's old Central High School. Dwarfed by the new developments, its red brick Victorian splendour now lies blackened by filth and neglect. Its walled gardens, once the playground of lost generations of school girls, now turn deaf ears to the grunts and groans of courting queens, sicken to the plastic-bag heroin addicts digging dirty needles in their delta of exposed veins, and cover with blossom the soporific tramps. Only the chipped gargoyles, pulling their bestial tongues in obvious displeasure, are left to weep for the things that were.

It was here that Shazia Ahmed first dated Damon Ruff. Bacardi Breezers on their tongues, they sat on one of the park benches and imagined orient and occident in perfect alignment. Anxious to impress. Reading the palm of atmosphere, the love-lines in the sky. Their conversation light with the froth of spring. Treading carefully over the mine-fields of the past. Her family. The hole in her womb. The loss of her baby. Not on a first date. There was too much at stake. Damon sobered up just in time to hear her say she loved him.

Now here she was again, with the shadows lengthening across the gardens, her heart now beating as fast in fear as it had once in expectation. So little appeared to have changed. The dark, imposing classrooms looked exactly the same. The bench where they'd sat, the bed of roses she'd thrown her gum into (there *were* such things as gum trees, Damon told her straight-faced). Nothing had moved. Yet it *had* changed.

It was nearly 9.30. She'd left the Rembrandt pub some five minutes after Amina, and melted like a cloud into the purple twilight. The swelling hosts along Canal Street spilled across roads and bridges, strung along by fours to the floor jungle rhythms, back beat of the Manchester night. Shazia wove in and out of the tables and chairs, bypassing the raised glasses and drunken scrums with the skill of the waitress. But her thoughts were disturbed. They kept returning to Amina. How long could it possibly take her? To get to the station. To bring Damon back? What if he hadn't got the message? She'd asked two men the time in the shadows of Prague Five. As the cars fizzed by, and the lights sank to sleep, she began to count the seconds down in her head, slowly and surely, ignoring the steady 150bpm thump of woofer and tweeter, and the 180bpm pounding of her heart.

Now, as she looked over the canal into the gardens of the old school, the fear came on her once more, the fear that Damon would never turn up. She made her way down to the narrow towpath by the canal's edge, and imagined herself as one of those Victorian maids she'd seen in pictures in the City Art Gallery, flitting down country lanes at dusk. She skipped over the cobbles as lightly as a wind. The towpath was deserted. Or so it seemed. Quite by chance, she looked back down the darkling way. And sensed movement. Something *was* there. *Oh, God.* A shadowy figure along the parapets. Scanning the ground. Her heart raced. Was it looking for her? She blinked in the twilight, terrified. But the figure had gone.

Had she imagined it? No. The demons were after her again. She quickened her step. The main road was near. Don't look back. Keep going. *Don't look back.* The steps were in sight. Just a few more. *Don't.* But Orpheus-like she did, fear clutching at her back. And her heart filled with a dread weight. The air *was* moving behind her. Tall and dark, a figure was running down the towpath. *Run, Shazia Ahmed, run. Run for your life.* And she bolted into the darkness, her arms pumping like pistons, on-wards, her lungs on overload, her heart thumping like a failing turbine.

Relief at hand, she ran faster. Faster. The cobbled stairs were approaching. She raced up them, frantic and desperate, two at a time, all the while imagining invisible hands on her, and burst into the crowds like a diver coming up for air. Gasping for it. Pushing through them, wading through their lacquer and treacle. Stumbling into the road where the wild klaxon of a private taxi nearly blew her head off. The Asian driver, his hairy arm hanging out, drummed the roof and stared at her. Winking.

'Need a lift, luv?' Broadest Oldham.

Shazia ignored him, ran down to the gates of the old school, all the time putting bodies between her and pursuit. Her hands grasped the heavy metal bars. Shook them madly. But the gates were locked. So she ran again, past the lines of black cabs, past the steady stream of fags commuting from their flats in India House, and tried to lose herself amongst them, coming to a stop underneath the old school's great Gothic arch. She slunk into its shadows, huddling on the cold, stone steps, her head bowed. She waited, nervously. Waited for Damon to show up. Waited for a figure to emerge from the gloom.

The seconds became minutes and her fingers drummed like rain on the cold stone uselessly. Though there was no clock near at hand, she imagined the hands turning inexorably from *past* to *to*. There was no Damon. Amina had failed. A terrible decision lay heavy on her heart. If Damon wasn't here soon, there'd be no time left. She looked down the road. It was empty. No tall stranger. No dark figure. She fingered the money in her pocket, the money Amina had left, the money she'd refused to take. There was enough. She could still make it to London herself.

The last flickers of sunlight bathed the city's rooftops. High up in the crow's nest of flats in India House, pan stick was being trowelled into deep crevices, cocaine sparkled like sherbet on Coco Chanel coffee tables, a bedlamite jumped from the service shaft of the upper floors, and, in the penthouse, gunshots had blown the face off a dilettante queen. The city's million secrets winked out of the firmament.

Shazia decided. She'd follow the rays of the sun. No point waiting for trouble. And she left the steps of the old school, fear her constant companion. If Damon was coming at all, he'd come this way. She'd meet him halfway. And if not, she'd risk the station herself. So she made her way back up Sackville Street, through the crowds, and down Canal Street, unaware she was being watched. The tall, dark figure had emerged from out of the gloom. For a few seconds it paused, as if weighing her fate, then followed quietly.

CHAPTER 34

It was 9:25 when Damon and Amina arrived at the Rembrandt pub. Her feet swelled and burnt as they pounded the twilit streets. Her heart swelled and burnt in sympathy. With his jacket slung over his shoulder, Levi's cool, and his T-shirt cellophane tight over his chest, she wasn't the only one purring. From the billowing cloud of joints inside, several heads turned to follow him upstairs. Several more raised quizzical eyebrows when he walked straight into the Ladies'. And when he emerged, consternation in his face, invisible eyes bored deeply into the pronounced U of his crotch, fly-fishing, their hands running invisible fingers through his hair. Not tonight, Josephines. Not this tackle.

'Well, she's gone,' he said.

His sense of purpose, more than the sore and aching limbs, some kind of manly certainty she'd never seen in him, stoked the fires of her passion. She just wanted to plant her trembling mouth on those bee-stung lips. He looked up and down the street, desperately hoping to catch a sight of Shazia. She seemed all but forgotten.

'You should have gone home, Amina,' he said, sadly.

The finality of it crushed her.

'I just can't think,' he said, 'I can't remember.'

Men never do.

Amina pursed her lips and tried not to think the possible. That Damon Ruff would miss his train. If Shazia and Damon left, she'd be on her own. Spending every weekend watching *Kabhi Khush Khabi Gham* and *Dil To Pagl Hai* with her sisters. Watching her mother and grandmother fight for the best seat on the sofa. Waiting for Mo. All her friends would quietly slip off the face of the earth, marry their culturally protected, parentally approved cousins, and she'd be left dreaming of the rain and the stars and fiery kisses coming down from heaven. The heart was mad, indeed.

'Look, Damon,' she said, 'I *can* still help. She can't have got far, you know.'

Damon frowned. The seconds slipped away.

'Then we'll have to split up. You wait here for her. See if she comes back. I'll scout round. You're probably right. She can't have got far. But, if I'm not back in fifteen minutes, Amina, you *must* go. You understand?'

He looked at her sternly, the way he'd probably look at their children in the future, with care and love, and authority.

It was too much for Amina Aslam. Within her grasp was the only thing she ever wanted; she wasn't about to let it go. Her moment had arrived.

She paused, then braved her heart.

'I love you, Damon,' she said, and darkened with shame.

His blue eyes crushed her. Through the techno air, alive with the screams of queens and the clinking of a thousand raised glasses, a small pocket of silence descended.

'I know,' he said, 'it's why I rang you back.'

Her heart shook from its moorings. *Dil Se.*

But when she lifted her head, he was gone, flitting down Canal Street like a shadow. A breath of the Manchester night touched her face and she looked up to see the crescent moon beginning to glow.

Of course he'd known. Known it the moment he first saw her. Eyes don't lie. She'd had her headlights on all day. If only Shazia's hadn't been on full beam. Things would have been so different. For both of them. Amina's family would surely not have tried to kill him.

He hurried down Canal Street, his eyes skirting every foreign path and cobbled way for sight of Shazia, madly and randomly. Then he saw it. Rising from the shadows, its turrets fortifying the sky. The veil was lifted from him. The old school. That's where they'd gone! Memories lurched back, then leapt on each other's shoulders. He'd taken her there when his money ran out. Listened to her plotting the colonisation of the west. If only she hadn't been so beautiful. And he so weak.

Darkness descended. It was now impossible to see anything clearly. Faces disappeared right in front of him. He broke into a run. He had to get there. On the bridge over the canal, however, he halted. Through the maddening crowds, something was waving. A pony-tail. Dancing in the air. A girl with a pony-tail. There she was again. Running, running. Then vanishing. Shazia?

He pushed through a group of media types and ran down to the old canal wall. Empty of life. Just a few broken glasses and empty cigarette packets. He peered over the parapets to the towpath below. Nothing. No-one. No, there. A figure, walking away. There was no time to waste. He threw himself down the old stone stairs as quickly as he could. The old school was only just round the corner. It must be her. Please. Too scared to shout, he ran, faster and faster. She was running, too, haring away from him. He sprinted, began gaining on her. But he was too late. When he reached the end of the narrow path, and took the steps up to Sackville Street, she was gone. A huge party of Hydrad women, all blonde chic and pierced navels, pushed him to the edges of the road. He couldn't see a thing.

Ruefully, he walked down to the school, his mind a sea of confusion, awash with love for Shazia and awash with something like love for Amina. Guilt at one balanced by expectation of the other. The crowds thinned, the music faded. He peered through the railings of the park. No-one. The gates were locked, too. Only the shadows of evening. Shazia was nowhere to be seen. He thought about continuing round to Whitworth Street, to the old Gothic entrance. She was fond of sitting under that. But no, they'd gone to the park. He made his way back up Sackville Street. To have one woman running the gauntlet for you was bad enough, to have two was disaster. Where had she gone?

The moment Damon left her, all Amina Aslam could hear was the echo of his parting words. 'I know. It's why I rang you back.' They lifted her high, higher than she'd ever been. Nothing stood between her and happiness now, it seemed. And she stood there on the pavement, exposed and isolated, and a million years, by her heart's chronometer, from the warmth of her family. She'd found another sun. But the darkness was approaching.

CHAPTER 35

Dru walked to the waiting taxi, flanked by Jamie and Billy. A strange sense of calm had settled over him. Candy's death, rather than pushing him to the terrible brink, had a numbing effect. Novocaine for the soul. If he was to live, he'd have to keep it that way. He counted down the steps to the driver's window.

Three.

Two.

One.

It wound down. *Fuck.* It wasn't who he thought it was. So much for tips. It was another surprise. The driver from last night! The calling card. Bloody hell. The Asian looked at him like he was coming for seconds. He got in. They got in. Sandwiched between them.

'Where you off to, boys?'

Dru looked at him, then at Billy. He desperately wanted to say, 'Take us to the DeepDrill', but dared not. Out spilled the name of Candy's club: *Scarlet Harlot's*. Scarlet fucking harlot, that's just how Candy had ended up, too. Blood all over the

289

floor, blood all over the ceiling. They'd be cleaning it up for weeks. Poor Candy.

The inside of the taxi was furnace hot. The black leather seat stuck to his pants like cling film. He found it difficult to breathe. The onset of claustrophobia. The agitation grew with every second. He was trapped. In the stifling heat he could smell his kidnappers. Stay calm. You're on stage. Look straight ahead. That's where your audience is. And there, above the driver's mirror, was what he was looking for. The pale green digits of the clock. 21:21. He was on in less than forty minutes.

Billy was beside him, delirious. He'd long since departed the land of the living. Strangely, though, Dru could connect to him this way. He'd grown up in spite of the world, as well, a member of no-man's club. The terrible visitations of violence, he understood that. They'd overwhelmed him the same way. He understood Billy, could sense the animal in him. Stoned as he was, there was still some terrible dark lurking there. He watched the dead eyes flicker in their sockets as he rolled his head round. They were just swimming. Suddenly, like oranges in a slot machine, they'd appear in line. Focused. All that entered that monstrous cranium was fear and loathing. He understood that perfectly.

The taxi was soon snarled up in traffic and the metaphysics of Manchester's one-way system. You couldn't get up Princess Street, the driver explained, catching Dru's eye in the rear-view mirror. He was tired and irritated. These short rides weren't worth the hassle. But, after last night, what had he got to complain about? He'd got out of jail free. The white boy in the back was living proof that his luck had changed again. The Ace of fucking Hearts! He still had to pinch himself. But when he found Sackville Street blocked by some giant street carnival, he groaned. The tailback stretched as far as Whitworth Street.

Dru's eyes came to rest on the man's ID: Intikhab Khan. How appropriate, he thought, for a taxi driver. He could use that tonight. Then they settled on the clock. He watched the digits change. 21:24. And knew that unless he got to *Scarlet Harlot's* fast, there'd be no performance tonight. Or, if there was, it'd be a short one-act revenge called 'Murder in the Cab'. Billy and Jamie didn't seem to care, happy to bide their time in the shadows. Suddenly, though, Billy tapped him. The oranges were lined up.

'I'm watching you, fucker.'

The cab doors were locked. Even if he could get to the handle, he'd never get out. No, the only thing he could do was pray. Pray that the crowds would part and that the taxi would get there on time. Pray that he'd get a chance to escape this black oven.

There were only a few hundred yards to go. They were going to make it. But a crowd of clubbers blocked the way. The taxi stopped. More delay.

Tick Tock. If you're going to live, you've got to keep calm. He had to risk it.

'You can drop us here, if you like,' he said to the driver. 'We can walk the rest of the way.'

A metal barrel was thrust invisibly into his ribs, as he knew it would be. Big mistake. The driver looked back at them.

'Here?'

Billy had woken.

'Drive the fucking car, Paki.'

The poison in his voice, like the poison of a serpent, stopped their ears. For one terrible moment, Dru thought Saddam was going to retort. And get every one of them blown up. Get them all pasted. He prayed very hard and breathed deeply.

So did Jamie Farrell. He sat on Dru's left side, thinking about the splatter of blood that was even now seeping across the mosaic tiles of Candy's flat. In an endless flow it poured, rising and rising till Candy's body was drowning in it. He looked out of the window. At all the shuffling lines of humanity. They were in some kind of frenzy. The thump of the dance floor seemed to hypnotise them. Some master shaman was at work in Manchester, speaking the language of the tribe. With drunken weary glances, girls in Gucci wrestled the flimsiest of dresses into a semblance of order, London media boys with classic James Dean jeans felt the hum along their zips, their cocks chomping at the clit. Glasses were raised in celebration, arms aloft in perspiration, morals sunk in condemnation. And the beat went on, till it began to hypnotise Jamie himself, and he almost forgot he was there.

Then Billy, weighing the violence of the earth in his hands, spoke his dreadful words, and Jamie's vision was wrested from the Gay Village of the Damned. The driver shrugged. He was still on a roll. And the taxi moved on. The faces coasted past, white and black, white on black. Then a break, and a view of cobbles and tables near the Rembrandt pub. The space concentrated Jamie's mind, focused his senses. A needle in a haystack. His eyes bored into the belly of the night with laparoscopic intensity. How could they not? There, standing on her own, beneath the awnings of the entrance of a strip joint, was the girl.

The girl. The fucking girl, the girl he'd crashed into, her hair parted like a curtain across her face. Her. Here? Beautiful. As beautiful a thing as he'd ever seen.

'Billy,' he shouted, 'she's there!' And agitation and excitement were in his voice.

But Billy was unmoved. His eyes were fixed on Dru's jaw, thinking how he'd soon break all the bastard's teeth.

He whispered.

'Who, Jamie-boy?'

'The girl, Billy. *The fuckin' girl.*'

Billy stared at him, his reptilian brain alive to threat and possibility, weighing Jamie's words up carefully.

He was quiet. They were becalmed. Dru prayed. Then came the tempest.

'Oi, Paki, turn your fuckin' car round!' Billy shouted, gesticulating wildly.

The whites of the driver's eyes flared in anger. Fucking white shit. He looked into his rear-view mirror and met Dru's. Like last night. Imperceptibly, Dru shook his head. A no of warning. Bold as he dared. As subtle as circumstance allowed. It worked. The driver cut through the darkling lanes. Dru could have wept. His chance had gone. Beside him, Jamie clawed at the windows of the cab, and Billy, Billy was in the zone again. He gripped the gun tighter than ever and waited to pull the trigger one more time.

'Jamie-boy,' he whispered, 'you're sure it was her, aren't you?'

The threat was clear.

Dru's fingers were twitching uncontrollably, itching for that mutant bastard's neck. He'd half asphyxiated strong bull queers before, Billy's scrawny pipe would be no problem. With one eye on the clock, now reading 9:42, Dru hoped his moment had come. The DeepDrill was near. They'd come full circle, the shaman had led his acolytes to the gates of oblivion. On the roof of Prague Five, a skeleton gyrated in slow motion, threshing with a scythe the field of bodies beneath it. Even Billy was impressed with that.

And for Jamie, too, the terrible moment was coming. The cab had pulled up on the bridge.

There, just as memory had left her, in her purple shalwar kameez, was the girl. Amina Aslam. Framed in the neon twilight, she was still as a corpse. The shaman's magic had failed. Pure as snow in northern Punjab, she remained undefiled.

Billy couldn't believe their luck. He strongly believed in witness tampering, especially *before* the police had interviewed them. It always saved a return visit.

'It's your lucky day, Jamie-boy,' he said. 'You're going to get the money and the girl.'

Jamie steeled himself.

Dru saw his chance had arrived.

CHAPTER 36

Damon Ruff fingered the tickets in his
pocket and knew that time was running
out. No Shazia, no train. He could barely
see through the thicket of arms and legs and
bodies before him. He needed a better vantage.
Braving the drop into the canal below, he vaulted
on to the stone wall of the bridge. It was too high.
He hated heights of any kind. Should someone as
much as raise their arm and distract him, he'd
find himself plunging into the silent depths.

From here he had a good view of the area. He
tried to pick out individual faces from the maelstrom sea of humanity, but their constant movement, their raucous screams and whistles, and the
deafening thud of techno, made it hard to concentrate. He felt time beating against him. She had
to be round here somewhere. With each passing
second his conviction became certainty. It *had*
been Shazia.

He looked over towards the Rembrandt pub,
hoping to catch sight of Amina. Worryingly, too,
she seemed to have gone. His eyes drifted across
the road to the junction of Canal Street. A steady

line of people obscured his view. He groaned. Now two of them to look for. He considered his next move. A few minutes pushing and shoving and he'd be there. God, not yet. Not while there was still time. He looked at his watch, nearly catapulting himself off the bridge in the process. He had to decide.

He thought about what he'd said. About Amina. It was true. He did love her. She was safe and new. The terrible unpredictability of life with Shazia had left him gasping for air. He loved her, he realised, for what they'd been, not for what they'd become. And, as if in confirmation of the thought, the crowds parted, and there she was, a porcelain doll etched into the very walls. Amina Aslam.

If he just made those very few steps, he could rewrite his history completely. All the tortuous lies he'd told Shazia, about all the contacts in London, about passing his exams, about being little more than a poor kid living with his mum in Walthamstow, all these would be forgotten. Ever since they'd met, she'd pinned expectations to him like he was a notice-board. What was he meant to say? No, Shazia, I love you, but I can't save you. He couldn't. Looking at Amina, now, her head turned to the west, all seemed clear. She didn't need saving. He'd go over to her and start again.

He made to climb down. Then stopped. The storm was approaching. Fate had intervened.

Not twenty yards from where he stood, he caught sight of it again. The pony-tail. Shazia's pony-tail. And there she was, picking her way through the rush and thunder. His heart was dumb. He followed her with his eyes, love on a wing, the way he'd followed her those few years ago. When they'd met. Waiting. And, while he waited, guilt washed over him. Poor Shazia. He felt he should jump now. Jump into oblivion. They would embrace, and kiss like old lovers, and he'd smooth her hair the way she liked. And they could make it to Piccadilly. There was still time. There was always time; time to live and breathe and time to regret, but seldom time to change things. Damon Ruff was granted such a moment. He could walk out of one life into another in the twinkle of an eye. Yet the tears and sorrow it caused would last a lifetime.

He looked out over at Amina Aslam, bathed in twilit red, and down at Shazia, flitting through the shadows. Two girls. One choice. Amina was waiting for him. For a beginning. No strings attached. Shazia, desperate, was the endgame, looking for everything, an everything he couldn't give. He paused, then plunged into the crowd. Shazia was within touching distance. He could make her out clearly now. Biting her bottom lip. The pain in her face appalled him. What terrible things had she gone through, just to get here? If she turned round now she'd see him, and that would be that. She'd take the decision right out of his hands.

But she paused, as if listening to some deep stirring in her heart. She was at the crossroads. A wrong turning now and she'd walk straight past Amina. The game would be up for all of them. Damon held his breath. And glanced skywards. By some strange quirk of the heavens, the three of them had ended up in perfect alignment underneath the stars. Shazia faced east, sinking into the shadows, Amina looked west into the setting sun. Damon, he was the fulcrum on which they balanced.

Decision time. He thought of his mother, facing a chill world alone without his dad, bringing him and his sister up penniless. She'd say Shazia, he was sure. And his dad, who'd fled from all responsibility the way he was trying to do, well, it was obvious. Go for Amina. You only have one life, kiddo. Decision time.

He fingered the tickets in his pockets, the seeds of a new life, and looked into his heart one last time. Then looking at the girls, at one end of the street and the other, he made his choice. And sadness nearly overwhelmed him. He heard the door of the past closing behind him. All out.

The time pushed a quarter to ten. Shazia Ahmed had pushed through another line of straggling party revellers, and still there seemed no end to them. She'd run out of 'excuse me's and was on to exasperated shoves. But, at least the fear of immediate pursuit had gone. Piccadilly was in sight. Only one wish remained. 'Damon, please be at the station.'

Damon? Damon Ruff? Amina Aslam's heart was fit to bursting with the thought of him. She hardly noticed the stream of passing faces, or the awnings of the strip joint behind her. Only one thing mattered.

'Damon, please come back.'

CHAPTER 37

Azad Riaz had just driven down the cobbled thoroughfare for the eighth time when it happened. Totally without warning. He thought his head would be blown clear right off.

'Stop the car!'

Aftab Akhtar, the palms of his hands pawing at the windows like an inmate, screamed murderously at him. All fire and insurrection, his eyes suddenly rabid, he peered through the tinted glass to get a better view.

'There she is,' he said. 'I can't believe it! Stop the fucking car, you daft Paki.'

Azad, relieved to be still alive, but sensing some terrible portent, turned his eyes on the street. Wreathed in smiles, which cut the air like razor blades, a thousand *sharabi*, driven to feverish frenzy by the hypnotic throb, glared back. Glazed eyes. It was near the witching hour, when boys became girls, when girls became ghouls. When every smackhead junkie roamed the street. All he could see was the broiling mass. What the hell was the guy looking at?

'Ah, my pretty,' Aftab whispered, audibly enough

for the nape hairs on Azad's neck to stand to immediate attention. 'Looking so sad. You should never have said goodbye.'

Uncontrollably, Azad began shaking. The sweat seeped through his pores and ran down his face. A gap appeared in the conveyor belt of humanity. He looked through, and his heart nearly gave out. Oh, Allah, it couldn't be. Her? Here? But it was. Aftab was looking straight at her, his words main-lining into his soul.

'Do you believe in second chances, my friend?' he whispered. 'Because I do. We all get what's coming to us. Allah can only be so merciful.'

And Azad prayed he would be. Prayed very hard. For he knew what was coming.

'You're going to stay right here, my friend,' Aftab said. 'I'll be back.'

And he pressed the barrel of his gun behind Azad's right ear.

'If you move, if you even think of moving, I'll kill you.'

And Azad didn't doubt it.

Aftab eased out of the taxi, ironed out the ruffles in his jacket, and quickly disappeared into the crowd. As he did so, as if sensing the rising temptation and doubt in Azad's mind, he turned to face him. Arms outstretched and pointing, he aimed an invisible gun at him. And held the pose regardless. Azad gulped. Temptation soared clear away. The crowds broke round Aftab like he was a statue, paying him no more heed than any other cokehead. And, in the blink of an eye, he was gone.

'Here's your chance, Jamie Farrell,' said Billy. 'Remember the game.'

The serpent in his voice uncoiled. He'd drawn his gun out again and was pointing it directly at the driver. In the blind spot. He couldn't see a thing.

'It's all you have to do, Jamie-boy. Just pull the trigger.'

Jamie Farrell looked at the girl. His mind whirred with doubt. A million excuses. And he remembered the Craze. Billy's eyes were boring on him, the way his eyes transfixed the blue of the innocent student, the brown of the innocent Paki, the grey of the wizened, old pensioner. Compelling, hypnotic, terrible.

'The Craze, Jamie-boy. Think of the Craze.'

He did. C was for cars which he'd nicked and crashed, R was for robbery, armed and fast, A was for arson, fire and theft, Z was for the cuts his switch-blade left, E was for drugs, the Whizz and Horse, which just left murder, the hardest, of course. This is where it led. The whole thing had been mapped out for him. Forget the fucking Kingsway. Forget everything. The Craze never stopped. Billy had known it all along. That's why the eyes bore down on him. Looking for doubt, looking for fear.

But Jamie wasn't afraid. Not any more. Not of Billy, anyway. He knew what Billy could do. He was afraid of himself, afraid that at any moment he was going to wake up in a cell with his father. The bullet reserved for the girl may as well have his name on it. He held his hand out.

'Okay,' he said, 'let's go.'

Billy snorted.

'It'll take more than a shot, Jamie. You'll need to bring her here.'

Despite himself, Jamie swallowed. Hard.

'And how do I do that? Whistle? She'll run as soon as she sees me.'

Billy, his gun still trained on the driver, reached into the left pocket of his baggy slacks. He brought out a knuckleduster and grinned.

'This should help,' he said. 'Break her fucking teeth.'

Jamie took it and climbed out of the taxi, his brain burning with cocaine and despair. Billy grinned broader. The clear air outside failed to lift the gloom. He melted into the night.

Back in the cab, the driver had finally seen the gun in his rearview mirror and was starting to panic. This *was* something to worry about.

'What are you doing with that, boss?' he said, frenziedly.

Billy spat at him, a great guzzle of tar and crack.

'Shut the fuck up, Paki.'

Dru stared at Billy, and measured the distance his fist would need to swing to connect with that zombie head. 9:45. Written in luminous green. One blow, just one blow. That's all it'd take. Ladies and gentlemen, will you please take your seats. The performance is about to begin. One blow. If he didn't strike now, all would be lost. The DeepDrill was just round the corner. His contract waiting to be signed.

There she was. She hadn't seen him. If he reached out, he could have touched her hair. Dancing, was it? He'd put an end to that. He imagined himself pulling her through some bazaar in Rawalpindi. No-one would give two rupees there. Just another squalid domestic. His fingers toyed with a fine metal chain in his jacket pocket. He'd save that for later. Through his dark glasses, Aftab Akhtar's world had gone black.

Black as the hole into which Jamie Farrell was looking. Amina Aslam was beneath the massage-parlour awning, looking frantically down Canal Street. He slipped behind a party of student types and walked amongst them unobserved. In the half-light, he felt protected. But this wasn't Northmoor Road. You had to be careful. He was behind her. Facing the west. Vaguely, he smelt her strange perfume. Olfactory systems a go-go. The cocaine had seen to that. He slipped the knuckleduster over his knotted fingers and hoped he wouldn't have to use it. Just reach your hand out, now. She won't bite.

★ ★ ★

Azad Riaz bit his lip, sweating, his fingers on the ignition. Allah was calling him. Calling him to arms. Was this all his doing? He couldn't let her go like this.

The driver shivered and slavered for his life, offered silent *namaz* that he'd see anybody again. The Ace of Hearts. The well of luck had really run dry. Dru looked at him piteously, and counted down the seconds. Three.

Shazia Ahmed could see the tunnel of people finally open. Two.

Amina Aslam, her hair fallen, finally looked round. One.

Bedlam.

When Amina Aslam felt the hand on her shoulder, she thought it must be Damon. Or Shazia. Or, cruelly, both of them. Their approach muffled by the thump of jungle drums. She turned quickly. And turned into a nightmare. For Damon's fringe was shorn off, and instead off looking into his kind face, she was staring at a monster. Shaven head, dead eyes, mouth contorted like an octopus's beak. Then all the pennies dropped at once. It was him! The gargoyle from Naz's take-away. *How?* Here, in this purple sea of faces, this twilight zone of humanity? She opened her mouth to scream, and waited for the air to rush out. But it was too late.

A right-hand vice gripped her throat. Her flailing hand tried to swat it back. She felt herself blacking out even as she tried to kick her assailant. Please, she called out, please someone help me, please Damon. But the words were empty.

Jamie Farrell had the nearest things to tears in his eyes. He couldn't blame the girl for trying. He hoped he wouldn't have to use the steel on that pretty face. His fingers threatened her windpipe, felt her delicate neck an inch from snapping. Just one turn here, and that would be that. All over. But his heart held back. As Billy had surely known it would. He dragged her through the undergrowth of people, and if one or two cast glazed eyes over the public kidnapping, none dared to question. He would have welcomed their intervention. It would have steeled his resolve.

Then, as he took his final steps towards the waiting funeral hearse of the taxi, he tripped on the cobbles and Amina fell to earth, choking and free. A small gasp of air and a strangled scream shot upwards into the night sky. Faces turned from their drinks for once, and a burly doorman made his way to them. Fuck.

But Jamie Farrell was used to this. The knuckleduster ripped upwards with terrible ferocity. The man didn't have a chance. Dealing with handbag-flaying fag boys on a Friday night did not prepare you for street war. His mouth erupted with blood and a couple of chipped teeth.

Jamie, facing a thickening circle of ghouls, grabbed the girl by her hair and dragged her to the waiting cab. The door was open. Amina Aslam was looking into the pit, fear, pure, naked fear emptying her bowels. Damon? Please Damon. Her hair was being torn from her head. Please save me.

The blow landed. Hard. The spring-loaded frustration of being cooped up unwound in that single punch. It knocked Billy Whizz sprawling on to the floor and dislodged the gun from his hand. Dru's mind was clear at last. To dive for the gun and shoot the bastard, or go for the door and run. Either way promised disaster.

He kicked Billy into the far door and tried the handle. Air, fresh evening air, greeted him. He gulped it in.

And watched as Jamie Farrell dragged the prostrate girl to her feet.

'Where the fuck are you going?' Jamie screamed.

Dru tried to push past her, elbowing his way through, breathing again. Jamie's fist met him full way in the face. He didn't see it coming. He staggered and reeled, teetering badly. Jamie was about to level another blow when he heard Billy.

'Get out the way, Jamie-boy.'

He froze. The Craze. Right before his eyes. So simple.

The crowd had drawn a wide circle round them. Dru had his audience at last. He hoped somebody was watching this. It would be unforgettable. He made his way up Canal Street, convinced he could still make the DeepDrill. *Knowing* he could. Then there was a dull thud, out of time with the thud of the music. He swayed like a broken marionette, then fell to earth, the back of his head haemorrhaging terribly. Blood shot out like a Catherine-wheel, brain raining across the barren ground. Billy Whizz was grinning from ear to ear.

A girl screamed near at hand, realising what had happened. Then pandemonium. The ghouls were scattering. The driver, his prayers answered, his paralysis of fear momentarily broken, made for the door. But Billy's command, and the flash of steel in his mirrors, had him mumbling again.

'Drive on, Paki, or you're next.'

Jamie had Amina in his arms. She was fighting like a fury. Why wouldn't Billy just shoot her? And even as he struggled with the thought, he knew the reason. That wasn't Billy's job. It was his! The fucking Craze. He looked inside the cab. Billy was staring at him. Staring hard. He felt the knuckle-duster in his hands and looked at Amina's tear-flung face. They had seconds to get away.

So had Shazia. Aftab Akhtar counted them down slowly. Then calmly clapped one powerful hand

309

over her mouth and whispered in her ear.

'We meet again, Shazia Ahmed.'

Shazia tried to turn, her brain quickening with fear. She recognised the voice immediately. Caught at last, just when it seemed she would get away. And she felt something being pressed into the small of her back. *Pray, Shazia Ahmed, pray*, but she knew it was over. Her soul was as good as lost.

She was marched through the crowds, away from Piccadilly, away from the ten o'clock train, away from hope. Aftab was leading her back, back to a waiting hearse. She sensed this time there would be no reprieve. The sky above had nearly closed over, the stars were being switched on all over the universe and not a soul paid heed. All except one.

Azad Riaz saw his niece coming towards him, and thoughts of running were banished. That was his flesh and blood. Almost. If he did nothing else on earth, and he realised he probably wouldn't, then this one act might redeem him from certain damnation. Poor Shazia. He watched Aftab emerge through the crowds and the sweat on his forehead glittered like the Milky Way above.

Damon Ruff had made his choice, too. And hoped it was the right one. When he saw events unfolding as quickly and terrifyingly as they did, though, he realised that his hope was badly misplaced. Like everyone else, he needed prayer.

CHAPTER 38

The taxi sped down Stockport Road a few minutes after ten o'clock. Through Ardwick and Longsight. The Devil's Run. There was still light in the sky, a scar of pink and red in the sinking firmament. The driver felt it on the right side of his face, burning what little was left of his conscience. He dared not look in his mirror. The awful silences, the sobbing moans. And that one terrible scream.

So he drove on, drove through the pain and sickening fear, past the familiar landmarks of this godforsaken zone: the crumbling Apollo, the Spinning Wheel pub, the miles and miles of squalid council housing, the parade of skinny white girls in their flimsy tops and plastic shoes, huddled at bus stops with their black, hood pimps. It rolled by in a dream. His eyes looked forward. Please don't hurt her. Please. And tears trickled down his swarthy face. Not like this.

At the junction of Plymouth Grove the taxi slowed to red and he heard movement in the back, and a voice through the grille.

'Drive on.'

The Craze. Cars were already pulling out. Drive on. Contact. *Jaldi, jaldi*.

The driver swerved. There was a screech of wheels, the klaxon blare of horns. Thud. A car mounted the A6, careered into the Pakistani Community Centre. And they were clear. The dark air closed in again.

'We need to dump her, friend. Quickly.'

The driver's brain whirred. Any second now he imagined the gun blasting a hole in his head. He mentally thumbed the long list of Manchester streets cabbies were told to avoid. One immediately sprang to mind. The rail depot off Kirkmanshulme Lane. Dark and deserted. One of his mates was driven there last week, car-jacked by three birdboys in Gorton. They got everything: fares, watch, even his bloody locket. Lucky to get out alive.

Minutes later, they were there. He turned the taxi up the old access road and approached the rail sidings. It was dark. The man told him to switch the engine off. Now the silence was even more pronounced, the moans a little quieter, the breathing a little heavier. He realised it was his own.

It's strange, the things you think before you die. The girl, sprawled on the floor of the taxi, thought her fear would prevent her from even thinking. But it didn't. Her mind spat and sparkled like a thousand solar flares. The black hood the man had placed over her head served merely to fuel them. Now, all was dark. Her face, still smarting from the clubbing right hand he'd given her, throbbed. She thought of the commotion they'd left behind. The screams in the night, the ring of gunfire. And she wondered what they were saying now, whether anyone would find her. Whether she was on the news. Old television programmes flickered through the channels of her memory, a schoolteacher asking her where her packed lunch was, a shopkeeper letting her off that one time. Trivial, random, unstoppable. He was going to kill her, she was sure. She'd read it in his eyes the moment he'd slipped the hood on. Murderous, vengeful intent.

After a few minutes, the taxi stopped swerving and turning. Pressed against the floor, her ears caught every bump and grate, the steady vibrations of the road. They were going straighter now. Faster. She thought she heard the wail of sirens, of police cars in hot pursuit, but they faded. Delirium. Nothing but the muttering darkness.

And the muttering was real. The man was talking to himself.

'Your time's coming, bitch.'

Then, it happened. The hood was taken off. Light. Light at last.

She looked up. And screamed. *Oh God.* It was him. But the moment she did so, the hammer of his fist smashed into her face again. And again. Harder. Blinding pain. Then his hand rummaged through her mouth and caught her tongue. Drew it out like dental floss. Her hands tied behind her back, she was helpless. Desperately she tried to retract it. But too late. She knew what was coming. Please no. But the knife sliced down, severing it from its root. Expertly done. The scream died in her mouth. Welled up with blood. She was going to die with the pain. The last thing she thought of was the fair. And the Big Wheel turning.

For a few minutes, there was nothing. Nothing said, nothing heard. Just the still night air and the crescent moon grinning sadistically down over the world. Azad Riaz just couldn't bring himself to look round. His heart would have given way.

'So, the deal is still on, my friend?'

Aftab Akhtar was in no rush. He was enjoying himself. He hadn't felt this way for ages. Not since the Jahangir job last year. Too many trips to England were making him miserable.

'You do want the little extra?'

He had one eye closed and was pointing the gun directly at Azad's head.

His voice darkened to a whisper of warning and threat. Azad trembled.

'I do think you should look, my friend.'

Getting darker. Azad felt his head taken in strange hands and the gun at his temple. He closed his eyes. A film of tears covered them. He turned.

'Open them.'

The shadow hid most of her but, in the semi-light, he could still see enough. Her face, turned to the side, seeping blood, was still recognisable. How could he have let this happen, to not have lifted a finger for her? He knelt desolate in abject failure, confronting his cowardice.

'What have you done?' he wailed. 'What have you done? Baby!'

Aftab Akhtar held up what looked like a slice or two of bacon. Bacon dripping. Very *haram*. Azad stared at it uncomprehendingly. Then it registered. And he was sick. The bastard. He cried piteously and hardly felt the blow to the back of his head, numbing him to unconsciousness.

Black out.

Hours passed in the balmy, night air. The world was hushed and fallen, disturbed only by the sound of passing trains and the rush of distant cars. Aftab remained unmoved in the back of the taxi and toyed with the girl. He ran his hands over her body and wondered what his chances were of getting anything at all to Khalid Ahmed. Damaged in transit. Even a dumb girl had her uses, though. She was pretty enough to dance for him, certainly. In the *nach ghar* for his 'political' friends. Or one of his many *kunjaree*. *The girl with no tongue*. Plenty of men would pay to fill that kind of mouth.

But then he thought better of it. The girl was bleeding everywhere. She wasn't going anywhere. Better to make a move. He got out the passenger side and surveyed the wasteland. It was a good place to dispose of a body. Like Katchi Abadis. Not a soul had passed their way. He kicked through the earth and found what he was looking for. A sheet of tarpaulin that would burn like a torch.

He returned to the taxi and stared at her. The light of the moon gave her an unearthly glow. Her hair fell about her like a river of raven night. Such beauty. Such waste. But there was no choice. He'd have to kill her. She was breathing uneasily. Everyone should have the right to see their end.

He opened the driver's door and shook Azad roughly. It was time he paid his dues.

'Are you ready, my friend? The *jinn* aren't about.'

Azad, coming up for air, surfaced from the somnambulant dark, struggling into consciousness. *Jinn?*

'What are you talking about?' he murmured, dribbling.

'Our deal, my friend. She's yours now.'

Azad flinched when he saw the gun again and half fell out. But Aftab's hand pulled him up. He placed him kneeling on the hard earth below.

'Suppose I just left you here, my friend,' Aftab whispered, 'what would you do?'

Azad stuttered and wept.

'What would you do?'

He couldn't answer. He was responsible. In that mad frenzy of activity, he'd had the chance to save her. And he'd failed. Now, here he was, choking on his own vomit, a sheet rain of tears sleeting over the soil. He was responsible. Aftab dragged him by the shoulder. Showed him the tarpaulin sheet, a lighter shadow in this lane of darkness. Ordered him to drag it to the taxi. The stench of grease and rubber rose up unpleasantly. He laid it out like a picnic rug. Aftab laid the moaning girl in its folds and creases. One flailing arm drooped out before the material closed over her. Aftab tried to push it back in. Noticed there was something on her finger. No time to waste. He drew a Pakistan army knife and cut into the bone. The mummy woke to pain, its scream stanched by the shroud. You never left anything to chance. He put the finger in his pocket. A useful memento to take back home. Khalid may even raise a smile.

Azad was sick again.

All thoughts of escape gone, he obeyed every instruction, sleepwalking into damnation. Not even his wife would forgive him this. He dragged the girl into the car and drove up a small incline, pulling up beside the sidings fence. It was drawing to one. No-one about. The shunters' yards were dark and deserted. Aftab, his gun drawn, watched Azad carry her. He slammed the passenger door behind him. It echoed too loudly across the tracks.

Then silence.

'It's down to you, my friend,' Aftab whispered, 'finish it off.'

He pulled out his wallet, withdrew a thick wad of fifty-pound notes, and placed them in Azad's palm.

'Buy your wife something nice.'

Azad looked at the money, then at the bundle of cloth. He wanted to die. He slumped on to all fours, hoping to sink into the ground.

'Please,' he said, 'I can't.'

Aftab sneered. Miserable Paki. They'd all gone soft. He rocked him with a savage blow to his head. Azad screamed, an echo of the girl's. The shout pierced the heavy air.

'*Kam karo*!'

The gun was there again. He flicked him a lighter. Told him to pour a half-empty can of diesel over her. Watched him carry the girl to the fence, then struggle with her up a narrow culvert beside the tracks. Watched him stagger and fall and spill the girl half on to the ground. The fucking daft bastard. Could he do nothing right? Then he heard the girl scream again, tongueless. He'd heard nothing like it. Even his nape hairs rose in horror. Fuck. Maybe the *jinn* were about!

Azad silenced the scream with his bare hand. She was better off dead, anyway. So was he. A torch flashed across the tracks. Then a voice. Fuck. The police? They'd followed him here. He panicked. Who'd ever believe him? The lighter flicked into open flame and the pyre was lit, arcing defiantly into the savage sky. The tarpaulin burned momentarily with the brilliance of the sun, then flickered gently, stuttering to smoky ruin. All life was like that.

He ran off, desperately, ignoring the shouts behind him. Of Aftab, there was no sign. He'd disappeared as suddenly as he'd come, slinking back into the night. Azad looked up. He had five hundred pounds and murder in his pocket. Allah save him.

The dream was different from the last ones she'd had. The figure had come into her room and sat on her bed as usual, but she could no longer feel her body. Her throat was numb. She couldn't speak. But Damon Ruff was looking down on her, sadly. And, as she burnt and her life was extinguished, that thought consoled her. He'd be staying with her forever.

CHAPTER 39

The ten o'clock from Piccadilly to London Euston left on time, its carriages surprisingly full. Returning students, businessmen, away-day families, the usual suspects. The noise of first boarding had abated and the passengers slept or stirred gently. Children hid in the arms of their parents. But, though he felt like joining them, Damon Ruff couldn't. Every time he closed his eyes, the nightmare returned.

He absently stroked the hair of the girl beside him. Her head was buried in the crook of his arms. She'd been sobbing for the better part of an hour. Now she was still, her eyes open, boring into their reflections in the near window. Into the doppelganger carriages. Looking through them into the vast darkness beyond. His words of empty comfort fell like rain on flooded plains, meaninglessly.

Suddenly she looked at him, and her eyes seeped with tears.

'I'm sorry, Damon,' she said, 'I'm sorry for everything.'

Damon Ruff looked at her and choked back his own. He kissed her gently on her lips. They were cold. He couldn't remember seeing her so beautiful, here on the edge of together. And yet his heart was heavy for the choice he'd made. He counted the cost of that choice silently. The mad rush up to Piccadilly, holding on to her hand for dear life, imploring her to run, though knowing she couldn't. The broken hand, pained from the blow he'd levelled at her attacker. The bruise on the side of the face where the man had lashed out. The sound of a rocket gun going off in the distance and the crowds screaming towards them, panic and drink fuelling their madness, the pounding music driving them onwards. All that kept them together was their fingertips. They'd been like that for years. The tide of bodies washed over them, trampling down the weak, drowning their assailant. His arms thrashing like a squid's, they had ridden the crest of the wild surf away.

Looking at her now, he realised how much she meant. He loved Shazia Ahmed. This was just the beginning. A chapter was closing behind them, for better or worse. He'd have questions to answer when they got to London. But not now. Now was for silence. He kissed her forehead.

'It was her, wasn't it?'

The train thundered on. The new honesty.

'Who?' he lied.

'Amina. It was her in the crowd.'

Damon pursed his lips. It was. But he couldn't speak.

Shazia stared out the window.

'I hope she's all right. She helped us both, Damon.'

He swallowed. The nightmare was returning.

Damon was asleep. Shazia Ahmed looked at him fondly. He'd come good just at the right moment. Her heart was bursting with what she knew was love. He'd come for her, where all the others had left. At the moment she needed them most. She sighed. When Aftab grabbed her from behind, all seemed lost. For once in her life she prepared to give up the ghost. Prayer was futile. Only flesh and blood could save her. And so it proved. Damon's punch broke the terrible spell. The fight returned. When the crowd engulfed them, she made sure her heel landed on Aftab's hand. Hard. They'd fled into the night.

The train thundered on and she thought of the fine times coming. A new life. And she gave up a silent prayer to Amina Aslam, for the help she'd given, and even to her mother, for the little she could afford. She'd never see them again, but they were in her heart forever.

There'd be just the two of them. Damon and her. There'd never be three. Or four. The abortion had seen to that. She couldn't conceive again. Somewhere down the line, she'd have to tell him. Not this line, not this journey, but soon. Very soon.

The train left the north and passed through the heart of England. The gleaming lights of London were still an hour away. Each copse and hedgerow was bathed in ashen light, the fields still and tall with wheat. The heavens, bright with stars, were clear. East and west were joined invisibly, and finally. Shazia Ahmed's soul floated high above the world, the way she'd dreamed it as a little girl, staring at the vapour trails. Rising and falling it felt free at last.

At last.

EPILOGUE

The door slammed hard behind him. The taxi tried to slew off hard to the right but the driver was so panicked by what was happening around him that he quickly lost control. It mounted the pavement, scattering what remained of the crowd. His head jolted sharply and hit the windscreen with a dull thud. It was the last he remembered.

There were only seconds left. Jamie knew it. He could sense the moment had come. The girl was struggling in his arms and there seemed no way to quieten her. Billy was grinning stupidly beside him, for all the world looking like the Devil. He held the gun by the barrel and made as if to smash its blunt end over the girl's temple.

A horn blared into sudden life, distracting them. It was coming from inside the car. The driver was slumped unconscious on the wheel. If they were going at all, they weren't going quietly. On the edge of vision, people melted fearfully into the shadows, like wolves around a campfire. It wouldn't be long before the brave ones came forward.

'Here, Jamie,' said Billy, giving him the gun. 'Take it. She's all yours.'

The girl whimpered when she saw it, redoubled her efforts to escape, but Billy grabbed her by her hair and yanked her back violently.

'Come on, Jamie,' he warned. 'Take the gun.'

Jamie Farrell looked at Billy and then down at the girl. One mocking. One cowering. How many times had he been here before? His mother, the police, his social worker, the fucking community rehabilitation officer. All of them taunting him. And the endless victims of his violence. All cowering fearfully before him. They knew there was no good in him. No good in anyone like him. No God in anyone like him. Never merciful.

The gun slid into his hand and felt warm.

They were all bad. The wicked are truly estranged from the womb, as soon as fertile Gorton bellies give birth; they go astray as soon as they be born, lost in the darkening Manchester estates; speaking lies, always lies. Terence was bad. Billy was bad. He was bad. They all deserved to die. His time had come. He was irredeemable.

It was strange how natural it felt. The feel of metal on flesh. Such a small thing, like a child's toy. What harm could come of using it?

The horn continued to blare, drowning out all objection. Billy's eyes urged him to it, to this one final act. All bad.

He looked at the girl and aimed the gun at her forehead. He expected her to close her eyes. He would've preferred it that way. But they were open. Wide open. Misty and clear, the way he'd first seen them. Like a goddess. All that stood between her and oblivion was an inch of air and a second of time.

Jamie knew the Craze would take him sometime. It took everyone. There was just no escaping it. The consequences of anything you do are nothing. Nothing times nothing equals nothing. He was going to see his dad. He pulled the trigger.

The face exploded before him. From such short range there was nothing left. Blood and brain splattered all over the back of the cab, jellied entrails hanging down like stalactites. Drip, drip, dripping on to the floor. All bad.

It was over.

'Get out,' he said quietly, 'get out the fucking car.'

She couldn't believe it. Jamie opened the door and pushed her out. And, as he clambered after her, Billy's body slumped on to the back seat, in a pool of his own blood. His time had been coming, too.

At the sight of Jamie Farrell emerging from the taxi, the wolves backed off. The screams started, and the frenzy began again. Thump, thump went the thick kick drum. The natives were on their way. In the fading light, Jamie looked like a ghost, cut off from the world as he had been most of his life. No excuses, though. He'd done what he could. He'd done what he had to. The Craze had ended.

Amina Aslam, her feet torn and bloodied, her head bashed and bruised, ran from the taxi like it was her last flight on earth. The safety of the crowd beckoned. If only she was amongst them, she'd be safe. Safe to run for the rest of her life. She heard the screams rain down like bloody thunder and ran faster.

She knew the white boy was behind her. Each and every second she ran, she expected to be cut down, to groan agonisingly on the ground. But the shot never came and she was free. Free at last. Drawn on in the fast-moving current of bodies. Down Canal Street forever. To freedom.

But, as she ran, another gunshot startled the sky. Nearer this time. The crowd screamed as one, veering in all directions. Another black taxi appeared before her. And, in the midst of the hysterical throng, she caught sight of him. There, struggling beside her. Damon Ruff. She called his name out wildly, not caring who heard.

But the crowds kept them apart, eased them away from each other. The vision died. Her calls were lost in the summer night air. Damon Ruff. It was in her head. She pulled herself out, weeping, and ran.

Straight into oblivion.

She hardly even saw him.

'I'm sor . . .' she began, but the words died on her lips.

She looked up. No. It couldn't?!

The fist caught her full in the face, a swift and brutal blow.

Aftab Akhtar, still nursing his hand after Shazia had trodden on it, was purple with frustration and rage. He opened the door of the taxi and pushed her in. She'd have to do.

The lights went out. The drums beat. The murder and the thudding.

A neon sign above Rocky's nightclub lit up red, yellow, and green. From somewhere far away, tinkling down from some forgotten karaoke, a sequinned queen chanteuse was singing.

Fly me to the moon.

It wound its way down to earth, falling, always falling, and settled on the city plains.

The taxi sped away. To Longsight. All hope gone. Behind it, a fading red sign burned dimly on the horizon and died.

The words flickered a final warning: **Welcome to Manchester**.

328

With special thanks to Oliver Johnson, Rachel Calder, and David Savage for reading and understanding the voice of one crying in the wilderness